Also by D.A. Graystone

The Schliemann Legacy

Two Graves

A Kesle City Homicide Novel

D. A. Graystone

Published by
Maaaddy Enterprises Inc.

Two Graves

This book is a work of fiction. The characters, locations, and incidents are products of the author's imagination or have been used fictitiously. Any resemblance to actual events, locations or persons, living or dead, is entirely coincidental.

Published by:
Maaaddy Enterprises Inc.
347 Millbank Dirive
London ON N6C 4W6
Canada

http://www.dagraystone.com

Dedication

*For all those who have ever been bullied
and dreamed of getting even.
Remember George Herbert's words
"Living well is the best revenge".*

*As always, for my parents and my wife…
I'm really not as strange as you might fear.*

Two Graves

Before you embark on a journey of revenge, dig two graves.

- Chinese Proverb

Chapter 1

The boy lunged. "Out of the way, loser!" he yelled.

Preston stumbled backwards off the sidewalk and plopped onto the damp grass. His butt hit hard; his hands barely stopped him from going flat on his back. He snapped an arm over his face, turning away from his attackers. But the four teenagers were already continuing down the sidewalk.

He was already forgotten.

Embarrassment flooded his system. The heat on his face contrasted with the cold of his ass as the dampness from the grass soaked through the seat of his pants. Struggling to his feet, he pulled at his jacket, hoping it would cover the wet stain. The red in his mottled cheeks deepened as he watched his would-be attackers saunter down the street.

The boys wore matching brown leather vests with a white crest painted on the back. They moved together – a pack of animals ready to take on anyone who crossed their path. Their laughter cut through him. Laughter directed at him – the geek, lard butt, weirdo, jerk, and tub. He was used to that. People had been laughing at him for forty years. He checked the retreating figures once more before turning away. He shuddered.

"Little bastards," he said to the night. "Just lucky I wasn't more prepared. Kick that dick into next week."

He *should* have done something to the delinquents, he thought. But, he had been outnumbered. Yet again, his subconscious had registered the unbalanced odds and stopped him.

"You got lucky this time," he said down the street after the retreating punks. He kept his voice pitched low – no need to disturb the neighborhood.

He looked down at his shaking hands. He shoved them deep in his jacket pockets, fixed his eyes on the sidewalk just ahead of his Hush Puppies and started toward the store again.

He had always walked this way. Concentrating on his feet, trying to will them straight. Duck feet. How many times had the other kids teased him about his splayed walk? His footprints in the snow prompted the comment, "Hey, at least one duck stayed for the winter!"

He envied the others with their cocky walks. They always stared straight ahead, welcoming, even *daring*, eye contact but not him. Too much risk, too much pain resulted from the briefest eye contact.

His life had been one long walk through terror.

He had been the brunt of every joke, on the receiving end of some form of terrorism all his life. Laughter, taunting, teasing or worse.

So very often, it was so much worse – bruises, cuts, broken bones. If he inventoried his body, he could remember each injury, each moment of pain, each humiliation.

Yes, he knew fear. He knew it intimately. He knew every heart pounding, sweaty moment of true terror.

Fear dominated his life. Stalking him, it was his constant companion.

Fear kept him safe. Fear was his protector but not his friend.

No, it was the other, darker emotion that he reveled in.

Rage.

Fear kept him safe but rage kept him sane.

At the store, he took a carton of orange juice up to the counter and felt the anger build. He let it grow, develop. He felt the heat form in his belly instead of his cheeks.

"Is that everything?" the young clerk asked.

"Obviously," he answered tersely, relishing the spill of anger.

If I wanted more, I'd put it on the Goddamn counter!

His mind played the entire conversation out as he tapped the counter, impatiently waiting for his change. He snatched the juice without waiting for a bag.

"You're welcome," came the sarcastic voice from behind him.

Mumbling obscenities through the closed door, he started for home. He felt the rage seething and roiling in his body. His pace quickened, his body hunched over, his eyes unseeing. His blood boiled with the rage.

Sweet, sweet rage.

His mind whirled with what he might have done to those boys. He imagined the satisfying crack of bone, the whoosh of air, the whimpering and the begging. And then there would be the blood. And that smart mouth clerk. He pictured how a few sharp staples would take care of him and his *you're welcome!*

He kicked at a stone, sending it into the side of a car. The small thud wasn't satisfying. He needed to hit, crush and inflict pain. His mind flicked to his neighbor's cat. The feel of the tiny bones under the heavy mat of fur, the slow squeeze...

"Hey!" He froze in mid stride, his head snapping up, suddenly face to face with the boy.

The rage drained instantly from his body, threatening to take his suddenly too full bladder with it. All-consuming fear instantly replaced the rage. Sweat clamped his shirt to his back and ran down his spine and into the crack of his ass. His palms grew slippery against the carton of juice. He felt his bowels suddenly loosen as he searched for safety.

The boy stood alone at a bus stop beside an all night gas station, an unlit cigarette dangling between his lips. He made no move to get out of the way. He just stood, waiting.

He fought the urge to run. His eyes flicked toward the station but the attendant was playing a guitar, paying no attention as the world went on around him. No cars were at the pumps and nothing but empty cars on the street and in the lot. He was alone.

* * * * *

Luis Gabel watched the blood drain from the fat cheeks of the loser in front of him and smiled. He couldn't believe his luck when he saw the blub waddling toward him.

This was the same wimp that had fallen on his ass when he scared him earlier. What a geek, Gabel thought as he watched the guy push his glasses back on his nose. God, the guy was sweating like a pig. There was actually steam coming off him.

This porker was ripe and Gabel was going to pick him clean. One glimpse of his blade and he'd be handing over his wallet. Gabel knew the type. He'd be too scared of him and his crew to ever call the cops.

"Christ man, you look like you gonna piss your pants," the boy said, putting his ace into his vest pocket. "We need to talk about a toll on my sidewalk."

The blub never looked him in the eye but tried to step around like some peasant avoiding the King. Gabel stepped onto the grass and grabbed his arm. The carton slipped and hit the ground. Orange juice shot up the Gabel's boots and jeans. In the half-light, it looked like he had wet himself. And then, the asshole actually laughed.

"Look watcha did to my boots! They're fucked. Now you are really gonna pay. Gonna shove my boot right up your ass!"

As he planted his foot to kick out, Gabel stepped on the half-empty carton. His foot went out from under him and he sailed into the air. Unprepared, he went down hard in the small garden on the boulevard, his breath rushing out of him.

Preston took one look at the prone figure and ran. He crossed the street and looked over his shoulder. Expecting to see the kid right behind him, the empty street surprised him and he stumbled into a parked car. Prepared for a ruse, he was ready to bolt at the first sign of movement. But there was nothing.

Seeing the helpless figure dispelled the fear. Rage flowed into the void. Checking left and right, he cautiously went back.

"Were you going to give me some of this?" he asked, pulling his foot back. The toe of his shoe connected just below the teenager's rib cage. The tentative kick barely moved him. Stumbling backwards, Preston saw no reaction, not even a moan. Bravado surged in him, giving flight to his rage.

"I can do better than that!" he said.

Taking a step, he slammed his foot into the boy's side. The force of the kick rolled him onto his stomach.

In the spill of the gas station lights, he could see blood, so dark it was almost black. It had soaked into the boy's stringy blond hair.

He had killed the little scum sucker.

RUN, his brain screamed at him. They're going to blame you.

He wiped his sweaty palms on his jeans and swallowed the bile rising in his throat.

THINK. You know they will blame this on you. You won't last in jail, not even for a single night.

Fighting the rising panic, he looked around. The kid in the booth still had his back to him, headphones on his ears and a guitar in his lap.

None of the houses had direct line of sight because of the trees. Suddenly, he was relieved for the empty street.

RUN.

Car.

"Turn, turn," he said, willing the car to turn down one of the side streets. "Damn," he said, unaware he was talking aloud.

The lights were getting close.

No time to run. Think, damn it.

He grabbed the boy by the vest and propped him against the bus sign. The punk fell over; his head sounded like a ripe melon when it hit the sidewalk. Preston started to giggle and fought for control. The second time, he got the body balanced against the sign. With seconds to spare, he stood facing away from the car and waited. The car didn't even slow as it passed.

Genius. God damn genius. Now RUN!

Ya, run, genius. Great idea. How many bodies do you think turn up at the side of this street? Did the driver get a good look at you? How much would he remember? You do stand out.

Hide the body. The longer it takes to find, the less chance of the driver making a connection. But where? He couldn't carry the kid very far.

A small sliver of light showed along the crack in the partially open door of the station restroom. "What better place for a piece of crap?" he said aloud and another giggle escaped.

He picked up the boy and wrapped an arm under his armpits. He felt the blood soaking into the sleeve of his jacket. He toted the teenager over to the washroom, just one friend helping another. The boots made the only sound as they bounced along the asphalt. Panting, he pushed the door open all the way and grunted as he pulled him over the lip of the threshold. He staggered and let the body drop just clear of the door.

He shut the door as quietly as possible and caught his breath. Dragging the boy across the floor, Preston pulled him up on the toilet seat. He pushed his head against the wall. The skull met the tiles with a satisfying, dull thud.

He grabbed a handful of hair and slammed the head against the wall again. This time, he heard a squishy crunch and smiled. Pounding the head against the wall in a primal rhythm, he spoke in a low voice.

"See what you made me do? All of you, always pushing, pushing, pushing! Never satisfied. You laugh at me, make jokes about me. Hurt me. Well, you pushed too far, didn't you? Now, you paid the price." In his mind, he could see all those who had terrorized him in the past.

Not conscious of his actions, he continued to pound the head against the wall until the skull was a chipped pulp. Suddenly, he realized how much noise he was making. Frightened, he released the hair. The body slumped forward off the toilet seat. He listened and could barely make out the chords of the guitar. He took several deep breaths to calm himself. He pulled the boy back up to the toilet seat.

Grabbing a wad of paper towels, he carefully wiped down the leather vest. CSI wouldn't get anything.

Turning to leave, his foot kicked something, sending it across the floor in a metallic skitter. Bending under the sink, he picked up a knife. He pressed the small button on the black and red handle and a six-inch blade sprang into view. The knife must have fallen from the boy's pocket when he fell off the toilet. Preston closed the knife and slipped it into his pant's pocket.

Standing in the bushes by the bathroom door, he scanned the area. The neighborhood was quiet. He took several deep breaths and started across the station lot.

As he passed, he picked up the empty juice carton. He tossed it and his bloody jacket into the garbage bin at the Chinese food place near his home. Smiling, he was confident he had left no clues.

* * * * *

Dan set his guitar down and stretched, rolling his head to relax his neck. Less than three hours and his shift would be over. He hated the 11 to 7 but at least he could practice his guitar. He stretched again and grabbed the key for the washroom. Carefully locking the door to the booth, he went around the building.

He opened the washroom door and immediately stepped back.

"Sorry man, didn't know you were in here. Hey, you okay, man?" Then he saw the blood, the matted hair and splintered skull. "Jesus Christ!" was all he got out before he threw up all over the crime scene.

Chapter 2

The incessant warble of the telephone dragged Gregg Mann out of a deep, dreamless sleep. He reached out with one arm and punched the speaker button on the top of the unit.

"Mann."

"Lieutenant?"

"Ya, hang on a minute."

Mann pressed the mute button and struggled to a sitting position. He focused on the clock radio. Five seventeen. What the hell, he would have been up in forty five minutes anyway. He coughed twice to clear his throat and scrubbed at his short salt and pepper hair. Flicking on the light, he gently shook the closest Pepsi can. Not much left but it would do. He had started into today's rations last night while watching the news. His conscience had got the better of him and he had left some in the can.

Quickly downing the last few mouthfuls, he released the mute. "What do you have?"

"Sorry to bother you, Lieutenant. I thought you would want to hear about this one."

Mann recognized Shane Kydd's soft, throaty voice. The only female in his homicide squad, the third grade detective brought to mind Kathleen Turner in *Body Heat*, with all the associated lust and desire. She was a good detective and deserved her gold. She'd make second grade before any of the others in his squad. If he had anything to do with it, she would make the grade in record time. Quotas or no, sexist sounding or not, the force needed female detectives. Their minds worked in different ways that often lead to a break in a case. They smelled a lot better, too.

"What have you got, Shane?" Unlike most of his detectives, he never called her by her last name – it made him feel too much like he was doing a bad Bogart impersonation.

"Tetrault and I are at the Fillup on Eighth and Euclid with a DB in the washroom. Male, Caucasian, seventeen. Head's bashed in. Might be gang related."

"Okay, I'll be down in twenty minutes. Who's on the scene?"

"CSU just rolled in. The ME is en route."

"Okay. Let the techs do their stuff but don't let them move the body until I get there. I'll be down as soon as I can."

Mann had been dressing as he talked and walked back across the room to press the disconnect button. That was all he needed, a gang killing. So far, they had been lucky with the gang situation. Some parts of Kesle were hip deep in gang related crimes but his three Divisions had been free of that curse for the most part. He prayed that this was just a related case.

Truth was, like the Mob hits of years past, not too many cops really cared if the gangs killed each other off. Most welcomed the cleaning of the gutters. But, unlike the Mob, who made precision hits, these idiots barely had the brains to use their guns as clubs. They didn't use a single .22 to the temple. These cowards just held down the trigger on their automatic weapons and hoped to hit their target. Whoever or whatever got in the way of the spray was just a couple extra bullets that they had stolen in the first place. Things usually escalated and innocents always got dragged into the fray. He didn't need this.

Mann left his third floor walkup and stopped in at the deli for a bagel and a Pepsi on his way to his car. He drove while he opened the twist cap one-handed with the bottle clamped between his legs. The streets were just beginning to get busy but he made good time. The station was on the edge of Southfield Division where it butted against Central. Two or three blocks between him and an extra forty-five minutes of sleep. Mann wheeled his Ford around the corner onto Eighth and took the wide Avenue up six blocks. He double-parked next to an Escort that he recognized from the Pool at the Division.

"Lieutenant!"

Mann acknowledged Tetrault and Kydd with a curt wave before leaning back into his car to get his bagel. He thought better of it and just grabbed the Pepsi. Mann ducked under the barrier tape and met the two detectives in the middle of the lot. Tetrault immediately launched into apologies.

"Sorry to get you out, Lou. I hope you haven't wasted your time," he said, giving Kydd a look. "Pretty routine, really."

An ass kisser destined for political greatness and detective mediocrity, Tetrault had relied on Mann being upset at the early callout. Yet another strike for Tetrault. Mann hated politics and despised the second grade detective. One of these days, he would get enough reason to transfer him out of the Division.

"It would have been your ass if you hadn't." Mann turned to Kydd and asked, "What've you got?"

Tetrault was still busy thinking of a way to claim credit when Kydd launched into her report.

"At four fifteen, the kid on the till called 911." Kydd pointed over to the enclosed cash area. "That's him over there, the tall one. The short, fat guy is the station manager. He got here a few minutes ago. Anyway, the kid says he's got a dead body in the john. Patrol responded and arrived at four-thirty-three, checked the body, called EMS and then us. EMS declared him at four forty two. We were on the scene at four fifty six.

"ID on the kid makes him one Luis Gabel, seventeen. He's wearing colors but I don't recognize the gang. He has 'Intimidators' on his vest and the back of his head is caved in. Appears that someone bashed his head against the wall while he was sitting on the toilet. No signs of a struggle and no weapons at the scene. No signs of theft and still had his wallet in his pants pocket. Not much in it, driver's license, school ID and twenty seven dollars in cash. He also had a home rolled smoke of questionable vintage in his vest pocket."

Mann waited a moment but Tetrault cleverly refrained from adding anything. Mann glanced over at the black car of the Medical Examiner. Kydd followed his glance. "ME got here about five minutes before you. I relayed your message. I was told to tell you that they would wait for half an hour, unless the body moved itself."

Mann smiled. Alf Buchanan was either starting early or just ending his night.

As Mann turned toward the washroom, a bright red jeep bounced its front tire over the curb and parked. Behind the wheel, he caught the flash of even redder hair and grimaced. Danett Wood. "Damn," he said aloud.

"News travels fast, eh Lou?" Kydd said.

"Too damn fast. Come on Shane, let's get rid of this nuisance first and then I'll see the body."

Kydd watched Danett Woods get out of the jeep and flip the seat forward. Danett, who worked for Channel Five, the local ABC affiliate, was one of the new breed of reporters. News for the MTV set, Kydd thought, remote newscasts with lots of blood, guts and rock & roll – FlashCams. They were basically a good-looking voice with a shoulder camera. The reporting usually had all the depth of a Roadrunner cartoon. But they had been around for a while and showed no signs of disappearing.

Danett pulled the heavy camera out of the back seat with one practiced lift. She's stronger than she looks, Kydd thought. Kydd glanced at Mann and saw him admiring Danett. One of the original FlashCams, Danett, at 35, was getting a little long in the tooth for the job. She was still very pretty, in a kind of severe way. And she still had a great ass.

And too good at her job, thought Kydd. Flashcam or not, she *was* an actual investigative reporter. If she was showing up, you could bet that tight little ass that she smelled the gang angle.

Kydd envied Danett's long legs as she easily stepped over the tape barrier. Long legs and a great ass, everything Kydd lacked. Bitch.

Danett had already spotted Mann and was heading in his direction. Mann waved the patrolman off as he hurried over to belatedly preserve the crime scene.

"Lieutenant Mann," she called over, "little early to be out and about, isn't it?"

No record light, yet. Maybe he was actually getting a break? "Barely enough time for my beauty sleep," Mann called back.

"It shows." Danett set the camera on her shoulder, tightened the focus and the red light blinked on. So much for a break. "Lieutenant Mann, what can you tell us about the murder?"

"I have only arrived on the scene myself. We will have an official statement in due course."

"Have you identified the body?"

"We have made a preliminary identification but are awaiting notification of next of kin," Mann said.

Danett obviously expected the answer and was already talking. "Our sources say that there is a suspected gang connection. Would you care to comment?"

Kydd heard Mann curse. The woman's connections were frustrating, her "anonymous" sources too reliable.

Conscious of the camera still rolling, Mann quickly formed the standard answer. "At this time, we are investigating all possibilities. Anything else we can give you, Detective Tetrault will be more than happy to provide."

Danett dropped the camera off her shoulder. "Come on, Mann. Give me something before everybody else gets here."

"Like I said, Detective Tetrault will give you everything we can."

Danett stared hard at Mann. As she shouldered the camera and turned it on Tetrault, she muttered "stupid flatfoot" just loud enough for Mann to hear.

Mann nodded Kydd toward the washroom. "Do you know the difference between a Flashcam and a vulture, Detective Kydd?"

"No, sir," Kydd answered dutifully.

"Nail polish."

Mann was rather pleased with himself. In one action, he had taken care of both the reporter and Tetrault. He knew that viewing the scene with Kydd, the junior detective of the team, was a slap in the face to Tetrault. However, it might make him realize that he had to actually do some detective work and not just kiss ass. Besides, he knew Danett despised Tetrault as much as he did.

"Jesus, what a stench," Mann swore. "Tell me that wasn't one of our guys!"

"Nope, that would be courtesy of the kid that found the recently deceased," replied Alfred Buchanan. The Chief Medical Examiner for the city was leaning over the body as Mann entered the washroom.

Mann scanned the floor between the door and the body. There were several circles drawn in chalk around brownish drops of dried liquid with the usual plastic tent signs marking the evidence. He looked over at the technician from CSU standing in the corner and raised his eyebrows. "Floors clean, Lieutenant. We vacuumed it first thing but it doesn't look promising. Way too many people through here since it was cleaned last decade."

Buchanan looked up as Mann approached. His half glasses were perched low on his nose and his face was red from bending over. Once again, Mann wondered how much longer the old man could last in his job. He should have retired years ago but refused to leave. The city did not press him; they couldn't afford to lose the best ME they'd ever had. Painfully, Buchanan straightened and came over to Mann, not offering his hand.

"This young lady get you out of bed?"

Reading the surprised look on Kydd's face, Buchanan smiled. "Well, it couldn't have been that other idiot."

Kydd blushed slightly so Mann stepped into the silence. "What are you doing working a scene like this?"

"I finally got Kendall's ass into the OR. I told him that I would cover for him personally so he would take the time off. Truth is, there isn't anyone else anyway."

Buchanan took a personal interest in all his technicians. Few complained about his *mother hen* management style and most gratefully accepted it, just for the opportunity to work with him.

"So, what have you got for me?"

"I have a dead boy whose name was Luis Gabel, 17."

"Heard all that. Tell me about his last minutes."

"Somebody beat his head against the wall."

"That killed him?"

"Didn't do him a lot of good. So, Dick Tracy, what's your read?"

"Doesn't look like a gang killing. I'd guess homosexual. No signs of a struggle. The kid's on the can, perp in front getting a BJ and grabs a handful of hair and thud. The perp's only worry would be not getting his pecker bit off."

"The man is a regular Sherlock Holmes," Buchanan said to Kydd. "I always was impressed with his keen mind even if his vocabulary is questionable."

"Uh-huh, so what did I miss?" Mann said, shaking his head.

"Not sure that the blows against the wall killed him. Take a look at the wall."

Mann moved around Buchanan and studied the wall. The tiles had cracked in several places where the skull had connected with the wall leaving bits of hair, flesh and brain trapped in the cracks. Mann shrugged. "Ya, so? What is it? Cement block under those tiles? Looks like a solid hit to me."

"Very solid. Too solid for the amount of blood. The first couple of blows should have bled like a bugger. Lots of splatter until the heart stopped. Then, there's the blood trail. Could be from the perp's pecker but I doubt it. Most likely it is the victim's blood."

"You figure a dump?"

Buchanan shrugged. "I'm still deciding. There are bits of what look like evergreen needles in his hair. And, look at the toes of his boots."

Mann bent down and studied the leather cowboy boots. They were fairly new except at the toes. The toes were scuffed. "Looks fresh."

"Very. My bet is someone carried him like a drunken buddy, holding him up straight. You want a stiff to look alive, carry him that way. Normally takes a fair bit of strength to hold up the dead weight but look at this kid. He's lucky if he runs 110."

Mann looked over at the CSU man. "Dust the vest."

Mann walked outside and took a drink of Pepsi. Kneeling down, he scanned the parking lot to see if he could see the blood trail. Dawn was still just a promise on the horizon and there wasn't enough light. The lot was full of cars so if the body came by car, the car would have been parked a fair distance from the washroom. But why here?

Mann watched the CSU team doing a sweep across the parking lot with flashlights. "How'd the guy get in?"

"The attendant says that nobody borrowed the key but the door is often left open."

Mann stood silently and watched the reporters gathering outside the inner barrier.

It didn't feel right for gang bangers. Not their style with the head beating and the dump in a washroom. Gang killings were public, noisy things. If they were sending a message, and they were always sending a message, you put the body on display.

No, it just smelled wrong. Or was that just wishful thinking?

Chapter 3

Safe.

Preston let the water beat down on him, adjusting it just a bit hotter so his skin took on a deepening flush. He relaxed and slumped against the side of the shower stall.

Suddenly, he straightened. Slapping the water off, he stood listening. He waited, sure that he had heard a banging on his front door. As silently as possible, he pulled the shower curtain aside and stepped out of the shower. Snatching up his glasses but ignoring a towel, he tiptoed out of his bathroom and down the front hall toward his apartment door. He looked through the peephole into the hallway.

Instead of what he expected, the hallway was empty. Listening carefully, he heard another thud farther down the hall. Stretching high on his toes to look down through the peephole he could barely make out the edge of the newspaper lying in front of his door. He exhaled loudly and sucked in another breath. He took another look through the peephole. Cracking the door open slightly, he reached through and grabbed the newspaper.

Holding the newspaper, he shivered and looked down at the puddle of water on the tile floor. He flipped through and pulled out the sports section. He laid it on the floor to soak up the water and took the rest of the paper to the dining room table. He glanced at the front page and was saddened to see the story was not there.

Realizing he was still dripping, he stepped back into the bathroom and quickly toweled dry. He slipped on a pair of hospital OR pants. Up until last night, that had been one of his bigger crimes, stealing the pants from the hospital. But everyone did it so it wasn't really a crime, right?

Returning to the dining room, he started to flip through the newspaper, scanning each page for the story. The first time, he flipped quickly through the paper. The second time, he spent longer scanning each page. The third time, he even went back to the front door and looked through the wet sports section.

How could the story not even be in the newspaper?

He rubbed his eyes and tried to focus on the newspaper. Sleep had eluded him last night. Not that he had wanted to sleep. He hadn't even tried.

He could feel the returning warmth and let his hand slip down to the crotch of his pants as he replayed the night.

He had killed someone. He had actually *killed* someone! Accident or not, that kid was Dead. Dead with a capital D. Dead by his *hand*.

He had hoped, but not really expected, to see the story on the front page but he was sure there would be a story.

He glanced down at the *Kesle Daily Post*. How could they just ignore his first killing? Like it hadn't even happened? Like the body wasn't even there?

Wasn't there – yet!

"Of course!" he said aloud, slapping his hands together. They didn't find the body yet or at least not in time for the newspaper.

He stepped into the living room – which meant he stepped off the linoleum and onto the carpet that marked the division between the dining room and the living room. He walked over to the couch and snatched up the remote. He flicked the television on and turned to the local television station. The early morning news show was already started so he settled back on the couch and waited, his free hand still down his pants.

He had to wait a few minutes but he was soon rewarded with a very short news story about the killing. They called it a suspected gang killing. The entire piece lasted less than thirty seconds.

He couldn't believe it, thirty seconds! Why was the story so short? Very disappointing. Didn't his first killing merit a longer story than that? Where were the fifteen minutes of fame Andy Warhol had promised?

Well, it is only your FIRST kill.

True. But still. *Suspected gang killing?* What the hell was that? But what did he expect from the dickhead cops anyway?

Be honest, you thought they were breaking down the door while you were in the shower.

"Okay, sure, maybe for like one second, I was worried."

He had been in a sweat when he got home. Ricocheting between total exhilaration and mind numbing fear but the panic had passed quickly. There was no link between him and the kid. There were no witnesses and no way to connect him with the body.

The perfect crime.

Glancing at the clock, he realized he had to hurry and get himself to work. God, how could he be expected to work when he had just killed someone? Didn't they usually give you time off for something like that?

"I need a better union," he said, chuckling to himself.

* * * * *

Preston settled into his chair and sipped his coffee. He slid down in his office chair as he heard someone walking by. He could hear the muffled footfalls on the carpeted floor as the person moved away from his cubicle. That is the way he always liked it – just let them walk on by. Maybe one of the cleaners? No, too late for that. Normally, not many of his co-workers got in as early as he did but he was later today. He usually arrived early and left late. He was conscientious about his work. And, yes, he admitted, it made it easier to avoid running into anyone. That eliminated the awkward goodbyes when the rest of the office was going for a drink and he wasn't invited.

Avoiding people had been his life.

How much of his life had he spent scurrying from one safe place to another?

But was anywhere safe?

Why not make your world safer?

Ignoring that voice, he slipped his lunch into his desk drawer beside the latest novel he was reading. Both his lunch and the book would reappear again precisely at noon. Since he wasn't doing outside inventories today, he would eat his sandwiches and read the book at his desk rather than risk the lunchroom. Eating with the others was just asking for trouble.

And he had enough trouble.

He closed his tired eyes but still felt the excitement of last night. He was just reliving the sound of the boy's head hitting the wall when he heard the loud voice.

"PeePee!"

Preston jumped and spilled coffee on his shirt and tie. He stared up at Jake "The Jakester" Wilson. The name never came out as PP in Preston's head. It always came out as PeePee, a name that had haunted him since Mrs. Muroka's Grade Two class. Stricken with a kidney infection and high fever, he had stood too long in the line at Mrs. Muroka's desk, waiting for permission to use the washroom. Right there, at the front of the class, he had wet his pants.

He had run to the washroom and never gone back to class. His teacher thought he had gone home. His father was too drunk to notice he wasn't there until his mother finished the afternoon shift. Eventually, a janitor found him slumped in the bathroom, the infection and a raging fever almost shutting down his kidneys.

And PeePee had chased him his entire life since.

* * * * *

"Jesus, Peterson, you in there?" Jake said, his unmistakable bray booming down the hallway between the cubicles.

Jake Wilson shook his head at the pathetic blubber sitting in front of him. Since Peterson had started, Wilson had targeted the useless prick. Some jerks, Jake had told his friends, just screamed to be taken advantage of. It was like the nature channel. There were the lions and there were the antelopes. Jake was a lion and Peterson was an antelope, a really lame antelope. And there was no herd to separate him from since he just didn't belong anywhere.

"Earth to Peterson!" Jake slapped Preston's cheek, hard enough to turn the flabby skin red and was rewarded with the usual little girl squeak. Jake remembered that first day when Preston had made some smart-ass comment, actually correcting Jake's grammar like some old schoolmarm. The fat twat just had to make out as if he was smarter than everyone else. Jake had feinted a punch and Peterson had actually ducked and let out a little girl scream. It was so perfect. Even the boss had spit out coffee, laughing so hard.

"Are you with me, Peterson?"

"Sorry, yes Jake. What do you need?"

"What I don't need is you on my softball team," Jake replied. "I mean, you can get the beer but I don't want you playing. Your leg is too sore, right?"

"My leg?" Preston asked.

"Jesus, are you stupid?" Jake asked. He kicked Peterson hard in the right shin. "There, that leg. Remember the injury now? Or do I have to remind you again?"

Jake could see Peterson fighting back the tears. "No, Jake. I remember now. I hurt my leg and couldn't possibly play. I'm really sorry to be letting the team down."

Jake laughed again. "Good little PeePee. But you'll remember the beer, right?"

"Yes, Jake."

Preston finally let himself rub his throbbing shin as Jake disappeared into the lunchroom. He felt his body relax as he realized he and his buddies would be in scarping down donuts and coffee for a while before starting work.

* * * * *

As the tension left his body, anger began to replace the fear. And the anger built until the familiar rage began to course through his body.

So are you angry with them or yourself? Mad Dog Killer...sure. Except you break out in a sweat when Jake walks in the room. Just like all the guys that have bullied you all your life.

But I have killed! I *am* a killer.

Mad Dog Killer...sure. Provided there is orange juice for someone to slip on.

He's still dead. I am responsible. It wasn't totally an accident.

Especially if he wasn't dead when you took him into the bathroom.

But he was sure dead after I beat his little pissant head against that wall. All those squishy thuds. God, he had enjoyed that sound. He had been fantasizing and masturbating for many years but he had never come like he did last night. He had finally got even with one of his tormentors.

He could feel the power surging through him. The power over life and death was in his hands.

Try anything like that with Jake and he would beat the crap out of you.

Preston looked down at his stomach and tried to tuck in the shirt that was always slipping out. That and the perpetual layer of fat had always made him look doughy.

But he didn't need strength. Strength was nothing against a superior brain. And he had the superior brain. Surprise and guile. They would never see him coming. The rest was simple. Some tape, some handcuffs. It would all be so easy.

He felt the hardness returning as he fantasized about what he could do to Jake.

And who would be top of the suspect list? Let's see, hmmmm, maybe Jake's tormented co-worker?

Preston could hear them all now. "Oh yes officer, he always hated Jake. I wouldn't be surprised if he finally just snapped."

Last night was the Perfect Crime because there was nothing to link him to the victim. How do you follow a trail that doesn't exist?

Of course, he couldn't kill anyone that he *knew*. That would be stupid. He was anything but stupid – not with an IQ in the genius range. Isn't that what they had said in High School?

What did that get you, genius? Just more bullying and torment along with a loser dead-end job?

"Now that's a group that deserves to die!"

For a second, Preston barely realized he had talked aloud. His deep, confident voice made him smile even if he barely recognized it.

Yes, if anyone deserved to die, it was the bullies from school. They had tormented him for years and years. Oh yes, they definitely deserved to die in painful and humiliating ways.

And none of them would be traced to you, right genius? All your old classmates start dropping dead and the trail leads right to the loser of the graduating class.

Still, there had to be a way to feel this power again and punish his tormentors.

Chapter 4

The constant buzzing barely roused Mann and he jabbed at the speaker button on the telephone. The dial tone added to the noise of the alarm and finally woke him. He reached up and shut off the alarm and the telephone before settling back in the pillow.

Yesterday had been a bitch. He hated early starts to begin with. But the body in the washroom had generated meetings with the brass. Nobody liked the idea of gangs coming into Southfield. That meant finding a solution that eliminated the gang angle. God save him from investigations directed from the top.

Then, they had fished a body out of the South Bay. Port Authority set speed records handing that one over to Southfield. And then just as quickly he lost it.

Three days before, a runner for a local coke dealer had his face blown away on a small yacht in the marina in High Bluffs. High Bluffs Division was one of the three divisions that Southfield Homicide covered. What should have been a routine case turned interesting when CSU turned up too much blood. The ME concluded that there should have been two bodies on that yacht.

When the Authority had pulled in the floater, they had notified Southfield. The floater's blood type matched the blood found on the upper deck. They would have to wait on the DNA for confirmation but they were pretty confident that they had found the second vic. Kesle didn't get that many bodies in the Bay with shotgun wounds.

Mann already had two shooters he thought were good for the killing. According to rumor, the cocaine runner and his partner had been cutting into the market behind Angelino's back. No doubt in Mann's mind that Angelino had ordered the hit and even less doubt who had done the job.

Mann's detectives had been searching for the duo when headquarters yanked the case out of their Division. The Mayor's favorite political cop had stepped in and the Special Organized Crime Unit got the case. Mann had fought to keep it. He owed Angelino and had vowed to bring the murdering bastard down. But what SOCU wanted, SOCU got.

Mann sighed and rolled over, sensing the weight in the bed beside him. Last night slowly came back to him. He had trouble remembering from one night to another if she was going to be there but you'd think he'd remember the next morning. She'd arrived late and brought Chinese. Fifteen minutes to devour the food and then they both fell into an exhausted sleep. Some romance.

A single apartment would help solve the problem. Four years of deciding whose place they use that night. His emergency clothes stashed in half a drawer at her place; half a closet of her clothes here.

Maybe they could get a house with a deck in the back yard. A place with a big BBQ that could handle a half dozen real steaks rather than that piece of tin crap on his balcony. Maybe even a pool. He could imagine her stepping out of the water, her bikini clinging to her body.

He shifted his weight as gently as possible and turned to face her. She was lying on her side and facing away from him, still asleep, her breathing regular. He reached out and stroked the soft hair that fell across the pillow. He could still smell her perfume, dark and warm after a night's sleep. He felt a stirring between his legs. He slipped his hand under the sheet and snaked his arm around her waist. He let the hand slide up and gently cupped her naked breast in his hand.

"Take it somewhere else, Mann."

Her voice startled him and he pulled his hand back. Then, he moved closer, spooning his body along hers. He parted her hair and kissed the nape of her neck. He whispered as he kissed. "Baby, don't you love me?"

Suddenly, she threw the sheets off both of them and stood up. She was only wearing a tiny thong. Her full breasts were firm, her nipples puckered in the chill air. She had a figure Mann had fantasized about all his teenage life. Even the shock of cold could not dampen his desire.

"Forget it. I'm still pissed about yesterday. Just tell your *little* friend we aren't playing. Dumping that dickweed Tetrault on me while you bounce off with Detective Tits. You can just suffer for a while." Danett turned and walked to the bathroom and shut the door.

* * * * *

Giving up on more sleep, Mann turned up the radio and wandered into the kitchen. He looked into the refrigerator for a Pepsi but there were none. He briefly considered a glass of water or juice. Instead, he just threw another case into the fridge. Taking a can out of the case, he popped the top and took a drink of the warm Pepsi as he headed back to the bedroom.

Dani's camera was sitting in its usual spot on the chair pointed toward the bed. Briefly, he wondered if the camera was ever on while they were making love.

Just the thought of his body on camera made him straighten and suck in his gut. His stomach was starting to run to the heavy side. Not much in the way of a six-pack left – probably because of the 12 pack of Pepsi he drank every day. Not exactly fat yet but he definitely headed that way. He should talk to Blaak and have him set up on some kind of program. Whatever program he used worked for the young detective. Course, Blaak was a good fifteen or so years younger. "Damn."

"Same to you." Dani appeared in the doorway wearing a robe. "Coffee?"

"I'm fine," he replied, holding up the Pepsi.

"I meant, did you make any?" Dani made a noise of disgust and left the room. "Why do I even bother?"

Mann forced himself to sit on the floor and started doing sit-ups. After three, he decided to wait for Blaak's program before getting too involved. He went into the bathroom to shave and shower instead. By the time he was done and sitting on the bed, Dani returned with a takeout coffee. His trench coat had replaced the robe. "You were out of coffee, as usual. I had to go to the store."

"Sorry."

"Are you still suffering?"

"I'll survive."

"Think so, do you? Maybe I should really punish you."

Dani dropped the trench coat. She was naked, very naked. With an animal cry, she pounced on him.

Later, they had another shower, together.

Chapter 5

Ed Buma, the Desk Sergeant at Southfield Division motioned to Mann as he came through the doors. He held up one finger and continued his telephone conversation. While he talked, he searched through a pile of papers on the desk. As he put the phone down, he said, "Buchanan called. Says he's free for an early lunch if you are. He's got a run down on the Gabel post."

It took Mann a minute to place the name of the kid from the gas station. "Thanks, Ed. Anything else?"

"Not here," he said, jerking his thumb upwards. "Lots upstairs."

Mann considered for a moment. Kydd and Tetrault had already requested four uniforms to continue the canvass of the neighborhood around the gas station. Now that he had lost the marina investigation, all other current investigations were covered. "Nothing yet. How's the wife?"

"Fine thanks. Doctor says she is going to be home by the end of the week."

"You give her my best. You still don't want any time? I can talk to Walsh for you."

"Thanks anyways. The wife's mother is coming in from Seattle. Me and her and a loaded gun? If I'm gonna see you guys at a crime scene anyway, I might as well work."

Mann smiled and waved his hand as the telephone rang again. Buma picked it up and Mann turned toward the elevator. That was the way with the true lifers, Mann thought. For some it was a job, others a career – a stepping-stone to something political or private. But for the real cops it was a life. Buma loved his wife but it would kill him to stay away from the station. Buma was a lifer. His wife knew it and accepted it. If she didn't, they would already be divorced like so many others.

Mann knew the symptoms. The job had cost him his marriage and his two boys.

His mood instantly soured at the thought of his two sons. It was seven years, no almost eight, since he had seen them and not so much as a letter. But some day, he would see them again. Somehow, he would redeem himself in their eyes. He couldn't believe he could fall from hero to hated so fast, so completely. And all it took was the quiet whispers of their mother and a very biased judge.

Mann stepped through the opening elevator doors and was immediately distracted from his depression by the wall of walking banker's boxes.

"Hey Gregg," came a deep voice from behind the stack of three boxes. Mann didn't have to see behind the boxes to recognize the voice. Only Sergeant Brant Davis had the strength and arm length to carry three of the heavy file boxes at once. Davis was second in command of Mann's homicide squad and Mann's best friend. At six foot five and all muscle, Davis could easily handle the boxes but Mann had to get the dig in.

"You know, we have these carts that you can use to move those things."

"Ya but one of the Robbery guys was using it and I didn't want to wait. It's only three boxes anyway. I'll tell you though, the way the boys worked me last night on the court, I maybe should have waited for the cart."

"Giving the old man some grief, are they?" Mann asked.

"Making me feel my age, that's for sure. I'm on the cusp of having my kids beat me for real…no more throwing the game to make them feel good."

The door slid open and Mann put his hand against the edge to hold it.

"It's okay; I'm going up to the conference room to put this out for the Deputy DA. He wants to prepare for the trial next week and make sure nothing is missing."

"All right. I'll catch up with you later to go over the Marina thing," Mann said, stepping out and walking through the door of the squad room.

Kesle PD Homicide Two was stenciled on the smoked glass. Kesle had 14 Divisions and Five Homicide squads divided between them. Mann was the Lieutenant in charge of the second busiest Homicide squad in the city. How he got there was still a mystery but somewhere he had an angel. That gave some balance to the devil that haunted him.

The squad room was almost empty when he walked in. He looked around at the empty desks. The unassigned board was blank. He needed to get some more bodies back in before they had another hit on the board. At the end of the room was a large urn of coffee. Likely an hour old, it already smelled strong and acidic. Thank God he never learned to like the stuff. Passing the coffee, he walked over to fridge and grabbed a Pepsi from his stash. Thinking about the warm Pepsi from this morning, he put another 12-pack in the fridge. Then, he remembered Blaak.

"Blaak, my office."

"Sure, thing, L T."

Mann smiled. Blaak was the only one on his squad who didn't call him Lou. Lou was the standard short form in the department. L T was more common in the military. Blaak had come to him via Military Intelligence. A good cop but he was Marine through and through. He still kept up the physical fitness regime of the Marines and was one of the best-conditioned detectives in the department. Not necessarily an incredible accomplishment considering the competition but he looked damn good.

Another mystery Mann had never solved – why Blaak had decided to get out of the military. If anyone was destined for the military it was Blaak. However, the military was not a subject you discussed with Blaak. He became a wall as soon as the subject came up.

"What can I do for you, sir?"

"Blaak, you work out a fair bit, right?"

"Yes, sir. A bit, sir."

Mann looked at the broad shoulders straining against the detective's shirt and smiled. "Think you could get me on a program?"

Blaak warmed immediately. "Absolutely. If you come down to the gym with me some time, I would love to set something up for you. You just name the time."

Mann was pleased. This was the first time Blaak had ever said anything to him without ending his sentence with "sir". Respect was one thing but enough was enough. "See, you can do it."

"Sir?"

"You got through three sentences without saying sir."

"Sorry, sir. Won't happen again, sir," Blaak replied, but he was smiling. He liked and respected Mann but some habits were hard to break. Besides, he did respect Mann and that was his way of showing it.

"By the way, are you still posing for the calendar?"

"Yes, sir, if you think that it's all right."

"Why not? It's good charity and not bad public relations – especially if we can beat the sales of the FD."

The department was putting together a beefcake calendar to try to better public relations and compete with the Fire Department. Blaak had been an obvious choice. Mann had immediately approved the request but was more interested in what Blaak's mystery woman thought. Rumor was, the detective was seeing an older woman, although nobody had ever seen her.

"What does your lady friend think about it?"

"She's quite proud of me, sir. As long as I keep some clothes on. I guess she figures it doesn't pay to advertise too much."

"Ya, right," Mann said. Pulling out the day sheet, he moved back to business. "What's doing?"

"I'm on that Visions stakeout. As a matter of fact, I should be leaving if that is all, sir."

"Sure, go ahead. I'll arrange some time in the gym with you in the next week or so."

"Don't leave it too long, sir," Blaak warned as he left.

Alone again, Mann sat behind his desk trying to decide what to do first. He poked at a stack of paperwork, almost hoping it would topple off his desk into the garbage can. God save him from paperwork and get him back on the street. The warm spring weather was making him restless. Maybe that was what had got into Dani this morning. He grinned at the pleasing memory. The smile quickly faded as he opened the first file.

Chapter 6

Mann slid into the booth and reached across the table to shake hands with Buchanan. "Thanks for taking time for me, Alf."

Buchanan shrugged. "I had to eat. I figured that you might have some questions that the report didn't cover – no offense to Kydd. She carried herself well and her voice is incredible."

"Really? I hadn't noticed."

"Bullshit. How's that redhead terror doing? She still putting up with you or was it just temporary insanity?"

"She's just fine, thanks. How's..."

The waitress interrupted Mann and they both ordered. As usual, Buchanan's order was full of calories, grease, and cholesterol. Mann tried for a salad and a Pepsi. He ignored Buchanan's questioning look and continued after the waitress left.

"How's Gretchen?"

"Gretchen? Oh, Gretchen. I haven't seen her in two weeks or more. I'm seeing a secretary from The Hill. We are going to go sailing in the summer."

"If it lasts that long." The old man amazed Mann. A widower who had desperately loved his wife, he had not wasted any time becoming active again. However, he didn't, as he put it, waste his time with young women. He much preferred mature women. According to him, they were more appreciative. He didn't bother with a woman unless she remembered that there had been another Bush in the White House.

"I heard they pulled the marina shooting. SOCU grab it? Got you pissed off?"

"I haven't shot anyone yet. What the hell, as long as somebody puts that Italian bastard away."

An older lady at the next table looked over and said something to the woman she was with. They both looked over again. Mann just stared back until the waitress came between them. When she left, the women had returned to their meal.

Mann pushed his salad around the plate. After sampling some of the cottage cheese, he reached across and speared one of Buchanan's fries. "What did you find when you opened the boy up?"

Mann's voice was just loud enough to carry to the next table. Buchanan glanced sideways and spoke at the same volume.

"First, what we didn't find. No major amount of drugs in his system, just trace amounts marijuana and cocaine. He wasn't high when he died. From the amounts, I would say he was in complete control of his faculties. As much as he probably ever was, anyway."

"Was there any evidence of homosexual activity?"

"None that I could see. No recent sexual activity as far as the boy is concerned. Rectum was normal, no signs of prolonged homosexual activity. I would say that the kid was either not active or straight and he tested negative for AIDS."

Mann heard the intake of breath from the table beside and smiled. "So it wasn't a gay bashing?"

"Straights have been bashed as gays before. There was even a case where a man and his wife – she had short hair and small breasts – were attacked as gays. Gabel was slight, longish hair, bit of a twink, I suppose. However, I don't have much faith in that explanation. For one thing, the beating wasn't severe, except for the head wounds. And that was definitely post-mortem. Usually, you see more damage with a gay bashing."

"Was this a gang killing?"

Buchanan gave up and shoved his plate of fries between him and Mann. "If it was, it was one of the strangest on record. He died from a blow to the back of the head. No knife wounds, not much bruising, nothing that would suggest that he tried to defend himself."

"Did someone whack him from behind before he knew what was going down?"

"Definitely not."

"You're that sure?"

"About that, yes. Let me lay it out for you."

Buchanan began to shift the plates around the table. The women were blatantly staring now. "This is the washroom. This is the south entrance on Euclid. This is the little garden patch."

Mann pictured the station lot in his mind. "I remember. Kydd said that you knew for sure that the body had been moved. You followed the blood trail?"

"Yes, but at the time, we didn't know for sure who's blood it was. Confirmed it was all the vic's. Anyway, let me show you how it worked."

Buchanan pointed at the plate representing the washroom. "The trail went from the garden to the washroom. CSU searched the garden and came up with our murder weapon – a rock."

"Somebody tossed it there?"

"No, it was buried with only about thirty percent above ground. It was in the dirt, solid and deep, so it hadn't been moved in years. But it had a good point on it and there was blood on the rock and surrounding ground. We even got some hair."

"You ruling this accidental or maybe a fight?"

"On the accident side, there appears to be fresh orange juice on the vic's boots and pants with some spatter on the sidewalk. Maybe he slipped in it or maybe he spilled it himself. We'll know if he was drinking any later today. If it was a fight, there wasn't much to it. No evidence of the vic having landed any blows. Whatever put him down did it fast and with enough force to put that rock into his skull. He didn't have a chance to throw a single punch. That sounds like a fall. I'd rule it accidental, except for what happened post-mortem."

"So the kid lands on the rock and death is instant. And then, the body was moved to the washroom?"

"Actually, given the position of the body in the bathroom, something happened before the body was moved. There was some damage to the upper torso. Most likely, the perp landed several kicks to the midsection resulting in bruised ribs and contusions. All those injuries were post-mortem."

Buchanan mopped up gravy with his roll and poured more tea. "The interesting thing is the wounds on the back of the head. As I said, the initial wound was low and punched through the cerebellum and into the brain stem. The wounds from the wall were much higher. The beating in the washroom was vicious. You saw the cracked tiles. That was nothing compared to the condition of the skull itself. Whoever did it was pissed.

These were very personal injuries."

Mann shoved his salad plate aside and drank some Pepsi. "So, the kid was killed accidentally, then kicked repeatedly, then dragged to the washroom and then the back of his head was bashed in?"

"That's about it. He might have been pushed but I see no evidence of it."

"What about the time of death?"

"I'd put it somewhere between ten and two, give or take an hour. Because the bathroom door was open after the body was discovered, we couldn't get an accurate ambient temp."

"Kydd said that the attendant came on at eleven. The guy he replaced used the john before he left. So, it was between then and two or three?"

"My best guess is the closer to eleven, the better."

"Anything else?"

"CSU got a footprint out of the garden. The top layer of the garden was peat. It was pretty deep but not much detail."

Mann could picture someone lifting the kid, his foot sinking into the soft soil because of the added weight. Peat was useless for prints. He stared at Buchanan, realizing he was still no farther ahead. "Was it gang related or not?"

"I'm guessing the powers on The Hill have already answered that question for you," Buchanan said, smiling.

Chapter 7

When Mann got back to the squad, Kydd was questioning a young man wearing tattered jeans and a black T-shirt with a blazing skull etched across it. His hair was spiked on top and shaved to the skin on one side and hung past his shoulder on the other and the back. He also had three earrings in his left ear. Pimples dotted his face and he had what was, for him, probably a month's growth of splotchy beard. Mann wandered over and motioned Kydd away. Kydd, in return, motioned him over.

"Lieutenant Mann, this is Detective Phil Garnham."

The two detectives laughed at the expression on Mann's face. In his early days, when undercover Narcs were first entering the schools, they usually looked like exactly what they were. This creature might look like a cop to the kids but he doubted it.

"Nice to meet you, Lou. Detective Kydd was telling me that you might have some gang trouble in your area."

"Sorry, pleased to meet you too, Detective. You'll have to excuse the asinine expression on my face."

"No problem, sir. You should see what my dad says."

"Where are you working out of?"

"Officially, I'm out of The Hill. SNU. I work anywhere they can get me into school. I just transferred out of the school that Gabel attended. The school he was registered at, anyway."

"What can you tell us about the Intimidators?"

"Lame," Garnham said as he eased back onto the desk. "Anything *but* intimidating. Gabel was the leader but the Ints aren't a gang. They're a little boy's club for wanna-be losers with only four hardcore members, well, three now. They've been friends since diapers. They were together because nobody else would have anything to do with them. Occasionally, they get one or two other members but they soon drift off. Like I said, lame."

"Violence?"

Garnham laughed. "Only on the receiving end. They made some moves on a rival gang about a year ago. All four ended up in the hospital. Total pussies."

"They have a sheet?"

"Small time. Mostly they sit around talking about what they're going to do and smoke 'fry daddies' and drink a bit of 'swamp juice'."

"Sorry?" Mann said, feeling his age.

"Cigarettes laced with Crack and gin with fruit juice, light on the crack and heavy on the gin. B&E and some auto but the auto was strictly joyriding. They might deal a little crack but everybody is doing that. Unfortunately, I got nine and ten year olds dealing more than these pukes."

"So, they're nothing."

"Less than nothing, they are totally off the map. Too bigga losers to bother fighting let alone wasting one of them. They're just ignored. A bunch of wimps that hang together because nobody else will have them. They wouldn't even qualify as an initiation kill. They... Oh, Christ."

Mann had seen it the same moment Garnham had. Mann grabbed Garnham's collar with both hands and lifted the detective to his feet. In one smooth movement, he threw the smaller man across Kydd's desk.

Garnham was up in a second and flew back across the desk at Mann. He landed a glancing right across Mann's jaw. Mann turned his head to avoid most of the punch and let himself fall backwards. He stumbled back two steps and Garnham was on top of him. They struggled until two patrol officers pulled Garnham off and pinned him to the desk. They were not gentle putting on the cuffs.

"Take him downstairs. Put him in holding until I can get something on paper." Mann swung around and faced the three Intimidators Tetrault had been leading into the squad room. They had been cheering on Garnham. "Who are these three? You dickheads with this one?"

Faced with Mann's rage, the three cowered back and Tetrault stepped forward. "No, sir. They are friends of Gabel. I brought them in for a statement."

"Take them to Interrogation. Get them the hell out of my face!"

"Yes, sir."

Tetrault led them away and Mann went back to Kydd's desk. She had picked everything off the floor and was trying to straighten some files. "I'm sorry, Lou. We agreed we wouldn't pick those three up until tonight. Give them some time on the street. If it was a hit, they'd be scared enough to talk. I thought it would be safe to bring Garnham in."

"Solid plan." Mann gently touched his lower lip, feeling the swelling start, checking for blood. "I'll have a talk with Tetrault. Did you get anything out of Garnham that I didn't hear?"

"Just what he told you. It's not a hit. There's nobody taking credit and no reason to hit anybody that low on the food chain. It just doesn't track."

Mann nodded. "What about Gabel's family? Why haven't we seen them down here?"

Kydd searched through the papers on her desk. "Gabel was on probation for a B&E. He was on a midnight curfew. That is why he left the rest of his crew."

"Under parents' supervision?"

"Just one parent, his father. Mother's gone. His father isn't exactly broken up about the kid. Says he has been no good all his life. He has two younger kids who he wants to try and keep straight. My feeling is, this makes for one less bad influence."

"Or a good object lesson for the kids?" Mann asked, thinking about what Alf said about it being personal.

"That too. Solid alibi though," Kydd added, anticipating Mann's thinking. "Haven't finished the final checks but it should clear."

"Okay. Go down and make sure the uniforms know that Garnham is one of ours. I'll go see what else Tetrault is screwing up. Good work reaching out to Garnham. I'm marking the case open and pending for now but I'm beginning to think that it is a no go. Opinions?"

"Let me do a little more digging into his background. I might turn up an enemy with a big enough beef. The Three Stooges in there might know someone."

"OK, keep digging for a while. Oh," added Mann, feeling the lip swelling even more, "when you cut Garnham loose, thank him for pulling that punch."

* * * * *

Mann stalked into the interrogation room and banged the door shut. He stared at the three boys lounging behind the table. Leave it to Tetrault to put them all in one room. He let his anger at Tetrault show on his face and the boys reacted to it instantly. Mann wished Davis were here. Now that would be some intimidation for these losers.

Mann stared at them, sizing them up. The muscle had positioned himself to protect the smaller boy on the right. The one on the left, slouched and trying to look bored, was the new leader.

"You," Mann shouted, pointing to the kid on the right. He had pitched his voice loud enough that all three boys jumped. Unfortunately, so did Tetrault. The detective tried to cover it by jumping to his feet and grabbing the smallest boy and yanking him to his feet. The muscle started to stand but Mann stopped him with a quiet "Don't."

The muscle eased back into his chair.

"Hey," the new leader said, trying to assert himself. "We want a lawyer."

"Why?" Mann asked.

"It's our right," he said, almost making it a question.

"You aren't under arrest. You are here voluntarily to help us find your friend's killer. If you don't want to help, we can arrest you. When we get around to talking to you, in a few days, then you can have your lawyer. Detective, cuff this suspect. He has become uncooperative. Check his alibi again. Leave him cuffed to the chair for now and I'll decide what to do with him in an hour or so."

Tetrault shoved the smallest boy toward Mann and moved behind the leader. Mann grabbed the kid and started walking him from the room.

Mann took the boy into the next room and shoved him toward a chair.

Mann sat across the table from him and stared.

"What's your name, kid?" Mann finally asked.

"Fox," the kid replied.

"Do you know who killed Luis?" Mann asked quietly.

"If we knew, he would already be down," Fox said. "Ajax would do him. No way somebody's doin' Swan and getting' away with it."

Mann thought for a second, thinking the names sounded familiar. When he finally placed them, he fought to keep the smile off his face. Garnham could have warned him that the gang had grabbed their names from *The Warriors*. Truly a bunch of wannabes.

"What were you doing that night?" Mann asked.

"You know, nothin'. Just hangin'. It was a nice night so we were just walkin' 'cause our wheels were fucked and Vermin didn't have the money to make it right."

"Any hassles that night?"

"Nope," Fox said, not entirely convincing.

"Nobody on your case?"

"Nobody gets on the Intimidators' case. We get on theirs."

"Were you on anybody's case that night?"

"Nothin' major. You know, just making sure everybody knew we were there," Fox said.

That meant scaring some civilians, maybe some half-assed graffiti. He had to go at this another way.

"Swan much of a fighter?" Mann asked.

"Hey, we all bop with the best, you know."

Mann thought back to the movie. "Ajax is the best, right?"

"Sure, he's great. Split a head easy but Swan could take care of himself."

"So anybody coming up on Swan would have to be pretty big, right?"

"You know it. Swan wasn't big but he could fight. Or he'd stick the guy, you know?"

"Swan was packing?" Mann asked.

"Uh, well," Fox said, backtracking a bit.

"Come on, a gang like yours, I know you'd be packing."

"Ya, we have blades. None of us go anywhere without them. 'Cept here."

"What was Swan carrying?"

"Same as us, he had a Blackie Collins Thin Red Line. We each have the same blade."

Mann knew a knife wasn't among the kid's effects. Maybe these losers were going to be useful after all. Mann kept the interview going for a while longer but got nothing. He cut all the Intimidators loose but told them he would be back at them if anything turned up.

Chapter 8

The three girls watched the dark haired man slide through the crowded bar. He smiled and nodded to a few people, expertly balancing his drink while dodging around the early evening patrons. He turned sideways to slip between two groups of drinkers, giving the girls a good view of his tight, jeans-clad butt.

"Ya, real hot. I'm still not looking anymore."

"It never hurts to look," Belinda said.

Christine's laugh was almost lost in the raucous noise. "Maybe. But why bother when you've got the hottest thing going waiting at home for you?"

However, she watched until the crowd swallowed him up. Belinda caught her eye when she looked back and Christine laughed guiltily.

Christine Yeck was out for one last drink as a single woman. In two days, she was to be married.

She suddenly smiled again and her small nose crinkled into what her fiancée called her *darling face*. God, she was happy.

"You're *really* going to go through with this?"

Christine turned her attention on Heidi. Twice married and twice divorced, Heidi was not a believer in marriage. "We've signed the lease on the apartment, the minister is sacrificing a goat or whatever they do in Jamaica, and our bags are packed. The day after we arrive in Montego, we hit the beach and we are husband and wife."

"Oh well, then you absolutely *have* to get married if you went to all that bother. But the rum better be good!" said Belinda.

Belinda waved for another round and Christine settled back in her chair. She could not stop smiling. Her life had never been better. She had been smiling since mid-morning when her boss had presented her with a wedding present – a promotion. She was now Divisional Head of the East Coast Section of Marketing and Sales. How would she fit all that on a business card?

"Will you please stop smiling?"

"You're just jealous, Bel."

Belinda pointed at the crowd of men at the bar. "I have a right to be jealous. Have you seen these losers? Christ, 99% of the population is gay, married or just too ugly for words!"

The three girls all stared at each other and then burst into uncontrollable laughter.

* * * * *

Preston was staring.

He tried to look casual but it was difficult.

How long had it been since he had seen her? He didn't want to think how many years it had been. She had hardly changed. She was still beautiful. She still looked as beautiful as the first day he fell in love with her.

As beautiful as the day she destroyed you.

He ignored that thought and watched her over the top of his drink. God, *Sandra Kew.* After all these years, there she was.

Squinting slightly, he could see her nose crinkle when she smiled. Just like before. Her nose had always crinkled when she laughed.

And, she always laughed at you.

How old had he been? High school? Almost, the summer before high school

* * * * *

He had spent the day at the library and got interested in a book. He was in the back where there were no clocks and little traffic – a place where he could go unnoticed. A place where he could hide. As if any of the Neanderthal jocks ever came into the library. But still – always better to be safe.

When the library lights flashed to signal closing time, he had been shocked. He should have left fifteen minutes earlier. The book had been so good. He loved books. He escaped in books. But this one had cost him. If he didn't hurry, it would cost him even more.

The fastest way home meant cutting through the schoolyard which was not his normal route, never his preferred route. The sight of the large red brick building pricked his senses. Tensing, he became more alert. He tried to stretch his senses as far as he could, watching for a flash of a coat. He listened for the pounding of the basketball. He couldn't see the courts but he should be able to hear the dull thud of the ball. He listened for the bicycles or laughter.

He heard them before he saw them.

Instinctively, he stopped and crouched behind a car at the curb. One of them came into view. He was on his bicycle, standing on the seat with one leg stuck out behind him.

Preston moved as fast as he could across the open space from one car to the next. His heart was beating. He only had seconds. He mustn't let his fear freeze him. Act now, he told himself. Using all the speed he had, he ran to the next car and stopped. He wondered if the explosion of laughter was directed at him. Carefully, he peeked over the car.

The group had appeared around the corner. There were six of them, four boys and two girls. The boys were on bikes, doing tricks for the girls. He heard "tether ball" drift across the street and knew where they were headed. He still had a chance, if he had the guts.

The tetherball pole was at this side of the school. If he looked to his right, he would be able to see it. They would play tether on their bikes. The girls would cheer them on and he could get by. He even had a choice.

The safest way would be to continue down the street to the gully. Once down the hill and in the trees, he would be safe. He could come up just two streets from his home. He would be home before he knew it. And, more importantly, before they knew it.

Except, it had rained for days. Today had been the first sun since Wednesday. The gully would be muddy and slippery. If he went home muddy, his father would not believe him about the library. His father would take one look at the mud and know he had been down in the gully. He could not tell his father *why* he had to go down in the gully. His father would call him a sissy. Then, his father would beat him.

Forget the gully.

That left the more dangerous route of the primary side of the school. He was really risking the bacon by going that way. All it would take would be for them to decide to go back around the school. Still, he had no other choice. He could go around the primary side and walk behind the bleachers. Once behind the bleachers, they wouldn't know it was him. He would be safe and almost home. He would arrive clean and no beatings tonight, thank you very much.

His keen mind, honed by years of hiding, had come to this conclusion in seconds. Before they could reach the tetherball and while they were still focused on their bike tricks, he moved. In a matter of heartbeats, he was safe with the school between him and them.

He listened carefully for anyone behind him. As he approached the final corner, the bleachers just yards ahead of him, he thought he heard a noise behind him. Looking behind, he was around the corner before he realized – and was looking straight at them.

Echoes. The echoes had betrayed him.

Panicking, he tried for the bleachers. He had barely leaned into his first step before the first bike skidded to a stop in front of him, kicking gravel onto his shoes. On his left was a huge puddle. He heard another bike coming up behind him and he started to spin around. He never even saw the foot aimed at is back.

He was jammed forward and went sprawling into the mud puddle, his glasses flying from his face. For a moment, he just stayed there, unable to move. He was covered in mud, his back ached from the kick and his chest hurt where he had landed on a rock.

"In the mud, right where you belong, porker!"

He slowly brought himself to his knees and searched the dirty water for his glasses. Putting them on his face, he tried to wipe the mud from the lenses but they just smeared. He didn't trust his voice – it would just crack and sound like he was going to cry. He struggled to his feet and started to walk. He just walked between two of the bikes and prayed. Then, he saw her – Sandra Kew.

He worshipped Sandra and knew that she loved him. Everyone was laughing but her. Amid the hoots and taunts, she was just standing there. Despite the pain, he straightened more. She would stick up for him and everything would be all right. She was popular and they would listen to her. All she had to do was admit that she loved him.

And then?

Then, even through the mud-streaked lenses of his thick glasses, he saw her nose. The nose that he loved so much began to crinkle. Just a bit, at first. Then more. Then, the laughter burst from her, spittle spraying from her mouth. Suddenly, she could barely stand, she was laughing so hard.

At you, always at you!

* * * * *

He looked over at Sandra's table.

He had welcomed the beating from his father that night because it helped to erase the sound of Sandra's laughter. The pounding of his heart in his ears helped to drown out the memory. Even the taste of the blood in his mouth was a relief from the bile that had risen since Sandra's betrayal. That little crinkle of her nose had crushed his world.

And now you can crush hers.

She looked over at him. He suddenly knew, with crystal clarity, that she had seen him. She had seen him and recognized him. And just like that day, she had turned against him. She was laughing at him, again. She was telling all her new friends about that day. She was telling them about the little mud baby. That is what her friend had been pointing at – him!

They were laughing at him. All his life, he had been laughed at.

His glasses. His weight. His walk. How smart he was. How bad he was at sports. It never ended.

Even Sandra. He loved Sandra and she ridiculed him. He could have given her so much. His very soul but she had crushed him.

How had she found him? How had she tracked him here? Why had she invaded this place, his one haven? The one place he didn't feel alone. He was always invisible but, at least here, he could almost feel like he belonged.

Now, he could never return.

It was always the same. The story would spread. Soon, people would be pointing him out and whispering. They would know about the puddle and the tears and the humiliation and they would laugh. He could never escape the laughter.

There is a way though, isn't there? A way to pay them back. A way to get even.

He clenched his fist. He clenched it so tight that his fingernails dug into his hand. He could feel the pain and something else.

He could feel the boy's hair in his fingers.

An electric chill passed down his back. Goosebumps broke out on his body. The sound of the wet thud and the crunch of bone erased the sound of laughter. Tiles cracking, bone splintering, blood and brains splattering. The power surged through his body.

Control, power and revenge, everything that had been denied him. His breath came rapidly and he felt light headed. Then, it happened. He slipped his hand into his jacket pocket and felt the knife. He held his breath. She stood talking to the others, her coat in her hand. They didn't move. With a final giggle, she turned away from the table. She was leaving and she was leaving alone.

The pissant boy had been good. He had felt so good.

But the boy wasn't real – just an accident.

True, it was an accident. He hadn't meant to kill the boy. He hadn't even known the boy.

He knew Sandra. It will be so much better this time.

The bar stool scraped loudly as he got up and left the bar while Sandra paid her tab.

Chapter 9

Cliff Degget was a happy man. He popped a beer and crossed the apartment to the narrow bed. Apartment, hell the place barely qualified as a room. Seven paces across. Two hundred and sixty-four trips across the room made a mile. And he had done his miles waiting for the call that was due tonight. He was finally going to connect with Angelino's number one guy. He was only one step from the boss of bosses. And that was closer than most criminals ever got to the man and light-years closer than any other cop!

Not bad for a poor black boy from the ghettos of Kingston, he thought, smiling at the invented persona.

Two long years of working his way through Kingston, Miami, and New Orleans and finally back to Kesle. He stretched out on the bed. Lucky he was short, he thought, as his feet hit the end of the bed. He drank down half the bottle of beer and let out a restless sigh.

Getting up again, he went over to his laptop and checked his latest bid on eBay. Somewhere in the long hours and endless nights, he had got himself hooked on eBay. He only won maybe one in fifty of his auctions but it passed the time. And besides, it wasn't as if he could afford to win more. But his eBay days were almost over.

He could see the end of this assignment. Everything was in place for the final play. And this play would guarantee him a Detective Second Grade once he brought Angelino in.

He fought when his boss had wanted to bring in the Special

Organized Crime Unit. This was supposed to be a Narcotics bust. But, now that they were involved, Degget had another option when the case was finished. Narcotics had been an incredible opportunity, especially right out of the Academy but it had its limits. SOCU might be the answer to his next step in the department.

Degget was so busy imagining which Division he would get himself assigned to, he almost missed the light step on the back stairs. He checked his watch. They were arriving early. They were also being quiet.

Too quiet.

After two years, Degget's paranoia was well earned and keenly developed. He reached for his gun and moved silently over behind the couch near the window.

They came in fast. Two men were in the apartment and spreading out as the door banged shut again. The first carried a shotgun and the second had a semi-automatic. Bullets sprayed the open kitchen and bed. He waited for them to move farther into the room.

The shotgun blew a large hole in the bathroom door. They started forward, forced to bunch together to get by the small dining table. Degget stood and pumped two rounds into each man. The shotgun went off as the first fell and Degget felt the hot air pass his left side. The second man went down silently.

Degget took a step toward the bodies as the front door burst open again. Degget launched himself backwards and fired. The bullet plowed through the heart of the third intruder as he was still trying to find a target. Degget continued backwards out of control. He heard the glass break behind him and felt himself suddenly suspended in nothingness.

Chapter 10

Without really thinking, Preston picked up the yellow plastic strap some careless paperboy had discarded after opening his bundle of papers. He supposed he picked it up because he hated litter. It might be useful though.

He crossed the street and walked quickly along the other side. Sandra was walking slowly as though she had all the time in the world. She was smiling. She must have enjoyed telling her friends about him.

Rage began to fuel every step. His vision was clear – observing every detail on the street.

He saw where he wanted to be and walked even faster. There weren't too many people around. Only the little neighborhood tavern was open at this time of night. With a little luck, it could work. He crossed back again.

Timing was everything. He set his pace to be at the precise spot when she arrived. She passed a couple walking in the opposite direction and said something. He couldn't quite make it out but was sure she said to go and hear the story at the bar. He wrapped an end of the strap around both hands.

A cab was coming down the street toward him. He watched Sandra turn and step toward the curb.

Her arm went up to signal the cab. But between her and the cab, the couple did the same. The cab swerved to the side in front of the couple and they got in.

As the cab did a U-turn and started back down the road, he watched

Sandra shrug and start back down the street.

He glanced behind to make sure he was still alone. The cab would be out of sight in seconds. A lone man walked in the opposite direction across the street. Preston adjusted his speed to make up for the interruption by the cab.

She passed him at the mouth of the alley and said hello.

He almost missed his chance.

She said hello right to his face but didn't seem to recognize him. For a moment, he was confused and then he realized it was just her way of saying how unimportant he was. The rage flared brighter.

The strap slipped easily around her neck and he snapped his hands back. Taken completely by surprise, she fell backwards. He dragged her into the alley and moved behind a huge garbage container. He used all his strength to pull the ties tighter around her neck.

She clawed at the strap.

A gurgle escaped.

He heard the sound and pulled the straps tighter.

Even as she died, she laughed at him.

Would he ever escape the laughter?

She stopped moving after a minute or so. He released the strap after five. She fell backwards into the garbage. Her tongue was sticking out at him, taunting him. He kicked her in the face. His foot connected just under the chin and almost totally severed her tongue.

Flexing his cramped hands, he felt the pain for the first time. He looked down at his bloody hands and realized it was his blood. The strap had cut into him. He sucked the blood and took a step back, careful that the garbage bin still hid him from the street.

Shoving one hand in his pocket, he felt the boy's knife. He pulled it out, looking at the black handle with the thin red stripe. He thumbed the button and the blade sprang out. Bending down, he finished cutting through her tongue until it fell onto her chest, landing right between her breasts.

Was that enough to stop her laughter? He looked at her throat, pale against the dark blood and bright yellow plastic. Why not be sure and take her voice with him? The Egyptians and the Vikings believed you brought your world with you into the afterlife. What if she went without her voice? Forever mute?

He stabbed the blade into her throat and cut around her larynx. He reached his fingers in and pulled out her voice box, silencing her for all eternity.

He stepped back and admired his work, his hand still wrapped around the bloody bit of flesh in his jacket pocket. He had done it. He had struck another blow for the used and abused. Once word got out, all those like him would feel uplifted and rise up in his support. They might not be capable of acting but they could live through him. They would take pleasure in his acts. Their support would be spiritual but support nonetheless.

But how will they know? She's just another slut in the trash. Who will understand? It isn't as if your last kill made any difference.

He had to leave a mark. But what mark could represent him? Whenever his mind played through his years of torture and terror, there was a single focus. His signature was obvious.

Like an artist examining a sculpture, he decided on the perfect spot.

Using his foot, he kicked her over. She landed with a wet plop in the soggy garbage. Too bad it isn't mud, he thought, surveying her smooth slim back.

Kneeling down, he started to cut.

Chapter 11

"Damn it all to hell. This crime scene is three days old! There isn't anything cordoned off let alone a body."

Mann stared down the alley and then backed up to look down the street, trying to picture the position of the body based on the photos. If he backed up enough, he could see the unlit sign of Jake's Tavern. "It shouldn't have taken so long to get to us."

"It's the knife," Tetrault explained unnecessarily. "They tossed us the case once it was IDed. If it wasn't for the new database the tax payers bitched so much about, we never would have tied it together and Central would still have it."

Kesle's divided its policing into fourteen Divisions. However, although each Division had a Detective squad handling most crimes, budget restrictions wouldn't allow for each Division to have its own Homicide squad. Mann's squad, operating out of Southfield Division, covered Southfield, High Park and the Bluffs.

Central Division, covering the oldest sections of the city, buffered Southfield from Downtown. Central's Homicide squad looked after Central and Downtown. Those two Divisions accounted for over thirty percent of the murders in Kesle, double any other Divisions. If there was an opportunity, they would dump a case in a second.

And they got their chance when they identified the knife buried to the hilt in the victim's back.

"OK, give me what you have," Mann said, still looking at the blank alley.

Tetrault consulted his notes. He had spent the day looking at the gang angle, which Central had ignored up until then, while Kydd stayed with Gabel.

"So far, nothing gang related in her background," Tetrault said. "She was straight as they get. Nothing connected her with the first victim. She lived in a different area, worked near here but not really in Gabel's turf. Gabel and his boys would have been toast if they had wandered this far east of Spinner."

Mann rubbed his eyes, looking from Tetrault to Kydd. "Same with your side?"

"Nothing more on the kid. If they knew each other, I don't know how they would. I can't find any common ground. Nothing but the fact that she had his knife in her back."

"Tetrault, what was she doing here?"

"She was having a drink with her girlfriends at Jake's. She was supposed to have left yesterday to get married in Jamaica."

"Was she a regular at Jake's?"

"Nope, never been there before. One of her girlfriends is and suggested it."

"What about the fiancée? Could he be involved in some way?"

"Central cleared him right away. He has an alibi for each killing. He's clean as far as the gangs go. Nothing there worth a second look."

"Take another look. There has to be something."

"Just the knife."

"What about the knife?"

"The rest of the Intimidators say that Gabel would have had the knife on him when he was killed," Kydd confirmed. "He was never without it. They even described the chipped blade. Happened during a game of Mumblety-peg."

"How does it get from Gabel's pocket into the girl?"

"The same killer whacked both," Tetrault said.

"Why?"

The question went unanswered and Mann stared down the alley. "What about the other three in Gabel's gang?"

"All have good alibis." Kydd shook her head. "And Garnham was right, they're wimps."

"And this is definitely right up there on the violence meter," Mann said, flipping through the crime scene photos. "Makes the bashing that

Gabel got look like he got bitch slapped and sent home to bed. What about the severed tongue? Could this be some sort of warning? We need to look into her business contacts. Could she have been blackmailing her way up the ladder? Was she some kind of a whistleblower?"

"ME says the tongue was partially severed by her teeth," Tetrault said. "Then the job was finished with a sharp object, likely the knife."

"She bit her tongue while she was being strangled? That doesn't sound right," Mann said.

"No, it was post. Looks like a blow to the chin. A kick would have done it."

"Does this get any worse? Any physical evidence?"

Tetrault flipped open the file in his hand. "No prints but CSU found another footprint in the blood. We are working on a match for the print in the garden. But the garden print was useless. This one is for a Hush Puppy. Who the hell wears Hush Puppies, for Christ's sake? They got some blood, type O positive, off the strap he used on the girl. It is definitely not her blood so we might get a hit on the DNA."

Mann looked at his own hands. "Make sure you ask the boyfriend for a swab. Make sure he knows about the blood. If he says no, we'll turn up the heat on him. Check his hands for cuts. It would be good to clear him. So, our boy didn't wear gloves but he did take the time to wipe everything. What about this yellow strap?"

"They use them to bundle the *Daily*. There is a drop between here and Jake's. There are a bunch of them in the gutter and next to the building. He likely picked it up on the way."

"No gloves and he used a piece of garbage for his weapon? It looks very spontaneous with not much planning. Any signs of rape?"

"No rape. And that doesn't make sense," said Kydd.

Mann motioned her to continue and Kydd shrugged. "I saw her picture – the before picture. She wasn't gorgeous but good looking. If this was a gang, they would have done her for sure. Pretty, white, twenty-something. She would be pretty hard to resist. They took time for everything else; they would have taken time for that. Especially if they were trying to leave a message for the boyfriend."

"She's got a point," Mann said. He turned to Tetrault. "What makes you so sure that it's a gang hit?"

"What else could it be with the knife, the kid and the sign?"

Mann had saved the sign for last. He flipped the file open and looked carefully at the design carved into the back of the girl. On the next sheet, the ME had sketched a rough version of the circle with a half circle intersecting the top. "You've ran this?"

"First thing Central did. Nothing. Not related to any gang in the country."

"Why wasn't it on the kid?" Mann stared at the ceiling again. "What's your theory, Shane?"

"No gang, sir. Except for the fact that Gabel was part of an insignificant gang, there is no other connection. Yeck had no connection at all with street gangs. My guess, she hardly even knew gangs existed. Except for what she saw on the news, gangs wouldn't even be in her world. Even this neighborhood isn't really gang banger turf."

Sensing her hesitancy, Mann prodded her. "And?"

"A psycho, sir."

Mann wasn't surprised, just worried.

"That, I don't need. I hope you're wrong but we need to consider the idea. For now, I want that design, whatever it is, kept quiet. I don't want to read about it in the papers. I'm not saying we do – and I don't want this repeated – but if we do have a psycho on our hands, we're going to get another body. I'll get on to Central and make sure it stays quiet. Too many have already seen it and it might be too late. But if we can contain it, let's do it. I want to be able to identify our man."

"Could be a woman."

"That might explain no rape," Tetrault agreed.

Mann stretched and rubbed the back of his neck. "Who had that case a few years back, the one where they thought it was devil worshipers?"

Kydd shrugged but Tetrault, who had been at Southfield for five years, spoke up. "The sacrifice thing? Greer. It wasn't a sacrifice though boss, just two girls getting rid of some rival on the cheerleading squad. Thought they could throw everything off them – good Christian girls that they were."

Mann looked at his watch. He was running late. Brant Davis wanted him to come to the hospital to discuss something about Davis' nephew, Cliff. Mann knew the boy had been tossed out of the police academy a couple years ago and disappeared. Davis had sounded pissed. If Cliff was back Mann thought he better get there before Davis got any angrier.

"OK. I'll just see if Greer recognizes anything. You two stay with what you have. Keep checking for any connections. Check out this boyfriend. Canvas the bar and the neighborhood. Come back tonight for the bar. Pull in the Intimidators and see if there is anything more there. But don't mention this latest victim, the sign or the knife. They'll mouth off all over the street if they find out that Gabel's knife was used. Just see how far their territory extends or at least how far they roam. I'll talk to Greer. I want to see if we should be worried about some kind of cult angle. If we've got a crazy on our hands, we had better move fast."

Really fast, Mann thought, before The Hill decides a gang killing is politically less damaging than a serial killer.

Chapter 12

Preston threw the paper down and cursed.

You killed the wrong one.

He looked at the paper on the floor. "Who the hell is Christine Yeck?"

That would be the woman you killed in the alley, idiot.

"I killed Sandra Kew," Preston shouted.

Louder, I'm not sure they heard you all the way downtown!

How could it not be Sandra? It looked so much like her. He would have sworn it was her.

He went to the bookshelf and pulled out a thin book. He carried it to the dining table where he sat staring at the book. His rush of anger quickly faded into fear. He never understood why he kept the book. It meant nothing but pain. But now, he was beginning to understand.

Rubbing his sweaty hands on his pants, he got up and walked to the kitchen. His eyes never left the book as though it would suddenly open and all his worst fears would spill out. He reached into the refrigerator and felt for the milk carton. He carried it back to the table but made no move to pour the milk.

He wiped his palms again and then slowly opened the book. The spine of the book let out a loud crack, startling him. He laughed uneasily. What did he expect? He had never opened the book since he got it the twenty-five years ago.

Who the hell would he want to sign his Year Book? He didn't even have a picture in the book. He had been sure to be absent that day since he had a swollen eye from one of his father's "lessons". His only picture was with the band holding his flute – the worst possible instrument.

Carefully, he paged past the message from the Principal and the pictures of all the teachers – useless bunch of turds. They could barely teach and they sure couldn't protect him from his tormentors. Most of them were as afraid of the bullies as he was. And the rest were even bigger bullies. His hand was shaking by the time he was at the page titled "Graduates".

The first pictures generated memories of fear and hiding – years of absolute hell. The hours he spent with the layout of the school, carefully planning alternate routes to avoid this hall or that area. His bladder nearly bursting but never daring to venture into the washroom. Always walking with his eyes down, praying he would not make eye contact. Nothing but pain. All because of THEM!

As he saw more pictures, the memories of the tortured years flooded back. The fear changed to anger. Anger became rage, rage for those wasted years. Rage for the happiness twisted into agony. Over twenty-five years later, he still felt the burning rage. Now it was a rage that could kill.

And now, he could make them pay. He had killed. He can kill, can't he? He can make them pay. Just like Sandra had paid.

But it wasn't Sandra, was it?

Sandra's picture was on the fourth page. He studied the picture carefully. He was sure it had been Sandra.

Looks just like her, doesn't it?

Yes, everything is the same.

What year is it, genius?

What does that have to do with anything? It is… Oh!

Ya, Oh! So who's the dumb one now?

Of course. She would be older now. He flipped back to his band picture and studied the changes. He was still himself but there were more changes than similarities. Even heavier, more lines, saggy and tighter all at the same time.

No, that hadn't been Sandra in the bar. It looked like her but Sandra would be older now. That woman wasn't Sandra.

That doesn't really matter, does it?

She had been laughing at me just like Sandra.

That's right. They're all the same, aren't they?

It might not have been Sandra but she was just as bad. They all had that same look. It was the look. He'd just forgotten to account for age.

The milk carton caught his attention. How long had it been since he saw those missing children's pictures on milk cartons? You never saw them anymore, did you? A whole generation of kids had gone missing since they stopped putting pictures on milk cartons. Not that it mattered; it was the technology that he needed!

Chapter 13

As Mann reached the hospital room, he could hear Davis' stern voice all the more dangerous for the low tones. He eased through the open door but Davis didn't even notice him.

Davis towered over the smaller man in the hospital bed. Mann had to look twice at the kid lying in the bed before he recognized Davis' nephew, Cliff Degget. He remembered Cliff as a fresh faced recruit in the police academy before he quit in some quiet scandal three years ago. Instead of the clean-shaven young man, Cliff had longish hair in half-assed dread locks. A scar now marred the right side of his face, running from below his eye to his jaw, making the scruffy beard Cliff now wore almost non-existent in a straight line on his right cheek.

"All I'm saying is, you could have trusted your family. You know what your Aunt has gone through the past three years?" Davis said.

"My trainers all drilled it into me, stay with my story all the time, mon. If I was going to be successful I had to be the guy they created for me," Cliff answered.

"And what the hell is with the Jamaican accent?"

"Sorry. I've been speaking that way for the past three years," Cliff said, obviously struggling to keep the accent out of his voice. "My trainers beat it into me. 'You live your legend or you don't live' is what they always said."

Mann coughed from the doorway and both Degget and Davis looked over at him.

"Uh, hi Cliff," Mann said. "Don't know if you remember me."

"Hi Lieutenant. Sure I remember you. How's it going? It's been a while."

Mann scanned for tubes. "You OK, kid?"

"Ya, sure. I just wrenched my back when I fell out a window."

"Don't change the subject," Davis interrupted before Mann could respond. "Who were these trainers? It sure as hell wasn't the Academy. I never believed that you cheated on that test. Breaking into the instructor's office the night before a test?"

"Of course, I didn't cheat on any test. This is all your fault, Uncle. This hasn't exactly been easy on me, you know. You and Auntie practically raised me. Because of you, I knew all the statutes while I was still in High School. Thanks to you, I was a better shot than most of my instructors. That's how they picked me for this. They washed me out and finished my training in Virginia."

"Virginia?"

"Langley."

"All part of the new happy family that 9-11 produced. They've been training deep undercover operatives for all the alphabet soup and some of the police forces too. They make me bandulu Lenworth, zeen?" Cliff said, dropping into his Jamaican. "I know Patois ca I flexing with my bredren from Ja for a lang time. Ya nuh see it? Tap bein Babylon. Ku pon dis. I brin Lambsbread to Angelino, mon. Til informa su-su to the fat jacket."

"What?" Mann asked.

Cliff smiled. "They turned me into Lenworth, a drug dealer from Jamaica. I learned Patois, Jamaican, when I was in school. A bunch of the guys on the track team were from Jamaica. I stopped being part of the police, Babylon. Look at me, would you even recognize me? I came back into the city and nobody even gave me a second look. I got this scar in Jamaica while I was still trying to establish myself. I was bringing in marijuana to Angelino's operation in a big way. And then someone turned on me and told him I was a cop."

"You know who?"

"No. But I am going to find out. I was under for two years without so much as a sniff. Only two guys in Narcotics even knew about me. Then, I get close to Angelino and my CO, decides it is getting too political. He brings in the SOCU just before my big meeting with Angelino and two nights later, I get three shooters in my apartment. I don't believe in coincidence. Somebody in SOCU is dirty."

Davis looked at Mann who shrugged and spoke. "Could have come from anywhere but the timing is suspicious."

"Unless somebody in Narcotics was just waiting to find a scapegoat."

"I swear, nobody but the two guys knew. They could have had me taken out anytime. It came from SOCU."

Davis nodded. "OK. What's your plan?"

"I need to be somewhere I can investigate SOCU and figure out who ratted me out. Basically, I need somewhere to lay low but I need access to the department main frame. I need information."

Davis raised his eyebrows at Mann. It was Mann's turn to nod.

"Ya, I want this guy as much as you do," Mann said. "And if we can take down Angelino at the same time, I got no problems with that. I can get him into Southfield somewhere. I'll talk to Walsh. Won't be our squad but we'll still be around to keep an eye on the boy."

"Bumboclot," Degget muttered.

Mann just looked puzzled, not realizing what Degget had said. "I'll set up a meeting with Olinyk. He's retired but he was in SOCU for about two years. He'll give it to you straight."

"Where are his loyalties?" Degget asked. "Sorry, but I'm a little paranoid."

"Don't worry. Nothing will get back to SOCU. There wasn't much love lost there. He didn't so much leave as was forced out. We'll set it up when your back is better and you are out of here."

Before Degget responded, a nurse walked in the room.

"Sorry gentleman, I need some time with my patient." She said, all but pushing Mann and Davis from the room.

"Wa'ppun goodaz," Degget said, falling back into his Jamaican accent.

Chapter 14

"Yes, si...si...sir, your pictures are ready," Bert Haynes stuttered out to the man in front of the counter. "I th...th...think your High School reunion group is going to be very happy with th...th...them."

He watched the man carefully flip through the eight by tens. Each had turned out even better than he had hoped. Aging pictures from old black and whites was always more difficult than color pictures with their lack of subtlety and depth. Normally, he did this for missing children but it was becoming more of a novelty item, especially for reunions. Attendees would compare their aged photo and see how different they were to reality. There were automated services online but they lacked his skill and finesse. Obviously, it was worth it to this customer to have the best. Haynes could see he was pleased.

Poor guy. Haynes recognized the type from when he was in High School. Overweight, sloppy, he was the geek always trying so hard to please. He likely had all the crap jobs, always the one setting up the AV equipment rather than doing the presentation, the prop guy instead of the star, picked to put away the sports equipment while the others celebrated the big game. Even now, he was running the errands. He wouldn't be on the stage at the big celebration. He'd be over by the punch bowl with the rest of the losers.

Haynes could understand. Stuttering all his life, he was always in the background. That's where his love of computers came from. And he had no regrets, not with Anne at his side. He smiled over at his wife. Sensing him, she looked over and smiled back.

"Th...th...this is an especially good one," Haynes said, pointing to the picture in his customer's hand.

The man looked up, obviously startled. He looked at the picture Haynes was pointing at of the petite little face, long red hair, gorgeous lips and sparkling eyes. Haynes saw the man's face turn red and guessed, incorrectly, that he was embarrassed. Out of sight behind the counter, Haynes couldn't see the man's right hand clench so hard it turned his knuckles white. Sweat broke out on the man's forehead and Haynes took pity and changed the subject.

"I'm s...s...sorry but I have to hurry off. Anne will make up the bill. I hope everything works out all right."

"It will," the Preston replied. "You have helped me a great deal."

Chapter 15

Mann took a look at the two murder boards that Tetrault and Kydd had set up behind their cubicles.

In the center top of one board was a head and shoulder shot of Luis Gabel on the coroner's table. Clustered off to the left were the names and aliases of the Intimidators. Mann shook his head again when he read the aliases. Beside each Intimidator was the notation "AC" for Alibi Cleared. A copy of Gabel's rap sheet was stuck to the board with a magnet. It was pretty short and filled with minor crimes – minor for any serious banger, anyway. Just enough to get Gabel a curfew. There was also a picture of a Blackie Collins Thin Red Line switchblade. There was a magic marker circle around a chip on the blade with a note stating members of the Intimidators identified it.

A short time line, mostly blank, attempted to narrow down the time of death. Kydd and Tetrault had narrowed down the time of death to be between 11:30 PM, when Gabel had left his fellow gang members, and 3:30 AM. A large question mark was at midnight with the notation, "Curfew never missed". The right side listed next of kin with a similar 'AC' notation. Under the heading of Enemies, the space was blank.

On the next board, there was a head and shoulder shot of Christine Yeck when she was very much alive. Apparently, her next of kin were more forthcoming with a photograph of the lovely young woman.

This murder board had similar notations to Gabel's with some additional information. No rape was prominent as was a description of the indignities that the killer had visited on her body. Strangulation, severed tongue, mutilated throat and the sign carved in her back, all with autopsy photos. Attached dead center of the board was a blowup of the sign. Beside the picture, Kydd had printed "Occult" and "Gang" with large question marks. Scanning the list of next of kin, Mann saw that all had been cleared.

He was still staring at the boards, sipping a Pepsi, when Tetrault and Kydd came back into the squad room.

"Anything new?" Mann asked.

Both detectives shook their heads. "Not a thing, Lou," Kydd added.

"Is there anything that isn't on the board?"

Tetrault flipped open his notebook. "Fiancée is clear. He wasn't even in town and that has been double checked."

"That's the truth," Kydd agreed. She picked up a paper on her desk and unfolded it. After scanning it, she waved the paper toward Mann. "And officially nothing on the DNA for the blood on the newspaper strap. The gang angle has nothing. Nobody is taking credit and it's just wrong for a gang. Garnham says he's heard nothing. Nobody has even taken any notice of her death. Nothing on the web, except for the usual chatter from her friends on Facebook and Twitter."

"Anything on motive?" Mann asked.

"I wish. Her purse was intact with lots of credit cards and about $300 in cash. There is nothing from her work, either. Everybody loves her and thinks she deserved the promotion. She handles the annual drive for Children's Hospital. Finances are good, other than some major credit card debt but that was for her wedding in Jamaica."

"Any ex-boyfriends out there that didn't want her getting married?"

"She's been with her fiancée for six years and before that, nothing serious, according to her mother. Certainly nobody that she thought was capable of this. Her mother said that she's the only one of her daughters that didn't go through the bad boy phase."

"Anything with this?" Mann asked, pointing at the sign.

"Nothing. Nobody in Gangs recognizes it. Some occult hits, having to do with a goat's head. The goat is a standard symbol for the Devil but nothing there so far. Greer is looking into it. Do you want us to go to the media with it?"

Mann considered it for a moment. "Do you think we are going to see more from this guy?"

Kydd looked at Tetrault who just shrugged playing it safe as usual.

Looking back at Mann, she nodded.

"Then, keep it under wraps for now. Do another canvas of the neighborhood. Recheck everything. Give it another few days, maybe you'll shake something loose."

Chapter 16

Nicholas Thorman let the ice clink against his teeth as the last drops of Scotch dribbled into his mouth. He held the glass there until his teeth began to ache. Finally, he set the glass back on the table.

Thorman struggled to his feet wincing at the pain in his head. He left the living room and walked down the hall to his den. He quietly eased the door shut and sat down at his desk.

Implements of his trade littered the mahogany surface. An HP laptop, pencils, binders, printouts, and the rest of the things he had used in his pursuit of the careful control and recording of numbers. Since his teens, when he first fell in love with numbers, he had been practicing what he considered the *art* of accounting.

It was only recently that he had perverted that art or rather it had been perverted for him. He had trusted his benefactor when his schooling had been paid. Thorman thought Angelino recognized his skill as an accurate and careful accountant. He had been so naïve to not realize what the Italian gangster had really been looking for. But Thorman's revenge was so close.

Taking a key from his pocket, he unlocked the centre drawer of his desk and slid it open. Pulling it out as far as it would go, he retrieved a length of stiff wire fashioned with a small hook at the end. He got up and went to the closet and unlocked that door. As though at an altar, he knelt on the floor.

With an ease that revealed much practice, he pulled out the old file boxes on the floor of the closet and piled them behind him, careful not to scratch the floor. Using the piece of wire, he pried up the floorboards. He had to force the cover at one point when it jammed against the side of the closet wall. Whether it was the lack of sleep or the Scotch, he didn't notice the small splinter of wood that peeled off the paneling.

Under the flooring, a large suitcase took up most of the space. He pulled it out and set it level on the floor. He removed yet another key and unlocked the suitcase. He took a deep, calming breath before he opened the lid.

The suitcase contained stacks of Bearer Bonds. Gently, Thorman ran his hands over the top of the stacks, feeling the slightly raised inks. He only wished it was actual cash, although they would spend almost as easily and were infinitely more transportable.

There was more money in front of him than he had made in the last ten years in his dirty job. More money than his father had ever made. Ten times as much money as his father had ever made. And it was all untraceable. He loved bonds.

And, this was just his walking around money!

Thorman lowered a flap on the suitcase and a sheaf of computer papers fell out –the listing of his stock holdings. Several bogus companies that he had set up owned them. The total of these securities alone was a hundred times what was contained in the suitcase.

On the last page he had written several dollar amounts. He had crossed out all but the last. This figure represented the total worth of his offshore accounts spread all over the world – a fortune in funds stolen from a despicable thief.

The last object in the case was his insurance policy – a DVD crammed full, of names, dates, amounts along with audio and video files. Amazing how people who are normally so paranoid about listening devices never thought about a laptop being a recorder. One quick touch and a hotkey combination starts recording every word. If it was pointed the right way, you get video, too. The discs contained the sum total of his boss's illegal activities over the past two years. Everything preserved in case he ever needed it.

He prayed every night that he never would.

Chapter 17

Preston pulled up several sheets of paper on the clipboard to uncover the glossy eight by ten photograph. He watched her balance her tray across the cafeteria. He had been sitting in the cafeteria for hours, reading a book and waiting. None of the security guards gave him a second glance. Long waits in the hospital were just too common. He was just another poor soul waiting. And now he had her.

He watched her sit down with her friends. One of them took out some knitting and started to knit but quickly made a sound of disgust. She was right there reassuring her.

"Let me show you," her words floated across the cafeteria.

"No," he said quietly to himself, "let me show *you!*" He tried to peek under the sweater at her uniform but couldn't get a good angle. Not to worry, the world would soon know the truth.

* * * * *

Finally finished at the hospital, Jeanne McIntosh walked through the small market and chose her vegetables. The meat for her special dinner was already in the cart. Choosing a head of Romaine lettuce, she inventoried the basket against her list. Satisfied that she had everything, she lined up at the register.

Glancing at her watch, she calculated how much time she had left.

Dr. "call me Peter" Michels was due to arrive at her apartment at seven for dinner. She had more than enough time.

She couldn't believe he had asked her out and then for her to invite him to her place for dinner? It was so totally unlike her. She had felt so shy and awkward, stumbling over her words, hardly able to look him in his eyes. And at the same time, unable to tear herself away from those amazing eyes. When he had touched her arm, she thought electricity had suddenly jolted through his hand. My god, how was she going to spend the evening with him and not come across like a love-struck teenager?

On the street, the day smelled of spring. She didn't even need a jacket. She had changed into her street clothes before leaving the hospital and enjoyed the feel of the light clothing. Her skirt ruffled in the breeze and she could not help but have a bounce in her step. Tonight was to be a special night.

* * * * *

He watched her come out of the grocery store. Once again, his eyes flicked to the picture. My god, Haynes was a genius. These pictures would make his mission so much easier. He knew he had been right when he saw her in the hospital but now he was certain. He had found her! All his planning hadn't been wasted.

She was not wearing her coat. She was bouncing along the street, purposefully making her walk seductive. She walked so that her tits bounced and jumped under the thin top. She was trying to make herself wanted. She needed him to want her. She was showing herself off for him.

As though he wouldn't remember. As though he'd fall for it again!

Jane Degenfeld. Jane. Baby Jane. Easy Jane. Yes, it was her. He had realized that days ago, from the first time he had followed her home.

It would have been so easy to take her – so easy to kill her. But he was learning, growing in his abilities.

The boy was an accident. Sandra had been too fast. The pleasure was gone in an instant. He wanted the pleasure to last this time. He wanted memories he could relive.

This time he had a plan. He knew her routine and he knew her building. He could have taken her in her apartment but the risk was too high.

You are still chicken-shit scared!

He wasn't scared; he was smart. But he was still going to enjoy seeing her die. Die in pain and humiliation like she deserved.

He had seen her with that doctor. She had been so blatant. She might as well have just taken off her clothes and done him right there. She was the same girl she had been in school – a Slut.

Everyone knew she was the easiest girl in the school. All the rumors said she lifted her skirt for any boy. All the boys talked about how they had screwed her. At first, he had thought they had exaggerated, but he came to understand that they were telling the truth. Easy Jane.

EJ would always give you a BJ.

Yes, she always put out. She never refused any boy. So when he had asked her out, she had accepted as he knew she would. She had not even thought about it, she had just said yes. He could still remember that date. He remembered it so well.

He sped up as Jane entered the Towers complex.

He even held the door for her as she entered the building. Together, they walked to the elevator and got in. He didn't need to pick up garbage this time. He was prepared.

He already had the rope out.

Chapter 18

Mann was staring at the large calendar on one of the evidence boards when Greer walked up beside him. "Hey, Lou. You got something?"

"I wish. I'm looking at the timing. Trying to find anything that might give me an idea when he's going to strike again."

A large red circle marked the fourth and another marked the eighth. "Only four days between the first and the second killing. Now it has been nine days and nothing. Is he finished? Just getting started? Why so quick to start and now a long gap?"

"There's usually a cooling off period between kills but it gets shorter, not longer," Greer observed. "While I was working the cheerleader case, I did a lot of reading on ritualized killing. Let's assume Gabel was his first kill."

"But he didn't kill him," Mann pointed out.

"No but he sure made certain he was dead," Greer pointed out.

Mann nodded and motioned Greer to continue. "OK, so Gabel is the first kill. Usually, there is a stressor, something that pushes the guy over the edge."

"Your talking like this guy is a serial killer."

"Technically, the FBI doesn't count it as serial until there are three kills but ya, I think this guy is just getting ramped up. Anyway, instead of a stressor, our guy accidentally kills Gabel and likes it. He liked it but it didn't satisfy him. Yeck was more of a ritual. Maybe it wasn't planned but with the beginnings of some ritual. Maybe Gabel didn't turn his crank and he needed something better. In the back of his mind, he knows it was an accident. Yeck gave him what he needed. Now, he can relive the kill and that gets him through the nights."

"For how long?"

"Who the hell knows? Truth? Without more kills we won't see the pattern, if we ever do. Maybe he just doesn't have anyone he wants to kill at the moment. He might be looking for a victim, right now. There is no way of knowing. It might be months before he kills again, maybe even years."

Mann turned away from the calendar and led Greer back to the small kitchen. Grabbing another Pepsi, he sat down at the small table.

"Tell me about the sign."

"Sorry, Lou. About all I can tell you is what it isn't."

"Which is?" Mann said, deflated.

"I have spent a lot of time on the computer. This is not a gang mark that shows up in any of the databases."

"Ya, Kydd already gave me that. What about a religious angle?"

"You know we have never had a satanic cult killing, right? That's all movie stuff. There have been individuals like Ramiez and Sean Sellers that say it was for the devil but these are rare. That said, the sign could have some satanic overtones. It could be a goat, common symbol for the Devil. Normally, the horns would have more of a curve at the end but the guy wasn't using a magic marker to draw the thing."

Mann just nodded and stared at the calendar.

Chapter 19

As she reached for the button, he slipped the rope around her neck and jerked her backwards. The groceries spilled on the floor as the doors slid shut. He released her long enough to push the button for the lower basement. She almost struggled away from him while he was distracted.

She was stronger than he remembered but it didn't matter. By the time the elevator doors opened, she was unconscious. She wasn't dead, yet. He couldn't let her be dead, yet. Just in case someone saw them, he wanted to be able to say that Jane passed out. Besides, he wanted her to see his eyes while she died. She needed to remember.

His heart slammed against his chest as the elevator lurched to a stop. The doors slowly slid open. Crouched beside the bag of groceries, he looked out at the hallway, willing it to be empty. As it had been each day this week, it was deserted.

Shoving the toppled lettuce back in the bag, he slipped one of her arms around his neck. Hefting her up, groceries dangling from the other hand, he struggled to stand. God, she was heavy. He staggered out of the elevator, the door hitting his shoulder and sliding open again.

In the hallway, he hitched her up on his hip and turned right. He moved as quickly as possible past the laundry room. The two women chatting loudly over the sound of the dryers did not even see him dragging her. At the end of the hall, he shoved Jane through a door. She fell in a heap on the floor. Taking one last look down the hall, he slipped into the room.

Preston stood, leaning against the door, trying to catch his breath. He wiped the sweat from his face and adjusted his glasses. When he could finally stand straight, he took a deep breath and removed a rubber wedge from his pocket. Preston kicked it under the door. He tugged hard on the door, pulling with all his weight. When he was satisfied that nobody could get in, he turned to the crumpled figure on the floor. She was beginning to come around.

Before she became fully conscious, he caught her left wrist in a slipknot in one end of the rope. Dragging her across the room, he propped her against a metal storage shelf. He looped the rope around the storage shelf and tied the other end to her right wrist, stretching her arms out straight with her back pressed tight against the shelves. The pain brought her around. Before she could scream, he tore off a piece of duct tape from the roll in his pocket and slapped it across her mouth. She thrashed and tried to trip him with her legs.

Preston kicked her in the ribs without hesitation.

Tears formed in her once defiant eyes and she pulled her knees up to protect herself.

"Don't do that again or I will really hurt you," he said, stepping back.

He stared between her legs, disappointed that she was wearing panties under the skirt. But it was more than he had seen in High School.

Staring down at the tears running down her face, he remembered his date with Jane.

"Guess you didn't think you'd see me again, did you Jane?" he asked.

She tried to say something, shaking her head violently. He almost thought she looked puzzled.

"Don't you recognize me, Jane? Well, I know you, Jane. Everybody knows Easy Jane."

He kicked at her legs suddenly back in his living room all those years ago, everything still fresh in his memory. "I just wanted what everyone else wanted. All I did was try to kiss you. You said you thought I was 'different'. Couldn't even be honest, could you? Why didn't you just say the truth? Call me different. Different? Weird is what you meant. I was too weird for you. Was a kiss and a feel too much? I only tried to touch your big boobs."

When she freaked, slapping him hard and running for the front door, he had lost control. Why shouldn't he have what every other guy in school had been given so freely and easily? Suddenly, he had been screaming at her, telling her he knew all about her reputation. He wanted to do it right then and there just like she had done it with all the other boys.

She had cried but he knew fake tears when he saw them. She had run from his house screaming so loud that the biddy next door had heard. The old broad ratted him out and his father had beaten him when he got home. But during the beating, he had figured it all out.

In a flash of pain-induced brilliance, it all made sense. And now, he could finally expose her secret to the world.

He pulled up his pant leg. Strapped to his calf was an eight inch hunting knife. He pulled it from the sheath. "Well, I guess we should see what I was missing all these years and see if what I guessed was right. I'll show you, you little slut. I'm not good enough for you, huh? Let's see what you really look like."

He grabbed her top and started to cut as she screamed against the duct tape.

* * * * *

He stepped carefully around the blood on the floor.

"You know what Jane?" he asked. "The say dead bodies don't bleed, but they sure leak like hell if the cuts are big enough."

He pulled the bra tight and snapped it together at the back. He had to be careful not to smear his signature. Then, he tried to pull her back over. He had to struggle. The large hole that used to be her stomach created a suction that held her to the floor. When she finally pulled away, he thought it was an interesting sucking noise.

He was no dummy and she had realized that. She wanted him but she knew he was too smart. She was afraid that he would discover her secret if he touched her. She just never suspected he was smart enough to discover her secret without even touching her.

Now, everyone would know her secret.

He reached in his pockets for the rest of the display.

Chapter 20

"Definitely the same mark," Kydd confirmed.

"Son of a bitch," was Mann's only response. CSU was still processing the scene and the constant flash of the camera hurt Mann's eyes, adding to his headache. As he rolled the body back over, he looked up at Tetrault. "What about the weapon?"

"No sign of it, sir. ME guesses a long bladed knife."

The door to the hallway opened and Brant Davis' wide shoulders filled the opening. He took a half step through and stopped. "Holy Lord."

"What do you have?" Mann asked.

Davis stepped carefully into the room and shut the door. "Jeanne McIntosh. She lives on the seventh floor. Keys fit the apartment door. CSU is going through it now but nothing. However, it doesn't look like she made it up there after work."

He paused when saw the body. Assigned the ID check and securing the victim's apartment, he had not had pleasure of viewing the murder scene yet. He took one look at the scattered body parts and swallowed hard. Then, he picked up the incongruity of the slashed woman, naked except for the white bra, now stained red with blood that had run from her mutilated throat. "Christ!"

Davis, for all his size and bluster, hated the really bloody kills.

"Sorry, Davis. I should have warned you."

"We talking Captain Crunch?"

Mann shrugged. "That's where I'm putting my money. You and I will be heading straight for The Hill from here."

Davis nodded, not wanting to sit in on that meeting at all.

"That," he said, pointing down at the floor, "used to be a thirty-five year old nurse named Jeanne McIntosh. She worked at Mercy. She worked yesterday and left somewhere around three thirty in the afternoon. She was off today."

"Anything from anybody she knows? Do they know what she was doing last night?"

"A girlfriend at the hospital had sent about a dozen texts to her phone. We caller ID'd her and we sent a squad to pick her up. I did get the name of a doctor who was supposed to have dinner with her. We're checking him out."

Mann looked down at the mutilated girl. "A doctor?"

Kydd looked up from where she was kneeling by the girl's body. "Lou? You need to check this out."

Mann stooped down and watched as one of the CSU techs pulled up the victim's bra to show blood soaked tissues.

"What the hell?" Mann said.

"You gotta be kidding? She stuffed herself?"

"Nope," said the CSU tech. "*Nobody* is that concerned about their breast size. The bra was put on postmortem or at least after he carved that design in her back."

"So the killer stuffed her bra full of Kleenex?"

"More than that," Davis said, holding up what was left of another bra from the pile of clothing shoved off to the side. "Looks like our boy brought his own bra with him."

Mann stood staring at the scene and everyone waited for his response.

"OK, lock this place down. Nothing to the media. Nothing. Especially about the mark. Kydd and Tetrault, you finish here. Get a canvas going, find out about security cameras, the works. Talk to everybody. And no access to this room until it has been cleaned. Use our crews."

"We are going to need some guys," Tetrault said.

"You'll have them in half an hour. I want somebody backtracking her from here to the hospital. Find out where she went, what she did from the second her shift ended. I'll get Greer on a canvas of the hospital and he can find someone to bring in this doctor."

Mann's cell rang and he had a short conversation. He clicked his cell phone shut and looked over at Davis. "It's confirmed, we're going straight to The Hill."

"And?"

"Walsh didn't say much but looks like the Mayor is already involved. We have an interrupt on arrival appointment with the Commissioner. Walsh is already there."

Mann looked at his watch. Rush hour would be over for the morning but it would still take close to half an hour to get to The Hill.

"We gonna get pulled on this one, Lou?" Kydd asked.

Mann shook his head, a determined look on his face. "Whoever is doing this is getting worse. I'm pushing for a task force – out of Southfield. This guy is ours!"

Chapter 21

Police Headquarters was located on the old site of Kesle's first luxury hotel. When the under-insured hotel had burned to the ground, the city had snapped up the land. The powers fought over the use for the prime property for years until a particularly pushy Commissioner all but forced the city to use the land for a new headquarters. He pulled several skeletons out of some pretty exclusive closets before the ink was dry on the new contracts. Because the building was set on a hill overlooking most of the surrounding area, the Kesle Police Department Headquarters simply became "The Hill".

By the time he and Davis had run up the steps of the building, Mann was beginning to feel winded. Blaak was right, he was out of shape. If the force ever implemented the fitness requirements for its lieutenants as it should, he would have some major work ahead of him. Somehow, he still hadn't seen Blaak about his workout routine. He would have to think about his diet too. Maybe even give up the Pepsi?

However, not if this was the psycho case he thought it was. He'd never survive a psycho without Pepsi.

After going through security, they took the elevator to the top floor. The elevator was full and the ride long. The Commissioner's office was to the left but when they got out, a young woman met them and motioned to the right. "This way please."

"Damn," Davis mumbled.

"Looks like we aren't alone."

The young woman smiled and led them to the hallway entrance of a conference room. The other entrance came from a well-camouflaged doorway in the Commissioner's office.

Mann was shocked to see his old Captain waiting outside the door. "Andy, what are you doing here?"

"Beats the hell out of me. I just got the official summons from on high about fifteen minutes ago," Captain Keough replied, shaking Mann's hand. Taking Davis' hand next, Keough greeted him. "He bring you into this snake pit?"

"Misery loves company," Davis replied.

"Well," Keough said, "let's get this over with. Got to admit, I'm pretty interested in why I'm here."

Inside the room, Mann wasn't surprised to see the usual suspects gathered. Along with Captain Walsh was the mayor's chief of staff, Don Parkside – no doubt to cover His Honor's ass.

As they were about to sit down at the long highly polished table, Commissioner James walked through the connecting door from his office. Mann caught a glimpse of someone sitting in front of the Commissioner's desk. All Mann could see was a pair of crossed legs in expensive men's slacks before the door closed quickly.

Before he even reached his chair, the Commissioner started the meeting. "Captain Walsh has been briefing us on the investigation. So, Lieutenant, do we have a serial killer on our hands?"

"Whoa, I'm sure it is too early in the investigation to jump to those conclusions," the mayor's chief of staff said. "God help us if the press gets a hold of something like this. We do not want to feed the fires of panic in the city."

Ignoring Parkside, Mann answered the Commissioner's question. "We have three murders with strong indications that they are the work of the same killer or killers. We don't have any indication at this point that there is more than one person involved so I am betting on just one killer."

"You are linking *three* killings?" asked James.

"I am. The tie to the first killing of the boy is weak but the knife definitely makes a trail."

"It isn't as if it is the only switchblade in the city. We know of at least three more like it," Parkside said, revealing how much he had read about the case. "There is nothing to definitively tie the knife to the boy."

"Actually, we can. Luis Gabel's crew identified it by a knick on the blade. There is no other logical explanation that puts the knife in the hands of a second killer so we have to assume one killer. The next two have a clear signature that absolutely connects them."

"OK," the Commissioner said, looking pointedly at Parkside, "let's accept three linked killings for now. Where does that put us? Captain Walsh said that this one was worse than the others?"

"The violence is escalating. This latest victim was mutilated – ripper kind of mutilation. He spread the organs all around the floor. We will have to wait on the autopsy to know about rape."

The Commissioner looked over at Parkside. The Mayor had just announced his candidacy in the coming election. Politically, this would be a landmine. As though completing the thought, the chief of staff spoke again. "Kesle does not need a serial killer at this point in time."

Mann opened his mouth to ask when it would be convenient and felt Captain Keogh's hand on his arm.

"As soon as this hits the press, the city will panic," Parkside continued. "I have been on the phone to the Mayor. He wants this guy caught before the press even knows he exists."

"Sir, given the frequency of the murders, we don't have much time," Mann said. "I would recommend a task force be formed immediately."

"A task force?" Parkside asked, the pleading clear in his voice. "That is definitely premature."

"The Lieutenant is correct," Keough cut in, beginning to fear he understood his role in all this. "The violence and frequency are escalating. And, if the Mayor wants the job done quickly, that is going to take organization and man power."

"Given the nature of the crimes and the current political climate," Parkside said, looking directly at the Commissioner and ignoring Keough, "I imagine the Mayor would agree with your decision to run the task force out of The Hill."

If he hadn't already turned to look at James, Mann would have missed the Commissioner's quick glace at the connecting door. It made Mann wonder whose legs he had seen in the office.

"No," said James, "Captain Keough will head the task force out of Southfield. Lieutenant Mann will continue to act as point on the investigation. I want some continuity if we are going to hit the ground running."

Mann wasn't sure if he, Keough or Parkside was more surprised.

"Lieutenant Mann, you are officially relieved of your duties on the Southfield squad," the Commissioner continued. "Captain Walsh will adjust the squad in your absence. The task force will operate out of Southfield for the time being. Get this nut case before I see him on television. That is all gentlemen."

The Commissioner got up and disappeared through the door into his office. Parkside already had his Blackberry to his ear as he left. The remaining four kept their seats and stared at each other in silence.

"Is he kidding? Do they really expect to keep this quiet?" Mann finally asked.

"Don't worry about them, Gregg," Keough said. "You continue to run the investigation. I'll run interference with the Commissioner and the Mayor's office as well as with the press, when they tumble to the case. I suspect that is what whoever dreamed up this idea had in mind. You concentrate on finding the killer."

"Thank you, sir." Mann turned to Walsh. "What happens at the squad?"

"Davis will handle the squad for the time being. Temporary pay raise, the works. I'm not bringing in anybody new if I don't have to."

"How many do I get?" Mann asked.

"For now, you can have four detectives and three Uniforms."

"I've got that now," Mann sighed. He stared up at the ceiling and thought aloud. "I want Kydd, Greer and Blaak. And I guess I had better take Tetrault so I don't have to bring anybody else up to speed. Just give me any uniforms you think deserve the duty. I'll need eight lines and at least four cars. But I'll need more guys to help with the canvass."

"We will be pulling in more uniforms from other divisions to fill the ranks," Keough said. "James will gladly reassign them."

"He's right," Walsh agreed, standing. "Well, I've got a Division to reorganize. Andy, you want to come with me and we'll get you set?"

"Gonna miss you, Mann, but I'll take the bump," Davis said, after they left. "But I gotta admit, I'm surprised you got the nod for this thing."

Mann knew what Davis meant and took no offense. "You and me both."

"But we always knew you had an angel out there somewhere," Davis said, motioning with his head at the connecting door.

"You saw?"

"Just expensive shoes."

"Damn," Mann said, glancing at the connecting door again. "I would have given good money to know who was in there."

Chapter 22

"Alf Buchanan, you know Captain Keough?"

"Sure. How are you doing Andy? Who'd you piss off?"

"I apparently wasn't doing anything worthwhile at the moment." Keough waved Buchanan to an empty chair. He had commandeered a cramped office but that was the way Keough liked it because it kept people out of his office and anyone who did venture in never stayed long.

"You're going to love this one," the coroner said, tossing photos on the desk. "I didn't do Yeck but I reviewed the notes. This is the same guy. But he went several steps farther this time. In fact, he really ratcheted it up."

"Holy Mother of Christ!"

"My thoughts exactly. He did a real job on the girl."

"COD?"

"Wait until I get her on the table for cause of death. It's scheduled for two hours from now. I want to be sure about this one. She was strangled twice, at least. From the bruising, I'd say once to subdue her and get her to the room and once to kill her, I think. But he might have been bringing her in and out of consciousness. Or, he might have strangled her to unconsciousness a few times. Two very distinct strangulation marks. One set was from a rope and the other one from his hands. But I'm not sure about COD. It could be strangulation or blood loss. From the spatter pattern, he cut her some before she died. Looks like he really wanted to hurt her. However, most of the mutilation was post."

"Strangulation matches the second victim," Mann said.

"Same MO but he came prepared this time. Highly unlikely he found the cord at the scene, according to the Super. She was definitely strangled and restrained with a small rope"

"What about the bra?"

"All of her clothes were cut from her body including her bra. This bra, the one she was wearing when she was found, wasn't hers. It was a full cup size and a couple inches larger than the other one. My guess is the killer brought it with him."

"What purpose?" asked Mann.

"Are you kidding? I don't have the slightest idea. We also found tissues stuffed in the bra."

"She stuffed herself?"

"No, that was done post-mortem and definitely the work of the killer. I mean, this was a nicely built girl and who uses tissues anymore? This wasn't some teenager. There are too many prosthetics that look better and are easy to get, especially for a nurse. Besides, her bra would have fit correctly without the stuffing. Nope this was definitely a message from the killer."

Mann was silent for a moment as he thumbed through the pictures. Keough, familiar with the way Mann worked, waited for the lieutenant. Finally, Mann looked back at Buchanan. "What do you think?"

"The theatrics of the scene strike me."

"Theatrics?"

"The scene was laid out carefully. The killer needed a place to do his deed but then he didn't try to hide the body. He had time. He had to be there for an hour, depending on how quick he was with the cutting. But for all that, he didn't hide the body or dispose of it in any way."

"What are you getting at?"

Buchanan picked up a picture and looked at it. "The internal organs are all arranged as though they are being inventoried. It was almost clinical, without any passion, as though it was more of a science project. It's the bra that is important. He wanted us to see a stuffed bra on that girl."

"Anything else?"

"He cut out the larynx."

"Their larynx?" Keough said, looking puzzled.

"The voice box. The Adam's Apple," Buchanan said, pointing at his throat.

"You don't mean he doesn't just slash their throats? You mean he actually cuts out their voice boxes?" Keough asked. "What does that tell you?"

"Not a thing, except the obvious that the mutilation tells me he might have some anatomical knowledge. He might be a doctor, another nurse, something like that. The basic organs, they come out with the slice and dice. But the voice box – who even thinks about it? And I'll tell you something else. He's taking them with him."

"He takes the larynx with him?"

"It wasn't at either scene. I just found out about it on the Yeck murder. The original autopsy listed only a deep mutilating knife wound, as though he had thrust the blade in and twisted it. My people screwed up. Once we had the second girl, we went back and checked. It was actually missing."

Mann was still focused on the doctor that was supposed to have made a house call at Jeanne McIntosh's apartment.

"Time of death?"

"Between four and nine, last night."

"Do you know if the CSU guys got lucky with prints?"

"Nope everything was wiped again."

"Wiped? You don't think he used gloves?" Keogh asked, surprised.

"He wants to be close to his victims," Mann said, almost to himself. "He wanted to touch them."

* * * * *

Hearing the soft rap on his door, Mann looked up from the pile of papers on his desk. Degget was standing in the doorway. He had cut his hair and shaved his beard which lessened the impact of the scar. He wore a suit and a tie with a picture of Bob Marley on it. Even standing in the squad room, Mann could sense tenseness in his stance. The watchfulness had nothing to do with nerves over a new transfer.

"Come in, Detective." Mann motioned the man to a seat.

"Thank you, sir. I hope I'm not bothering you." He handed Mann a file folder.

"Not at all. I understand that I have pulled you for a while," Mann said, flipping through the personnel folder. Davis had greased the transfer, dealing with Walsh as an uncle more than as a cop.

"Yes, sir. They were looking for somewhere to dump me."

"Go see Detective Kydd. She'll set you up. Any problems, you see me," Mann stressed.

"Thank you, sir."

Degget stood up and left the office. Degget had found his hiding place and Mann was one step closer to Angelino.

Chapter 23

"Please wait over there, Ms. Seymour," the voice from the darkness said.

Andrea joined three other women and two men. Two of the women were chatting but everyone else stood quietly, staring down at the stage or out at the audience. Squinting through the footlights, Andrea could barely make out the three people sitting in the theater.

Glancing at the three women, she tried to decide which parts the other women had won. The older woman was obviously the mother. That left her and the other two women for the sisters. Two unimportant roles and Gwen, the character who was in virtually every scene and all but carried the play.

"*Don't even think it,*" she mentally cautioned herself.

"OK," came a voice from the audience, "can we have some chairs please?"

Stagehands quickly put out nine chairs in a circle on the stage. One of the men and the older woman walked over to the chairs. Hesitantly, the other four followed. On the seat of each chair was a copy of the script. None of the actors touched the scripts or made any effort to sit down. They were all deciding what to do when the three from the audience appeared from the wings and walked over.

"OK," the tallest of the three men said, "let's get started on this. Sit for Christ's sake. I hope you have all heard of me or are smart enough not to admit it."

"Hi Henry," the older woman said, laughing.

"Hi Martha. Martha and I are old friends. I have had the honor to direct her in several plays and she knows exactly how to get on my good side so just follow her lead and you'll be fine. These other two suits are the money men. With any luck, you won't see them again until opening night."

The two men looked at the director, neither sure whether he was kidding or not.

"We are going to do a quick read through today. I want to hear how this thing sounds before I decide on any rewrites. I'll have that done by mid-week and then you have until Monday to get your lines down before we start into major rehearsal."

Jack pulled a paper out of his jacket pocket and unfolded it. "OK. Parts."

Each actor tensed as Jack began to list out who would play which role.

"Michael, Smitty. Martha, the mother. June, Debra. Alex, David. Andrea, Gwen. Diane, Isabel."

Andrea suddenly remembered to breathe and let out a great rush of air.

Martha laughed and the director looked over at her. "You have just been given the lead in what is sure to be this year's Tony award winning play and that's the best you can do?"

Chapter 24

"So, I can trust Mann?" Degget sat across the kitchen table from Brant Davis.

"Of course, you can, you stupid boy!" Ruby said from where she stood doing up the dishes.

"I'm sorry, Aunt Ruby, but it is hard to tell who to trust," Degget said. "Everybody seems to have a hidden motive. All these years, you've never really talked about the Lieutenant."

"Oh, Gregg's got an agenda, all right, but it isn't hidden. He wants Angelino, probably more than you do." Ruby tossed a dishtowel to her husband. "Dry these dishes and tell him about the video tape"

Davis heaved to his full height and picked up a plate out of the rack. "You know Mann made his name when he was still in the bag, right? He had been on patrol for about six years. I was about three months in and still riding with my first partner."

"I sort of heard the story. He arrested some dirty cops but there were some questions about it, wasn't there? Something about him being dirty or involved?"

"No," Davis said, "there was no question about it. It was a good bust. Mann just had the bad luck to bust a very connected cop. Mann was clean. Unlucky, and a little stupid, but never doubt that Mann is a righteous cop. All the bullshit that settled on Mann came from the Commissioner at the time trying to cover his ass. The rest came from Mann's obsession to nail Angelino."

"Tell him how it really happened," Ruby said.

"On the day in question, Mann was on his day off," Davis began.

* * * * *

Gregg Mann was down at the Beaches with his wife and two sons. The baby, Wayne, was still in the stroller but Rick was running around as they wandered along the boardwalk that bordered the sand. Gregg had his new video camera out and was trying unsuccessfully to get some video of his wife. "Just concentrate on the boys," she insisted.

Mann stepped onto the hot sand and started to video tape Rick as he jumped along the boardwalk, trying to only hit every third board. As Mann swept the camera across the boardwalk, three men caught his eye. Two of the men were pushing the third into a warehouse across the street. Just before they disappeared into the building, Mann caught a glimpse of the guns.

Mann reached for his pocket but he had forgotten his new cell phone back at the apartment. He quickly scanned the boardwalk. He finally saw the patrolling officers well up on the pier that jutted out into the lake.

"Honey, there's something going on in that warehouse," he said to his wife.

"What are you talking about?"

"There are a couple guys with guns that just took a third guy into that warehouse. Go get those guys," Mann said, pointing out to the pier. "Give them my badge number and tell them I'm in plainclothes and unarmed."

Mann ran across the road and looked at the side of the building. A stairway ran up the side of the building to a door and a window. Another door from the alley was set twenty feet back from the bottom of the stairs. He tried the lower door but it was locked. A transom window was open a few feet down the alley. He dragged a couple crates over and slipped through into the warehouse.

Mann could hear the voices and the scrape of a chair on cement. To his left, a staircase ran up to a loft area with storage and a small office. He went for the high ground, silently mounting the stairs. Almost at the top, he crouched down and watched the men. Bringing the video camera up, he used the zoom to get a closer look. He clicked on the record at the same time.

One of the men, Mann labeled him Number One in his head, had a revolver pointed at a kid sitting in a chair. The kid looked about twenty years old and was crying. The guy with the gun was talking too low to be heard but the tone was as menacing as the gun. The second man, Number Two, had his gun out but seemed nervous and kept looking toward the front door. He reached out and pulled on the arm of Number One who just shook it off.

"Where the hell is my coke you little snot?" Number One suddenly shouted. "I know you grabbed it up and ran. I want it back."

The kid in the chair sniveled some response that Mann couldn't catch.

"Are you bullshitting me? You better be telling me the truth."

The kid said something else and reached into his pocket.

"Easy," said Number One. He motioned to Number Two who dug in the kid's pocket and pulled out a small object. Mann thought it was a key.

"OK, we got it. Let's get out of here," Number Two said, almost pleading.

"Yup, we're out of here. But first we get rid of this problem."

The kid must have realized what was going to happen because he tried to launch himself off the chair to his right. The gun went off and hit the kid in the left shoulder, spinning him around and knocking the chair over.

Without thinking, Mann stood up and shouted, "Stop, Police!"

Both men opened fire on him. He ran up the stairs and tried the office door but the knob wouldn't turn. As a bullet lodged in the door beside him, he made a decision and threw himself at the window to the right of the door. He crashed through the glass and hit the railing. He tucked himself around the video camera and rolled down the stairs.

Hitting the pavement knocked the wind out of him. Two men burst out through the side door under the stairs. Expecting a bullet any second, Mann heard running feet and two voices.

"Freeze, police!"

Mann heard the two men from the warehouse shout, "Police, undercover."

The two uniforms weren't having any of it. "Put your guns down now!"

The suspects put their guns on the pavement and raised their hands. "Its OK, We're undercover. That's our suspect," Number One said, pointing at Mann. "I'm going to reach for my badge."

"Don't move!" the older of the uniforms shouted, coming forward quickly. "Keep your hands on your heads."

A third cop skidded to a stop at the top of the alley. While the newcomer pulled his gun, the older patrolman approached the two guys and holstered his. "Davis, you cover these guys. Jefferson, cover the guy at the bottom of the stairs."

"I've got them, Mike." Davis assured his partner.

The two guys were kneeling on the ground when Mann's wife arrived with the boys in tow. She started into the alley and Jefferson blocked her way. "That's my husband! He's a cop. Is he hurt?"

Mann finally got his breathing under control. "We need an ambulance. There's a guy shot in the warehouse."

Mike looked at Mann's wife and kids. Making a quick decision, he stepped back from the suspects on their knees. "Jefferson, check it out."

Jefferson ran into the warehouse and they heard him shout, "Man down!"

Davis used his shoulder radio to call for an ambulance. Davis' partner walked up to him. He showed him the ID from the two kneeling suspects and pointed to one name. "Get the Lieutenant down here. We are deep in it. This is going to be way beyond our pay grade."

Before the Lieutenant could arrive, Mann started to give his story. When he mentioned the video tape, Number One started shouting.

"That video is part of our investigation. I don't want anyone touching it, in case they erase it. You understand, Officer?" he asked pointedly, looking directly at the older man in uniform. "I don't want anyone to accidentally erase that tape."

"I understand totally," replied the older cop.

He popped out the tape. "Officer Davis, are you witnessing this?"

"Uh, sure Mike," Davis said, clearly not understanding what he was witnessing.

"Officer Mann. Do I understand correctly that removing this small tab will prevent the tape from being erased?"

"Yes, sir," Mann said.

Mike snapped the small piece of plastic off the tape. "There, that should take care of any of your concerns."

"Do you know who and what you are screwing with?" Number One asked.

"I know exactly who you are. And I am guessing this tape will prove exactly what you are."

* * * * *

"Mike showed me what it took to be a cop, that day," Davis said. "Luckily, he missed most of the fallout. That was reserved for Mann."

"That was Commissioner Anders' son, wasn't it?" Degget asked.

"Yup. Mann had gone and videotaped the Commissioner's son shooting a kid over a drug deal. Felony attempted murder. Would have been murder if Mann hadn't told us about the kid in the warehouse when he did. As it was, the vic almost bled out before the ambulance got there. Jefferson saved him."

"What happened to Mann?"

"The Commissioner tried to do everything he could to discredit Mann. Perhaps, he thought that would help get his son off or maybe he was just pissed. But nothing was getting his son off. He went down and did some serious time. By the time the investigation was finished, the Feds were involved and he ended up doing Federal time too. But the damage had been done, Mann was tainted. That wasn't the worst of it.

"Anders' partner, Billy Jones, knew he was going down. He wasn't the brightest bulb in the box but he did know if anyone was going to fall hard, it wasn't going to be the Commissioner's kid. And there wasn't much defence against the video tape. Billy wasn't a bad guy, just greedy and easy for Anders to manipulate. He rolled over on Anders and the whole operation. That meant that Angelino's new organization was going to take a big hit. He had just come to power, having eliminated most of the competition. There were still some very fresh corpses around and Jones knew too much. Angelino had Billy killed."

"That hit Gregg hard," Ruby said.

"Why? The guy was dirty, right?"

"Guess you had to know Billy," Davis tried to explain. "Like I said, he really wasn't a bad guy. He just got in way over his head and didn't know how to get out. Gregg felt responsible in some bizarre way. Don't get me wrong, Billy wasn't an innocent but he shouldn't have been killed like that. Gregg was really pissed off that it happened. He has wanted to get even with Angelino ever since. He knows the dirty cops, the deaths, they all stem from the drug money. Angelino is the one that Gregg will chase forever. It cost him a lot."

"And what the Italian bastard didn't take, the bitch Gregg was married to did," Ruby said. "She figured Mann should have played the game so he could have moved up into the big jobs. She saw herself as the

Commissioner's wife some day and wanted Mann to play along so he could move up. When they got together, Mann talked about being Commissioner some day. For Mann, it was just talk. He was a cop but she wanted a bureaucrat. She soon realized he was never moving very far…not far enough for her. She took the boys and poisoned their minds."

"But none of that matters to you," Davis said. "All you need to know is that you can trust Mann and his motives. Stick with Mann and he will help you. You want the same thing and he might even keep you alive while you get Angelino. I got you on that task force so you can get back in the game. Don't waste it."

Degget nodded. "And I appreciate it."

"Just be careful," Davis cautioned. "And remember you don't have to do this all by yourself. You're family and that matters more than anything."

Chapter 25

Where is the dwelling of the lions and the feeding place of the young lions, where the lion, even the old lion, walked, and the lion's whelp, and none made them afraid?

He wandered through the financial district along the busy streets. Everywhere he went, people shoved and jostled him as they rushed past him. Each of them hell bent on getting ahead of the other guy. They walked like they did everything – with no regard for their fellow human beings. They produce nothing. They create nothing. They thrived by tricking others into buying things for more than they paid for them, having added no value them.

They lived in a world of lies, destruction and greed. And greed, Mr. Gekko, is *not* a good thing.

Greed and envy breeds bullies.

To find the lion, you must enter unto the den of the lions.

Businesses were finishing for the day and people were hurrying home or to the nearest bar. Brokers and investors wore frowns of despair. The market had been unusually volatile making investors unsure where they would stand at the opening bell tomorrow. The brokers secretly smiled knowing that they would make their commissions either way and blessed the flurry of trading that marked the uncertain times.

Truly, this was the den of the lions.

In this place of greed and avarice, he would find his foe. Among these bullies, uncaring souls, rapists and pillagers, he would find those who had tormented him for so long. They created nothing and destroyed everything. They cheat and lie. They spread false hope – only profiting by someone's misfortune.

He flowed with the crowd and entered a bar. He tried to move slowly, trying not draw attention to himself. He did not belong. Others would sense that. The lions quickly smelled out and slaughtered the sheep.

But this sheep had claws!

* * * * *

Three hours later, he still sat at the bar – ignoring his own advice. Strategically located beside a large potted plant where most of his nine drinks had ended up, he made himself invisible. This was Kesle and nobody approached a lone man slumped over his drink. But the hours of waiting had not been in vain.

He consulted his small book and compared the picture with his target across the room. There he stood – his next target.

The scum was holding court, surrounded by a crowd of admirers. The arrogant worm gestured extravagantly, voice booming, while those around stared in wonder and awe.

Preston had found perfection and felt himself harden. He got up and wandered over toward the tight knot of people. Suddenly, the crowd erupted with laughter and he regained his senses.

Just how badly do you want to get caught?

He immediately veered to the left, almost knocking the drink from the hand of a designer suit. Ignoring the icy stare and mumbling an apology, he headed for the door. What was he thinking? Where was his brain? His cock was too big. His erection had drained all the blood from his brain. Be invisible.

He immediately left the bar and walked across the street. Standing in the recess of a shop door, he began to wait for his prey.

He was excited. He had actually found David Kraemer.

Now he needed to make a purchase.

Chapter 26

Giovanni "The Hinge" Angelino considered himself one of the new breed. Gone were the days of fat old men sitting in cigar-filled rooms with torpedoes lounging around waiting for the next hit. The game had changed. Angelino had capitalized on that change.

Two generations ago, his predecessors would have been scandalized at the extent of his legitimate enterprises. His empire included publishing, advertising, computer technology, medicine, food services, and flashlights. Each business was legal and very profitable. Every year, his organization made millions from these companies. He also contributed to art galleries, children's hospitals, and wildlife concerns. In fact, he sat on the boards of three different charities.

His office, located in his own building, was the height of respectability. He looked down on Fifth Avenue far below and, without even straining, the marinas at South Bay. He had three secretaries – none of whom he was sleeping with – and a collection of lawyers and accountants working to close deals, not keep him out of jail. The office itself was a masterpiece.

One of Kesle's top designers had designed it. The desk was the state of the art, brought in from Japan. He could access the computer of any one of his companies by pressing a couple of buttons. The rest of the office was just as modern but not sterile like so many he had seen. For some reason, space age meant uncomfortable to most designers. For him, space age meant more leisure time and greater comfort.

Comfort and security – his office gave him all that. He looked at the paintings on the walls and the fresh flowers in the vase. Then, he turned around in his chair. When he passed his hand over a patch on the wall, a light flared in a recessed section. A huge crystal glittered in the lighted alcove.

The crystal was over a foot in diameter and almost three and a half feet high. Greens and blues, evidence of chromium and aluminum, sparkled in the lower half. The upper spires cast red shadows as the light caught the iron traces in the crystal. Perfectly balanced, the crystal was power, strength, and intelligence. He gently stroked it and felt the power suffuse his body.

He swung back to the desk, picked up the small racquetball and patiently squeezed. He could feel the muscles in his forearm press against his fitted shirt. Power, strength, and intelligence were the key to his success – the perfect blend.

Angelino had always been a large boy. Since his early years in school, he was bigger and tougher than the other boys. And he always hung with the roughest crowd. Most of the fathers were connected in some way or another. Being the only child of a widow, he lacked the influence of a father. He made up for this by making deals with the other boys. He supplied protection in return for contact with their fathers and the business.

Most of the other kids, and their fathers, assumed he was stupid. Stupidity went with size and brawn; everyone knew that. He didn't fight the insult; he used it. Thinking him too stupid to understand, his friends would discuss things in front of him that he shouldn't have heard. Each little nugget of information, he filed away.

Angelino wanted what those kids had. The kids always ended up with something that fell off some truck. But, he had more ambition than his friends. He didn't want the little gift that fell off the truck. He wanted the whole freaking truck.

Brainpower wasn't exactly legendary among his friends' fathers. Like most of their ilk, they lived from job to job. Most had never finished fifth grade. Spending money was their favorite pastime. As soon as the money came in, it was gone. Nothing planned beyond the next score. Make a score, spend the money.

Meanwhile, Angelino spent his time plotting and planning. He read everything he could – philosophy, art, psychology, mathematics, physics and history, especially the history of war and conquest. He led a careful double life, hiding his books the way some of them hid their drugs and money.

He planned while they took stupid risks out of boredom and some ridiculous macho code. Yung taught him that self worth came from within. Angelino was not interested in their approval beyond entrance to the inner circle. He impressed them with his ruthlessness and quick violence. They missed his intelligence in the flurry of beatings, blades and bullets. A three-year stint, knocked down to nine months with good behavior, proved his loyalty

Meanwhile, he quietly finished College courses in business.

He created his business plan complete with organizational charts of competitors' operations. He had a long-term plan that he executed flawlessly, adjusting and adapting like any good general.

Within ten years and three times that many bloody, unsolved killings, Angelino controlled most of Kesle. Nothing moved without his blessing. And no profit realized without him getting his cut.

Since that time, he continued to gather power around him. He stayed in good physical shape – no pasta and wine belly for him. He still worked out two hours a day. He used hired muscle for protection like everyone else but he was his own best protection. His athletic body and razor sharp reflexes had saved him more than once.

And he still read everything he could get his hands on. His ever-active mind also kept his minions under control as well.

He stabbed at several buttons on the computer console. A spreadsheet flickered onto the screen. He leaned back and looked at the monitor.

He knew thieves surrounded him. No matter how legitimate he became, crime was his main business. Hundreds of millions of dollars flowed through his organization over the year and everybody skimmed. It was a tolerated bonus system– up to a point.

Letting the spreadsheets cycle through, he watched the proof mount.

That someone was stealing wasn't surprising but the amounts were staggering. He marveled that anyone could be smart enough to implement such an intricate theft and still stupid enough to try it. Working for him, a smart, hard-working person could become very rich. Why steal from him when Angelino allowed himself to be used? People who blatantly stole from him only made themselves dead – very dead.

Angelino squeezed the small ball, controlling anger directed mainly at himself. He considered himself as a keen judge of character. But Thorman had truly surprised him. Of all his employees, he had rated

Thorman as one of the most trustworthy or maybe just most easily frightened. He had brought Thorman along, recognizing his ability early, and hiring him at a ridiculous rate straight out of school.

Then, the boy stole from him.

Still, Angelino had made the right decision about Thorman's brainpower. The man was an accounting genius. Too bad he was a freaking idiot, too.

William Hill walked across the light blue carpeting and sank into the chair in front of Angelino's desk. He hadn't bothered to shake hands with Angelino; he never did. He pulled out a pack of cigarettes and lit one with a silver lighter. He still hadn't spoken and Angelino just stared at him, not bothering to mention it was a no smoking building.

As it had in the past, Angelino's mind wrestled with the conflicting signals it was receiving. Hill's eyes were warm and sincere. Slightly sagging jowls gave him a soft, vulnerable look that welcomed trust.

Everything about him screamed middle-class burnout. There was no hint of the trained remorseless killer that hid behind those soft eyes.

"I have a problem with one of my accountants," Angelino finally said.

"Of the most serious nature?"

"Ya, right," Angelino said, hating this stupid kind of talk. His techs had swept the office just before this meeting but Hill would always be careful. "There is a complication. This has to be handled exactly as I lay out and might take some time."

"You're paying the money, friend. Of course, everything has its price and this one is now double my usual fee. I hate this city. This city is bad luck."

Angelino shrugged. He wasn't just making a lesson with this hit. Thorman had embezzled a great deal of money and Angelino wanted it back. He laid the circumstances out to Hill.

"So, I don't make a move until you say so. I just cover him until you find the bucks. It's a done deal, though? I can go ahead with the planning?"

"Believe me, there is no doubt how it will end. Just the when. But if he tries to run, he's all yours, money or no. I want him brought to me, if possible. If not, take him. He doesn't get to spend another dime."

"Use the usual transfer codes. And I'll expect a daily transfer of an extra ten percent for every day I am stuck here. Work fast, I really hate this city."

Chapter 27

No one remembered how East Wharf got its name. There was no West Wharf and East Wharf was on the north edge of the bay. During the day, the area was loud with the noises of large ships and dockworkers. The surrounding neighborhood, mostly shops, gut wrenching restaurants, and pornographic theatres did a slow business during the day. At night, that dark world came alive with junkies, hookers, and assorted unrighteous individuals who crawled up from whatever holes hid them during the day. Millions of dollars in goods, both legal and illegal, moved across the docks every day. At night, the trade ran almost exclusively to the illegal end.

The night people crowded the sidewalk in the early summer heat. Prostitutes leaned into car windows, occasionally getting into the car to disappear for a few minutes. A street vendor hawked a watch to an unsuspecting visitor to the city. Street people shuffled along, trying to find somewhere safe to spend the night.

Degget wore jeans, T-shirt, and an old fedora that had once belonged to his grandfather. A leather jacket covered his holster and gun. He moved with ease through the bustling streets.

Degget had been assigned to investigate street gangs for the task force. He was supposed to concentrate on the black gangs, naturally. It would help, if he could get close enough to one of the gangs to make conversation. So instead, he was working on his own investigation. He passed by the porn theatres with both video and live shows. Muscular men with potbellies tried to sweep both men and women off the sidewalk and into the shows. Occasionally, he would stop and talk to the barkers. For the most part, the street people shunned Degget. Word had already spread.

Degget needed a more willing participant.

From a distance he saw a quick deal go down. Stevie had just scored and would be heading for one of the local shooting galleries. Even from this distance, Degget could see Stevie was hurting.

Making an educated guess, Degget brushed past one of the bouncers at a sleazy nightclub and started through to the back. With the shortcut, he would intercept Stevie just outside the burned out hotel.

Degget had been dogging it on the task force. It wasn't as if that was hard to do. All he needed was a uniform who wanted his gold shield. He'd been happy to cover Degget's ass. It wasn't as if he was really involved in the active investigation. Once they got their heads out of their asses and stopped looking for a gang connection, he would involve himself more thoroughly. For now, he would use his time more productively on his own investigation.

Unfortunately, that was going in the same direction as the serial case – nowhere!

The leak had to be in SOCU. Flem waltzes in from SOCU and the shooters arrive. But Degget couldn't see Flem as the snitch. The Inspector was up for the Commissioner's job. The mayor would have checked him from his flat feet to his balding fat head. So, who did Flem tell? Who sold him out to Angelino?

He released some of his pent-up anger as he grabbed Stevie. He slammed him against a wall with one hand and snatched the baggie from the junkie with the other. Degget stayed clear of the addict's rotted teeth and bleeding gums. Stevie was sure to be positive and Degget wouldn't risk a bite.

"Who set me up, mon?" Degget asked, his Jamaican accent returning.

Stevie took time to focus. He had been thinking exclusively of the Horse in his hand. The last thing he expected was Degget. When recognition finally dawned, he literally wet his pants. He was either too frightened or hurting too much to notice.

"Jesus man, I don't fucking know."

"How bad you need this, Stevie?" Degget asked, holding the baggie in front of Stevie's face. When Stevie made a grab for the bag, Degget pocketed it out of the junkie's reach. He slammed Stevie against the wall again to get his attention.

"Hey, man," Stevie pleaded. "I don't know shit like that. I mean, Christ all mighty, I'm nobody."

"But you do talk to people. Pass the word. I'm looking for whoever put the finger on me. Tell them that I'm real pissed. You got that?"

Stevie nodded and Degget stepped back, tossing the baggie to the man. Stevie juggled the baggie for half a second and then darted toward the darkened doorway of the old hotel that served as a shooting gallery for local addicts.

* * * * *

Degget had come up with nothing. All his sources had dried up and blown away. But just being out on the street might prompt some action.

Odds were Angelino was still gunning for him. It was an honor thing with The Hinge. And if the Guinea bastard was still after him, so was the traitor who had exposed him. If he made enough noise and rattled enough cages, the traitor might get nervous. And that might mean exposure.

Degget turned up an alley. About half way to the next street, he heard the scrape of a shoe. He swung around, his hand going inside his jacket.

Two men stood just inside the alley. A sawed off shotgun was clearing the overcoat of the man on the left. The drunk staggered out of doorway and reached for the man on the right. The shotgun swung to the right and went off. The blast blew the drunk backwards into a pile of garbage. The man started to pump another cartridge into the chamber as Degget fired. The bullet hit square in the chest. The man flew back and landed on his back rather than crumpled. Degget recognized the look of that fall.

As the man on the right drew a pistol from beneath his jacket, Degget shifted his aim to the right and higher. The two headshots brought the second man down as the gun cleared the holster. Before the second man was down, the shotgun was coming up again. Knowing the man was wearing a vest, Degget went for another head shot. This time, the first man went down permanently.

Degget pulled out his cell phone and called in the officer involved shooting as he ran over to the drunk. A quick look told Degget there was no rush for an ambulance. Holstering his gun, he sat down on a box and waited. He could already hear the wail of the sirens approaching.

Chapter 28

Hill sat in his car outside Angelino's office. Already, his mind was working on the hit and the implications of the unusual stipulations. He flipped open his laptop and typed in a few commands. He waited for the connections to go through his encrypted sat-modem. As soon as he was connected he checked his balance. The initial deposit was already there.

Angelino was serious, he thought to himself.

Angelino had not named a figure but this Thorman must be into him for huge bucks. Normally, the lesson was of key importance since that saved more money in the end. To let the accountant walk around while he tried to trace the money was stupidity. Angelino's ego was working full tilt, risking everyone around him so he didn't come off as such an idiot.

If the money was worth it to Angelino, then it would be more than worth it to Hill. He was getting old and ready to retire. His reflexes were slower and he felt the pressure. The jobs were getting harder, more complicated. He longed for the old days of a .22 in the ear. Now they wanted "natural causes", not hits. Too much work, risk and stress weren't worth the money anymore.

And with enough money in the bank, he would just get rid of Angelino. Kesle would be reeling for years from the power vacuum and nobody would ever think to worry about looking for him.

Hill wondered how many men Angelino had on the job. He would be keeping it quiet, using only one or two and Hill could guess who those would be.

They could be useful, Hill thought, as his plan started to come together.

Chapter 29

Dale Lewery looked at the computer screen. In his hand, he had a hard copy of his original story. Munro had cut it in half and he was fuming. He got up from his desk and stalked up to his editor.

"Munro. What's with my story? Christ, you cut me in half."

"I had reason."

"Pull it up. Slug McIntosh slash serial."

"I know," Munro said, making no move toward his computer. "You don't have enough to go with the serial angle. I'm not going to print trash because you think you have a story. And, the gang kid? What's that?"

"Look, this is good. Really good."

"Words, those are all just words. I need proof. Show me proof."

"It's simple. The kid gets killed in the washroom."

"Gang related," interrupted Munro.

"I don't think so."

"Did I ever mention I hate when my reporters say 'think'?"

"Ya, ya. Listen, the kid is killed and Southfield gets the call, right? It's their division but just barely. A couple more blocks and it's in Central."

"So?"

"Then Yeck is killed."

"Strangled, I might add, as opposed to beaten to death."

"Yeck is killed on Friday, right? Central gets the squeal. But, three days later, Southfield picks up the case."

"Central tossed it? It happens. They get more cases than they can handle so they dump everything they can justify."

"Exactly! What's the justification? From what I hear, there's some connection, some link to the kid."

"You have 'heard', 'some connection'. These are not words that fill me with confidence. We are talking some middle class, drug free, bride-to-be and some low-life gang banger kid. What's the connection?"

"I tell you, there is a link. I don't know how. Not yet. But they have connected the killings somehow. That's why they tossed Southfield the case, first rights. You know how it works. You get a connected case; the original detectives get the call. But this time, whatever connected them, didn't come out for days."

"What about this task force?"

"I told you, the Commissioner formed a task force today to investigate a *serial killer*. McIntosh is the latest victim. I know there's a link between Yeck and McIntosh. They got the same detectives on it."

"Southfield got the call because it was in High Park," Munro said. "That's their division. No mystery there. And you know there aren't enough detectives to go around. They all get multiple cases."

"But they aren't up yet. And, there's more to it. I tell you, there is a task force."

Your information is good?"

"Golden. And I'll tell you, this last one was a bad one. I was there and some of those cops looked real green coming out. And, the cops cleaned it up themselves."

"What?" Munro said, sitting straighter. The cops rarely clean a site. Gather evidence, make a bigger mess, but you had to clean it up yourself or hire a blood crew.

"Yup, they sent their own guys in."

"OK," Munro said, drumming a little beat on his desk. "I'm getting a little more interested. But you can't connect this kid?"

"Not yet."

"Ya, not yet. OK, who's running the task force? How many they got on the task force? What divisions are involved?"

"I don't have too much. My information is, they pulled Keough in to head it and it is out of Southfield."

"Keough? I can go with that. He is on his way out and would make a good scapegoat if the investigation goes bad. Two killings aren't much to warrant a task force. There has to be more."

Lewery sensed Munro starting to weaken and kept pushing. "I know.

That's where the kid and especially the clean up comes in."

"Maybe. Anyway, Keough is a good administrator but who's going on lead? Are they going to use someone in Southfield?" Munro asked.

"I don't know. I've been trying to find out. No way it's Mann."

Munro nodded. "No, they wouldn't put Mann in. He's pissed in too many ponds to catch anything like this. This could be a career maker and his career was screwed years ago. He isn't exactly a political player."

Munro stared at Lewery, who knew enough to stay quiet for a change. The Mayor would piss tacks knowing there was a leak about a serial killer especially after just announcing his candidacy. However, he didn't want to go out too far, yet. But damn, that would sell some papers.

Munro rubbed his hands together and then sighed deeply. "What you got is weak."

Munro held up his hand when Lewery tried to speak. "Shut up and just listen. You're weak, very weak. But if your source is good, go with another rewrite. Use your original but go slow on the serial killer angle. For now, write it up as possible connections between the two killings. Nothing stronger than that. And don't mention the task force yet. Got it?"

Lewery was about to argue and stopped. He would play Munro's way for now. He would dig some more and see if he could get something more for the next few days. As long as he was keeping the flame burning, he could wait to throw on some gasoline.

Chapter 30

"It seems you have been busy," Mann said, his irritation obvious. He had just seen the bodies of the two shooters Degget had killed. On one hand, he had finally located his prime suspects for the Marina killing. On the other hand, they weren't going to be doing anymore talking. Literally another dead end on Angelino.

Degget looked up at Mann. "Yes, sir."

Mann stared hard at Degget. They were in one of the interrogation rooms at Central. Mann got the call because Degget was currently under his command on the Task Force. On the way down, Mann had been considering Degget. He knew Degget had sloughed off some of his work on one of the uniforms. Mann might have considered cutting him loose but, Davis aside, Degget was the best bet Mann had had at Angelino in years.

Degget glanced up at the camera in the corner of the room. Then he looked behind to see if there was a one-way mirror. There was just a cement wall but Mann knew what he was looking for. Mann walked over and pulled the plug on the video and sound feeds. Then he took a seat across from Degget.

"You know you just killed my best suspects in a shooting that I was planning on tracing back to Angelino."

"Sorry, Lou. Next time I'll let them waste my ass so I don't screw up your case. At least I must be shaking something loose to have them after me but I sure don't know what it is unless Angelino is just cleaning up."

"Angelino is pretty vindictive. But there might be an easier answer," Mann said.

Degget raised his eyebrows. "Ya?"

"You remember the guy with the shotgun tonight? He was the cousin of one of the guys you killed in your apartment."

Degget thought for a moment. "That makes sense 'cause I sure don't have shit."

"What have you been doing? Arnie wasn't any help?"

"When I couldn't even draw my gun without screaming, I figured my doctor was right and I should just heal. I spent last week on my back buying and selling stuff on Ebay. As for your buddy, he's in Arizona until next week. I'm hoping to hook up with him on Monday."

"And then?"

"I've already got an organizational chart of SOCU. I'm going to start looking into each member of the squad."

Mann nodded. "You know what kind of target you are painting on yourself?"

"Apparently," Degget said, a wry smile on his face that didn't reach his eyes. Mann could see determination in those eyes. Degget wasn't going to stop – which meant he needed protection. Damn it, Mann thought to himself, did he have to make a son out of every detective on his watch? Probably. Besides, this one was related to Davis. That did make him family.

"OK'" Mann said, "But I need everybody concentrating on this task force. You're working for me or I transfer you out. I want this nut off the streets. We have some leads coming in that are going to be more solid than the gang bull."

"I never really thought it was a gang," Degget said, trying to keep up with Mann's sudden shift. "That's why I was cool with dogging it while I, uh, followed other avenues."

"It's not a gang," Mann admitted. "However, the Mayor has his reasons not to be convinced. He would like nothing better than the gang angle. That means I have to waste time on it. So, since the ivory tower says keep working the gang angle, that is your assignment until further notice. You are working for me. You report to me. Understood?"

"Yes, sir." Degget replied.

"However," Mann added, walking toward the corner of the room, "keep me informed of any developments. When the time comes, you don't have to be alone in that alley. And if you are right, you damn well don't want to be."

Mann plugged the feeds back in and went to the door. "Get cleaned up. The OIS pukes will have some more questions but they'll clear you on this tonight. Get back to work in the morning. And let me know if Arnie gives you anything."

Chapter 31

Removing the envelope from his inside coat pocket with a piece of tissue, Preston dropped it in the mailbox.

Digging in his pocket, he brought out a caffeine pill. He popped the small, pink pill into his mouth and dry swallowed it. He needed the pills to keep awake.

He was tired most of the time, now. He spent all his free time hunting. For the first time in his life, he was the hunter! Casting his eye along the sidewalk, he watched people jostle each other, rudely pushing ahead to gain an extra three seconds, only to be stopped at the next crosswalk.

Beware, I am watching. I am vengeance! And my power will be that of legend.

But he was tired.

He needed a plan. This hit and miss approach was getting him nowhere. He had been lucky in the past but that luck might not hold. Obviously, it hadn't. Three days and he had not found a single match. He had to think!

His gift was brains.

Think! Hard to think when he was so tired.

He quickly thumbed through the book of pictures. A light rage filled his thoughts as he remembered the years of torment. Then, he remembered the killings. He remembered the revenge…the power. A satisfied warmth passed through him and he smiled a harsh, unfeeling smile. He shifted his jacket to cover the growing erection in his pants.

He had another almost ready. He'd spent so many late nights following him, learning his routine, and planning. This one was going to be incredible. He was almost ready. He had most of his supplies. All he needed was a delivery and a quick trip to the country.

He glanced at the mailbox one more time. He expected the contents of his little package to cause quite a stir when they arrived.

Chapter 32

While he waited for Greer, Mann scanned Buchanan's postmortem report. There was very little physical evidence once again. No fingerprints. The killer had wiped everything down. They hadn't even found a strand of hair.

Mann sat back in his chair and rubbed his eyes. He looked up at the sound of a knock. He motioned Greer into the office.

"Evening, Lou."

Mann thought Greer looked tired. He probably had been following the doctor most of the night. "What do you have on the doctor?"

Greer already had his notebook out. "I questioned Dr. Michels again today."

"And?"

"He says that he went to her apartment. He rang her buzzer but didn't get any answer. He said he was pissed off and went for a drive. You know, big doctor stood up by the lowly nurse. Then, he thought maybe she had been in the shower or something so he went back. He still got nothing so he went home."

"No alibi?"

"He says that he doesn't remember anybody that saw him. He did call his service from his cell. We checked with his provider and he did make the call. They are backtracking the tower but he says he did it from the parking lot of the vic's apartment so we know where that's headed – parking lot or the basement, same difference."

Mann thought for a moment. The doctor was the perfect suspect. He had the opportunity and definitely had the means. If he was a psycho, the motive could be anything. However, they would have to go slow if they wanted to build a case with very little physical evidence.

"He won't voluntarily give a DNA sample," Greer added.

"He give you a reason?"

"He felt it was an intrusion on his rights to be catalogued in the system," Greer said.

"OK, give him some rope," Mann decided. "I want you to do some more checking on him. Go back and get some alibis for the other two killings. That will give us something more. If he's our boy, he's going to do it again. Monitor him. I think that we might want to put a tail on him. I'll clear it with Keough and get some more bodies."

"It's just subjective opinion," Greer said slowly, "but he seemed really freaked by the whole thing. I think he's feeling guilty for being pissed off at her."

"Stay on him but go slow for now. If we get anything from the other killings, we'll go for a warrant for the DNA."

Chapter 33

The room was pitch black.

From the other room, he could hear the steady drip of water. Drip, plop, ping. Drip, plop, ping. Drip, plop, ping. You'd think he'd fix it. Kraemer was destroying his Zen. He always had.

Of all the bullies, David Kraemer was the worst. A blond, blue eyed Adonis who lived to terrorize the defenseless, he was perpetually tanned and wealthy. He used his money and his muscle to attract the girls who flocked to him. They threw themselves at him, the sluts. They didn't care what he was like; just that he had money and power.

Kraemer was an athlete. He was good at everything! Name it and he was the best the school had – at least, for the sports that mattered. And Kraemer knew it. He parlayed his strength and ability into becoming a God among the lesser humans. He used his strength to impress the girls out of their pants. To him, sex was a reward, a badge of honor earned by virtue of his greatness and his wealth.

The world owed David Kraemer and David Kraemer was going to collect.

How Preston hated him.

But, Kraemer only had brute strength with little intelligence. As Quarterback, he stretched his mental ability to the limit. The coach always sent in the plays. The superman was lost if he could not use his physical prowess. Denied brute force, the scum was scrambling for an answer.

As with all bullies, he demeaned what he lacked. Intelligence had no place in his world of muscle and sweat. Nothing but sports mattered. In Kraemer's world, anyone who didn't score touchdowns, baskets or goals was useless.

He thumbed the switch and the small lamp illuminated the scene. He smiled at the vision provided by the circle of light. He could hardly wait for Kraemer to arrive. He would learn that brains always beat brawn.

He rubbed his right wrist. Even after all these years, the lump of bone and the scar remained. In the cold or damp, it ached – a constant reminder of the humiliation of that day.

* * * * *

David Kraemer was horny.

Jerking off that morning had done nothing to ease the ache. He wanted to get laid. There was a new girl in town who called herself Sunni. Sunni, with an 'i'. He couldn't stop thinking about her and that tanned body that just wouldn't quit. She was here from California visiting her cousin. She was going home tomorrow so this was his last chance at some Cali putang. He had spent most of the day hitting on her and getting nothing. Then, the wimp had waddled by. The Gods were smiling.

"Hey, wimp. I thought I told you never to come around here again." David turned to Sunni. "I keep telling this geek not to come around but he won't stay away. I swear he likes to get hit."

Preston couldn't move, barely fighting down the panic. He had been stupid to come this way after the music lesson but his mind had been on his science project. He tried to just keep walking. Clutching his music case, he angled toward the pillars to get out.

Kraemer had no intention of letting him go. Too good to be true, he couldn't let the opportunity pass. Sunni would love to watch this little wimp get his. Besides, the fat slob just plain deserved it. The short, fat, brainiac lived to be beaten. And David was born to do the beating. He moved up face to face with the little wimp while his three friends moved in behind, cutting off his escape.

"Gonna run home and cry to your mommy, geek?"

"Just leave me alone, David. I'm not bothering you."

His voice came out with a slight quiver that David exaggerated. "*I'm not bothering you.* You fruit. No wonder you play the fucking *flute.* You like playing the flute, gay boy? Bet you like playing the skin flute too, don't you?"

Sunni and the other girls giggled, encouraging David. His three friends stepped forward and formed a semi-circle behind Preston, eager for the action.

"You ARE bothering me, wimp. Your face bothers me. You bother anyone who has to look at you. I've warned you and warned you. Now, I guess I'll just have to show you. Give me your flute and I'll show you what you can do with it!"

Panic finally overruled all else and he started to run.

Kraemer grabbed him from behind before he had finished the second step. Then the taller boy, reaching for the music case, swung Preston around and into one of the pillars. He hit his nose, not hard enough to break it but blood began to gush. When he was pulled back to face the girls, Sunni vomited.

When David saw Sunni tossing up her lunch, he went into a rage. His planned afternoon down by the pond was ruined. He couldn't kiss her with barf breath. He wasn't even sure if he wanted a blow job with barf breath.

David turned on him and came forward. "Stupid, fucking wimp!" The animal look burned on his tanned face. He was crouched and his hard blue eyes were mere slits – one hand clenched into a vicious fist and the other hooked into a claw.

Preston desperately looked for an escape. Kraemer's friends had backed off when they saw the look in their leader's eyes. They were almost as frightened as Preston was. Preston realized that if he turned and ran, they wouldn't stop him. He started the motion but ran into the pillar again and slammed against the wall.

David tried to land punches but the wall and the pillar impeded his swing. He started to drag Preston away from the wall.

Preston began to cry. Desperate for any protection, he reached between the pillar and the wall to anchor himself.

Frustrated, David grabbed his arm just below the elbow and pulled.

The sound of the cracking wrist echoed through the enclosure and Preston screamed. He slowly pulled his arm out of the hole in the bricks. His arm was suddenly numb and he felt the world spin as he stared at the bone sticking through the skin. Sunni threw up again.

David backed up, suddenly frightened. His friends were already cowering far in the back of the enclosure.

Tears streaming down his face, Preston cradled his arm against his body and staggered toward home. Behind him, David was recovering. Summoning up his remaining bravado, he started to chant, "Baby tears, baby tears." Soon, the others had picked up the chant and were laughing at his retreating figure.

* * * * *

Tired and a little drunk, Lionel Hart opened his apartment door and was surprised to find darkness. Normally, he left the hall light on. He felt along the wall and flipped the light switch. It was already in the up position. "Not again."

Since he had bought the loft, the building power had gone out twice. He started into the apartment and stopped. He turned around and looked at the light in the hall. The lighting wasn't bright, just barely penetrating the apartment, but it was on. He had taken the elevator up as well.

Circuit breaker?

Hart started into the apartment again. Moving slowly, he groped toward the kitchen and the flashlight on the fridge. When the door started to ease shut, he didn't notice. Then, the light came on.

Hart hardly noticed the small lamp on the floor. Instead, he looked at the rope suspended from the ceiling. The light shone brightly on the hangman's noose and then faded until it disappeared before the rope met the rafters. He was so enthralled by the sight; he didn't hear the footstep behind him.

He never saw his attacker. The rubber hose, weighted with lead shot, struck him in the back of the head and he collapsed.

When he came to, he was suspended by his hands. His arms ached and he kicked his legs, trying to find some support but they wouldn't move. He had tape across his mouth. Through blurred vision, he could see someone moving in front of him.

"Do you remember me, Kraemer?"

Hart blinked at the man, trying to recognize the voice. His vision was still blurred and he couldn't see clearly. He shook his head and felt something around his neck.

"Don't remember me? You'll feel the pain anyway. And you know what, David? I brought my flute."

Chapter 34

Thorman stood in the doorway. Tinker Bell shone brightly, the little nightlight helping him pick his way to the bed. He bent over his sleeping daughter. Her small form looked so innocent and delicate.

She had kicked the sheets down so he pulled them up around her neck. She sighed in her sleep and turned to face him. He waited until she was settled and bent to kiss her. He drank in her little girl scent until his back started to ache.

As he backed up, he stepped on one of her toys. She stirred again when the small creature squeaked. He waited until her breathing returned to normal. Then, paying more attention to where he was going, he walked out of the room.

He continued past his own bedroom and his sleeping wife. He would not be able to sleep so there was no sense in disturbing her. Instead, he returned to the bar in the living room and started to pour another drink.

Looking at the decanter, he thought about how much he was drinking. He tried to remember when he had last filled the decanter. Had Jill filled it since then? Christ, could he hang on long enough? He poured the drink.

Should he just go upstairs and wake Jill? They needed nothing from the house but the one suitcase. In hours, they could be in the air and out of the country forever. He took out his cell phone and speed dialed the airline.

"When your next flight to London, England?"

He listened to the courteous voice on the other end. "Nothing earlier than that?"

That was a stupid question and he could hear the impatience creep into the woman's voice. "What about Paris?"

Thorman listened for another couple of seconds and then closed the phone and sipped at his drink. London, Paris, either flight would do. Jill would fly there with Alison and he would take the train somewhere to the west. The sixth big city he found, he would jump on a plane to Chicago. From Chicago, he would fly to Los Angeles. From Los Angeles, he would head back East through Mexico to Jamaica. From there a chartered boat would quietly take him from Jamaica to the Caymans.

Meanwhile, Jill would be driving across Europe until they lost themselves. Then, she would continue east until they ended up in the French Polynesian Islands. He would meet them there. If they took enough planes, trains, buses, and cars, they could just get lost. The world was so big.

But, the big score was coming. This was the one that would tell Angelino that he had corrupted the wrong man. He would get even with Angelino for perverting the art of accounting and turning him into an accounting whore. He only had to hang on for a couple more weeks, three at the most. He could almost double the money if he just waited. He'd have enough to buy an entire island. If he could hang on, he would never have to worry about money again. But, did he have the guts?

* * * * *

From his hiding spot behind Thorman's house, Hill watched Thorman sitting in his home office. He had picked this vantage point early in his surveillance because the houses on either side didn't have dogs. The natural rise of the Bluffs gave him the perfect view of both the house and the road. Dressed in black, wedged into the hedge, he was virtually invisible once night arrived, unlike the two idiots that Angelino had watching Thorman from their car parked on the street.

Thanks to the listening devices and cameras placed strategically throughout the house, Hill had heard the conversation with the airline. Thorman was starting to panic. If Hill played it just right, Thorman would be wound tight. That would make him act even more suspiciously. Even those idiots down there would notice and report to Angelino.

Hill needed Thorman in a state of visible distress if his plan was going to seem plausible. Already, Thorman wasn't sleeping, drinking too much, and then taking pills to stay awake. He was becoming paranoid and susceptible. The proper threats should push him over the edge.

And then, the two idiots in the green sedan could play their final part. God knows, the world would never miss them.

Chapter 35

"Commissioner? How many murders is this man responsible for? How many times has this man killed?"

Mayor Dalton, sitting beside the Commissioner, looked down from the podium at Dale Lewery. Lewery always hit for the fence. God, how he hated that man. Likely James had prepared answers to questions in the order that he thought they would come. Lewery never bothered with logical order. Lewery had proven that the *Daily* had been on top of the story all along. Every word he wrote hinted at a serial killer without actually coming out and saying it. Now that they had been forced to admit the existence of a serial killer, Lewery would run with everything he had. Nothing increased circulation like a maniac stalking the streets.

Mayor Dalton glanced sideways at the Commissioner. He willed the man to hurry up and answer. Each moment reduced the credibility of his reply. Finally, James cleared his throat.

"At this time, we feel that there have been two victims." He glanced at the sheet of paper in front of him. "Christine Yeck and Jeanne McIntosh."

Shouted questions sounded through the small room but Lewery would not yield the floor. "Commissioner! What about Luis Gabel?"

The Commissioner's face clearly registered disbelief for a two count before shifting to anger. He glanced over at Keough and Mann, a clear message that there would be a long discussion about snitches within the department.

Gathering what poise he could muster, James turned back to the pack of reporters. "At this time, we have no conclusive evidence that Luis Gabel was killed by the same killer as the other two victims."

James quickly pointed toward another reporter. He did not recognize her but anything was better than Lewery.

"Commissioner, wasn't Luis Gabel a known gang member? Does that mean that these killings could be gang related? Are you investigating a gang connection?"

Mayor Dalton saw James start to shake his head. He almost swore aloud and quickly stood up beside the idiot. Leaning toward the microphone, he interrupted James. "At this time, we do not have enough information to dismiss that avenue of investigation. There is certainly evidence to point in that direction. However, we are not limiting ourselves for this investigation. We have already set up a task force to investigate these chilling murders. Although we see a swift resolution, we are prepared to expand that force as necessary."

"And how do you answer the charges that the public should have been informed of the danger?"

"We are informing the public," Mayor Dalton said, looking Lewery square in the eye. "A panicked public, no matter how well informed, is at a disadvantage. We are sparing nothing to bring these killers to justice. I trust that you will do your utmost to inform the public of the facts and not attempt to sell newspapers or increase ratings by sensationalizing these murders. We are going to bring these vicious murderers to justice before they have a chance to kill again!"

The brief silence following the Mayor's comments was shattered by the sound of a cell phone going off. Mann reached to look at the text message as Keough's sounded. In the space of three heartbeats, half a dozen cell phones were going off, including the Commissioner's. Mann jumped to his feet and began to leave the podium before the rest of the group had their cell phones out of their pockets.

The Mayor looked at Mann's retreating figure and quickly turned to the reporters gathered in front of him. "That is all for today. Thank you for coming."

Dalton walked through the curtains at the back of the room and James followed. When they were out of earshot, Dalton turned on James. "What the hell was all that about?"

"They found another body," James said, trying not to make the statement sound too obvious.

"God damn it. Was someone just waiting until I was in front of the cameras? And tell me you weren't going to deny the gang angle."

"The evidence doesn't point toward a gang. There is nothing to the gang theory, no matter how politically convenient it might be."

Dalton looked around to see who might have overheard the comment. "God protect me from idiots. I don't care who says what. If you have an option between a single crazed killer or a run of the mill gang, which do you think would be better for the public? Christ on a cracker, they've already accepted gangs. Nobody likes them but they don't really think about them anymore."

James nodded, although he obviously didn't agree. What the Mayor was really saying was that nobody was going to run against him on an anti-gang platform since nobody could do anything about them anyway.

"As for Keough, I want him replaced. A captain shouldn't be in charge of something like this. I want at least a Deputy Inspector. If your detectives can't show some movement in the investigation, at least I will be seen as taking it seriously."

James had been expecting this. It would look better for the media. He had been trying to find a replacement for two days. Problem was, nobody wanted the job. Every detective in the department was falling all over themselves to be assigned to the task force. There was no downside and a hell of an upside if they broke anything. But finding a bureaucrat to be responsible for the case? That was an entirely different matter.

"There are not many available at this time due to the recent budgetary cutbacks," James said. "It might take some time."

"We will make the announcement this afternoon at four to make the evening news. If you can't find someone by then, maybe you would like to head this investigation yourself? That would look good in the press."

"I disagree. If I involve myself directly, I will be showing a lack of faith in my own men. Better that I delegate the duties until it becomes absolutely necessary that I take over."

Dalton looked at James for a long time. Slowly, a smile spread across the Mayor's face. He reached out and lightly patted the Commissioners cheek. "I'll make a politician out of you yet. Now get out of here and get me some information on the latest victim. And for the love of Christ, turn off your blessed cell phones during the next press conference."

* * * * *

Mann stared up at the naked body hanging from the rafters in the loft and shuddered. There was a limpness to the body that looked unnatural. The body didn't hang right. Mann couldn't quite figure out what was wrong.

"I understand the reporters couldn't hear the Mayor because of all the cell phones at the press conference," Buchanan said from behind Mann.

Mann smiled in spite of the scene in front of him. The rumors certainly sped around the department. "I think His Honor had a stroke when he looked around. I didn't wait to hear the fallout. Let the Commissioner have that pleasure, he gets paid way more than I do."

"Ain't that the truth," the Medical Examiner said. "Then again, he doesn't have to look at things like this."

"No doubt on this one," Mann said, more of a statement than a question.

"Nope," Buchanan said, shining a flashlight on the chest where the killer's symbol was carefully carved in the skin. Mann had that same feeling. The chest didn't look right, even accounting for the carving.

"You had your look?" Mann asked.

"I just got here a few minutes ago. Want to do a walk through together?" Buchanan asked.

"Lead on, Master."

Buchanan stepped over the threshold. Out of habit, he checked to see if Mann was wearing gloves. He pointed to the light switch on the wall. "We had to tighten the bulb to get this to work. I suspect the killer loosened it himself. Want to see it the way the killer wanted us to?"

"Ya, I want to try and see it through his eyes. I still can't figure this guy out. Why a male victim this time?"

"This one was definitely chosen. He knew this victim or chose him for some reason. Everything screams planning. He knew the apartment layout. I highly suspect he brought the rope with him. He knew about the rafters. He had been here before."

The lamp positioned under the body cast strange shadows over the body but clearly showed the vicious violence. Two ropes ran from the rafters, suspending the body by the hands. The legs were tied to ropes and anchored to two large piles of weights. He appeared to be doing a jumping jack in the air, like some perverse cheerleader. His mouth was taped with duct tape. More duct tape was running from around his head to both arms to hold his head up. Both eyes were swollen shut; one ear was dangling by a bit of skin. Blood ran down both arms from where his wrists were tied.

The now familiar sign was carved high on his chest. Below that bloody mark, the man's stomach had a large gash from sternum to groin that had been sewn back up with thick black thread. He didn't have any genitals.

"His name was Lionel Hart, Lou," Mann heard from behind him. "Lives alone."

Mann kept looking at the scene as Lanyon read the report from the doorway. "Super found him because the door was open. He had seen the door open early this morning but figured Hart had just taken some trash down or something. When he saw it again later this morning, he opened the door and found the body."

"He mention the mark?" Mann asked.

"Don't think he noticed. He didn't go in the apartment. It isn't really noticeable from the door because of the way the lamp is positioned."

"The lamp isn't really set to display the body well. Was it moved?" Mann asked.

"Nope, right where he left it to highlight what he really thought was important," Buchanan said, walking behind the body.

"What the hell is that?" Mann asked, as he came around the body.

"A flute."

"A what?" Mann's mind adjusted to the upside down picture and the scene came into focus. There was about six inches of flute sticking out of the victim's rectum. "How long is a flute?" Mann asked.

"I don't know, maybe two feet," Buchanan said.

Chapter 36

"So you're Davis' nephew," Arnold Olinyk said, leaning against the counter.

"Ruby is my aunt, Mr. Olinyk," Degget said, looking around the small kitchen. It was surprisingly clean for a retired cop's place. Everything was in place, no dishes in the sink. Degget wondered if that was because his uncle's friend had just returned from an extended vacation or if it was always this neat.

"That much is obvious. You don't exactly have your uncle's size," Olinyk said.

"No sir, I'm afraid my one cousin's already taller than I am. And he's only fifteen."

"Call me Arnie. How about a beer?" Arnie said, motioning to the kitchen table. "All I got is Bud Light, if that is good with you."

"My favorite," Degget said.

"Good man. Never turn down a man's beer, even if it tastes like cold horse piss."

Olinyk dug out a couple cf beers and pop the caps. "Davis told me about you being under for two years and about you getting burned. Two separate tries on your life? Christ, I never even fired my gun once in the line of duty. How you doing kid?"

Degget looked into the older man's eyes and saw genuine concern. "I'm five and O at the moment. Five of them in the ground and I'm still kicking. I lived with these shits for two years. I know what they are so I'm not having too much trouble with having blown them away, if that is what you're asking."

"Bloody right," Olinyk agreed. "Bad guy draws down on you, somebody is going away and it sweet Jesus better not be you."

Degget clinked Arnie's upraised beer bottle in response.

"And you think SOCU is where the leak came from?"

Degget paused, still concerned about Olinyk's loyalty, and Arnie just laughed. "Don't worry, son. There ain't no love lost between me and that bunch of desk-riding suits at SOCU. I can't say any of them is bent but they sure aren't cops."

"How so?"

"Like I said, I'm not saying they are hinked but they sure aren't what I was figuring when I got assigned there. I mean, I was the token old guy. When the Mayor formed SOCU, he needed some gray hair to give the new squad some legitimacy. I was a decorated detective with a solid arrest record. But I already had my twenty. I was hanging around 'cause I loved the job. I liked putting away the bad guys and I thought this was going to be some kind of kick ass Untouchables thing."

"The Mayor sure makes it sound like it. Our last best defense, right?"

"It's a small squad, only like a dozen guys that work very independently on the surface. You figure a flying squad like this should do some real damage, right? Nobody stands in their way and they get the job done. Not the way it works. I'll tell you, Flem is no Elliot Ness and the squad ain't the Untouchables. More like LA Law."

Arnie finished off his beer and got up to get another. Degget waved off his offer of another and Arnie continued. "I'm a street cop. They put me in a suit and gave me my gold but I was still a street cop. But I was through with the little guys. You arrest one of them and ten guys are lined up to take his place. I was after something big and I thought that was what SOCU was all about. I was expecting big cases, big takedowns and lots of warehouse raids. Two years and I never went on a raid, never broke down a door. Christ, I hardly pulled my gun."

"That's not necessarily a bad thing," Degget said, remembering the past few weeks.

"No but all of these arrests were so bloody civilized. And they didn't really mean snot. Everything was political and designed for good press. All there was were lots of spreadsheets and org charts, meetings and discussions, conversations with the Mayor. Independent my ass. The Mayor had his hand up Flem's tight puppet ass from the start. Everything was for show."

"You mean they weren't good arrests?"

"Oh they were good. Too good. Everything always stood up in court with an amazing conviction rate. We got some major drugs and guns off the street but that was it. All the arrests were for show. If it looked good on the news, it was what the Mayor wanted. And the conviction rate? If you ignore anything that might not get a conviction, even if it takes somebody down only for a while, you are going to keep your record intact. Only bet on the sure thing, you are going to win but you don't win big."

Degget thought about it for a moment. "But you never suspected that anyone was dirty?"

"Everybody's probably dirty. Hang around with the kind of money we touched and the bloody Pope would be tempted. But get a cop killed kinda dirty? No way. I wouldn't have pegged anybody on the squad for that kinda dirty. These aren't real cops; they are just fast tracking for the political posts. Christ, most of them have their nose so far up Flem's ass, their snot is brown."

"Nothing that stands out? No excessive violence? Citizen complaints? IA investigations?"

Olinyk snorted. "You'd actually have to face someone to rough him up and that might wrinkle your suit. No, these guys were picked because they were part of the political machine, not because they could stand toe to toe with anybody."

Degget stayed for a while longer talking with Arnie but didn't really come away with anything useful.

Chapter 37

Deputy Inspector Stephen Livermore sat back in the creaking wooden chair behind Keough's desk at the task force headquarters. Sitting on the other side beside Mann, Keough slid a cup of coffee across the desk.

"Andy, I'm sorry that they pulled you back on this," Livermore said.

Keough shrugged. "I was expecting it. Four killings are too much for a lowly Captain. As far as I'm concerned, you're welcome to it. I hate the psycho cases."

"Just as long as you understand that this is just a political thing. A Deputy Inspector looks better at the press conferences. If James could have come up with an Inspector, I would still be reading about this case in the papers."

Mann grinned. If they had to have more brass involved, he was happy with the choice. Livermore wasn't particularly concerned with his political career. The Mayor was doing his best to deny the psycho. Eventually, even he would have to admit the truth. Meanwhile, Livermore would keep the politics away from the investigation and let Mann take it in whatever direction was necessary.

"I've read most of the reports. I was up all night skimming what has been accomplished so far. I want to hear personal opinions."

"The gang angle is in the toilet," Keough said.

"That about covers it," Mann confirmed. "We haven't come up with anything. Every major club has disavowed. Even the small-time guys are smart enough to know they don't want this heat. They've normally got what three, maybe four, percent of the budget aimed at them? They know the task force is going to bring major heat so the smart ones have been cooperating – as much as cooperating means to those low-lifes."

Livermore agreed. "What about a cult?"

"That holds a little more hope," Mann replied. "The whole thing stinks of devil worship. I've got people on it now but so far, we have come up empty. We have some evidence that it is a single killer or at least no evidence that there is more than one. I'm leaning that way."

"What do you have on the sign?"

"Everything and nothing. Could be anything. The guys on the cult angle see it as some sort of goat. Fairly traditional symbol for the devil."

"Opinion?"

"A single man," Mann said firmly. "A real bad ass, totally screwed up, psycho who is going to go totally ape-shit before long."

Keough nodded his agreement. "And, he's not limiting himself to women. You haven't found a pattern yet? His next target could be anyone? The press is going to have a field day with this one."

"We have come up with one lead."

Mann showed Livermore two pictures of a matchbook. The open cover was black with *Night Dance* written in sparkling gold letters. Inside the cover was a telephone number.

"We found this at Hart's place. We found another one at Jeanne McIntosh's apartment."

Livermore looked at the second picture. "This is McIntosh's phone number?"

"No, life couldn't be that easy. It belongs to another woman. We are checking her out but I think she is unrelated."

"Do you think they might have been left by the killer?" asked Livermore.

"No. It was found in a drawer of Hart's bedside table. It has Hart's fingerprints on it and is in his writing. McIntosh's was in her apartment and the killer never got that far."

"Do you think McIntosh and Hart knew each other?"

Mann held up the palms of both hands. "His number was not in her address book. We are cross checking phone records. We are going to have to redo all our interviews with her friends. We already know she went to the *Night Dance* so they could have met there. Hart's name wasn't on any of our lists from our investigation into McIntosh but that isn't surprising."

Livermore rubbed the back of his neck. "Jealousy, maybe revenge?"

"Maybe," Keough said. "We'll know more when we find out whether they ever dated. If they were sleeping together, we might be able to tie a third acquaintance to them. If we can do that, then we might have our psycho. The Yeck kill could have been a cover-up."

"More likely," Mann added, "the *Night Dance* is a hunting ground. Thing is, the *Night Dance* was fighting the no smoking ban and handed out about a million of these matchbooks."

Livermore was silent for a moment before he continued. "What does Buchanan have on the Hart kill?"

Mann flipped a file open and slid it around so Livermore could see the pictures. The first one was of Hart hanging by his hands.

"Alf says this is getting worse and I can confirm that," Mann said. "Hart was severely beaten. He was beaten for hours. Whoever did this was meticulous. Virtually every bone is his body was broken. Hart was alive for most of it, too."

Mann thought about his initial impression of the body. Now he knew why the body looked so wrong. Every bone had been broken. His chest had been caved in from severe blows, likely from a metal baseball bat. "For one person to do this kind of damage, they had to have beaten him, rested, beaten him more, and rested and so on. We found evidence that he stopped and had a couple power drinks that Hart had in his fridge."

Livermore flipped the pictures while Mann continued. "The killer cut him from sternum to groin. His internal organs had been removed. This time, we found them in the trash rather than spread around. The empty space remaining between his broken ribs had been scraped clean – like a pumpkin. He then filled the cavity with cow manure and sewed him back up."

"Cow manure?"

"Pretty clear message. The man was literally full of bull shit."

"Is it being analyzed?"

"Yes," replied Mann, knowing where Livermore was headed. "Looks like it was fresh. I don't think this is going to be tracked back to a supplier. I think he just went out in a field and picked it up. We're working that angle to see if we can find anyone who saw anything. But it is a big area to canvass. We're getting help from the Troopers."

Livermore let a shudder pass through him and turned to the next picture. "What the hell?"

"It's a flute. He used a rubber mallet to get it up there. Buchanan says it wasn't post mortem."

"Jesus. What else can Buchanan tell from this?" Livermore's voice was weak and he cleared his throat. "Did he get anything more on the psycho?"

"Alf is sure that he is left handed. The direction of the blows and the way the knots are tied point that way. Otherwise, the apartment was clean. No prints and no DNA, so far. The killer also took the larynx again."

Chapter 38

"I see a juicy, rare steak that takes two waiters to carry. A baked potato. Steamed cauliflower with a wine and cheese sauce. A good wine – something expensive. I'll let the steward pick it out. Desert might never end – decadent is how they will describe it. God, I can taste it already."

Munro looked over at Lewery. "You are the only person I know that could be happy that a psycho is loose in the city."

"I'm not happy about that. I'm only happy I was right."

"That I can understand. After all, when was the last time it happened?"

Lewery let the comment pass and looked back at the computer screen. He had finished the last rewrite of his story hours ago but he had not come up with a headline. Sprinkled through the body of the text, KNAME stood out in red.

The rest of the office was empty. The night crew was on a break before the final crush of press time. Still, neither he nor Munro could come up with a name for the killer.

"Without a name, the whole thing falls apart. We need a name to pull the article together. What's a serial killer with a distinctive tag to hang on him?"

Munro stared off into space. "We don't know enough about him."

"What's to know? He strangles his victims and then cuts them up."

Munro nodded. "Okay. What about the Kesle Killer or Kesle Jack?"

"Good but he seems to have settled around the South area. What about the Southside Strangler or the Southbay Slasher?"

"Slashing is what will sell papers and we have a higher circ in the South end. Southside Slasher. Good alliteration and not too difficult to say. Agree?"

Lewery leaned over his terminal and tapped at the keys. SOUTHSIDE SLASHER TERRORIZES CITY appeared across the top of his screen. He did a couple quick commands and the KNAME automatically became Southside Slasher throughout the article. He pressed another series of commands and watched the rest of the front page format. Munro reached over and hit the send button.

"Well," Munro said, looking at the clock, "that just made deadline."

Chapter 39

George Logan sipped his coffee and looked at the map spread out across his table. A donut on a piece of wax paper held down one corner of the map which threatened to blow away every time someone walked in the door of the donut shop. He placed his finger on a red dot on the map. He traced his finger along the many straight streets to a blue circle. He knew the route without looking at the map. Twenty minutes in the worst of the rush hour traffic. The subway might be faster depending on the time of day.

He looked at his watch. Gathering up the map, he left the donut shop and walked to his car. He pressed a button on his watch starting the timer. As quickly as he dared, he drove through the wet streets of the city. When he turned into the parking lot, he glanced at the stop watch and smiled. He found a parking spot and turned off the car. He immediately got out of the car and sprinted for the entrance.

* * * * *

Tina Logan watched her husband catch his breath. She shifted uncomfortably in the hospital bed and held her hand over her stomach. The baby kicked as he too searched for a more comfortable position. "You're going to kill yourself. Why do you have to rush around so?"

Logan still couldn't talk without gasping. "I want to be sure I can make it."

"I'm not due for a week. Besides, if you don't make it, it won't be the end of the world. I want you alive to see your son."

"Shhhh, everyone will hear you." Logan looked around at the other beds in the quad room hating that everything was packed in so close. No privacy. Looking at his wife's expression, he knew she was annoyed with their old argument about him wanting a private room for the first night the baby was born. She raised her eyebrows.

"OK, not going to talk about that, promise. But I'm not going to miss our first child being born either."

Tina had been in the hospital for the past month and George had visited her every night. She looked forward to his visits but his worrying tired her. She just wished that the baby would come so she could go back home. The miracle of birth was amazing but it was also a total pain in the ass. The waiting would be the death of her.

Tina didn't have long to wait – for birth and death.

Chapter 40

Lewery slit open the padded envelope and shook out the contents onto his desk without even looking. He was watching the ball game on the newsroom television as he opened his correspondence from the last few days. Well, maybe more than a few days. He'd been too busy with the Slasher case to really worry about it. Since naming the Southside Slasher two days ago, Munro had let him really run with the story. The latest story about the *Night Dance* had been brilliant. But the mail did pile up. He really needed an assistant to look after this paper.

He glanced down at the contents of the envelope and then looked back at the television. It took a full thirty seconds before his baseball focused mind realized what he had seen sitting on his desk. He turned his head slowly down, almost afraid to look in case the object wasn't what he thought.

He stared for another full minute, goose bumps breaking out on his body. Finally able to bring himself out of his stupor, he took his letter opener and his pen and moved the object aside. Carefully, he opened the letter that had also come in the envelope. He read it twice before he shot out of his desk chair.

"Lewery what are you screaming about?" Munro shouted as he crossed the newsroom

"Munro, you have to see this," Lewery yelled. "I wish we could have stopped the presses. I've always wanted to say that."

Munro stood behind Lewery's desk. "Ya, that's going to happen, right after they promote you to my job. You've been watching way too many movies."

"After they see what is in this envelope," Lewery said, "they just might give me that promotion."

Munro looked down on the desk blotter and instantly recognized Jeanne McIntosh's driver's license. As soon as he saw the small piece of plastic, he picked up the entire blotter and started toward his office. Lewery didn't have any choice but to follow.

"Shut the door," Munro ordered.

Munro opened his desk drawer and took out a clear page protector and a pair of tweezers. Carefully, he picked up the letter by one corner with the tweezers and slipped it into the plastic cover. "Tell me you didn't touch any of this."

"I'm not an amateur," Lewery said. "But this could really change the front page."

"Not tomorrow's," Munro said, sitting down and staring at the letter. Now shut up and let me read this."

Lewery moved behind the desk so he could read over Munro's shoulder. He still couldn't believe his luck. He had toyed with the idea of writing a book about this case. It was the story of a lifetime and having the scoop on the serial angle already gave him a boost. With this, the publishers would be bidding fast and furious and he would have a guaranteed best seller.

Dear Mr. Lewery,

I am writing to you because I have always admired your writing, your determination and your unswerving pursuit of the truth. I sense a kindred spirit. One who has survived similar tortures and trials. Powerless and weak, we have decided to strike back. I have been freed by life-changing events and I wish to free others.

You are the voice that I cannot provide. There are those who would try to muzzle me because they cannot risk being exposed. But your words can be seen by millions and together we can make people understand the danger we all face. I know that you won't be satisfied with the filthy lies that will be told about me. Their violence, their hate, their harassment must be stopped.

I understand and can forgive your unknowing mistake in calling these dead people "victims". Writing from the outside, deceived by the liars, you can be allowed this error of judgment this once. I will bring you inside, expanding your knowledge and vision. You will understand that I am the victim. I have always been the victim. We all have. We are all subjected to untold and unforgivable torment by these vicious creatures. Creatures, yes…they are less than human.

I'm sure you will get many pretenders contacting you. But you will know me by my mark. And by the driver's license of the liar I have already exposed. Yes, I have exposed her to the world and shown her for the filthy liar and tease that she always was. Now the world knows what I have always known. Rejoice in the revelations that I bring to the world and pass my word to those who hide in the darkness and lurk in the background. Those afraid to show their faces will soon be able to come into the light.

I remain in the dark, where I have always been forced to hide. But now I am a warrior. Retribution embodied. Revenge is at hand for all. Death and exposure finally comes to those who have terrorized me for so long. I hide in fear no longer but remain hidden in order to strike and survive. I will punish them for the injustice and the pain they have caused. Not just for me and my pain but for all of us.

Yours sincerely,
A friend and fellow victim who has refused to take it anymore.

"This is gold, absolute GOLD! Talk about a whack job. You might have really pissed him off with tomorrow's article."

"I didn't really talk too much about him," Lewery said, suddenly feeling very unsure.

"You all but called him a faggot!"

"Better not let the lefties hear you call our gay population that. Besides, I only mentioned the fact that he had moved on to a male victim who happened to be found nude. Just accurate reporting. Besides, screw him," Lewery said, regaining some of his confidence. "I call them as I see them. And I see this letter on the front page of the paper."

"Slow down, Ace," Munro said. "We have some figuring to do about all this."

"What's to figure? We print the letter on the front page of tomorrow's paper."

"Which is why you will never have my job," Munro said.

He flipped his Rolodex until he found the number he needed. Picking up the phone, he dialed. "It's Munro. I know but I got a big problem and I need it solved immediately. I'm going to need you down here in half an hour. We need to go talk to some policemen about something Lewery has got."

Munro paused and then laughed. "Ya, I know. Let him rot but he didn't get himself arrested. We got a letter from the Southside Slasher. Ya, not a bad handle, eh? Anyway, we need to make some quick magic deals with the powers so we can run with this thing. Livermore, Keough and Mann. I agree. Good, I'll see you in fifteen, then."

"What're you doing?" Lewery asked after Munro. "We're taking this to the cops?"

"Of course, we are going to bloody well take it to the cops," Munro said, picking up the phone again. "Get me someone to shoot a letter and a driver's license in my office right now. It isn't going anywhere. I don't care about lighting. You have five minutes."

Munro slammed down the phone and looked at the letter again. Finally, he looked up at Lewery again. "You don't really think we're going to hold this back from the cops, for Christ sake? Of course, we are going to give it to them. This psycho is killing people and we aren't going to do anything to make it easier for him."

"But…"

"Relax, will you. We're also going to make one mother of a deal for this paper and you are going to have so much access and so many exclusives, you are going to be able to fill that book you have been salivating over since you heard about the second body."

Lewery had the decency to cast his eyes at the floor for a brief second. But when he looked back up, his eyes were gleaming.

Chapter 41

"What about the *Night Dance?*" Livermore asked.

Mann visibly winced. The *Night Dance* had been a promising lead that had gone sour.

"We are still looking into the possibility that he used the *Night Dance* as a place to pick his victims."

"Yes, I know."

Mann had already heard the tone in Livermore's voice. He knew what was coming and dreaded it.

"You've all seen the *Daily,*" Livermore continued. He put on his reading glasses. "I quote from the illustrious rag that passes for a newspaper in this city. The headline reads: 'Is the *Night Dance* the local hangout for the Southside Slasher?' The body of the story runs for two columns but this small bit tells the entire story. 'Police seem to think so. The establishment and the employees are under investigation after a connection was discovered between the victims of the Southside Slasher and the after-hours bar.' The article continues to warn people who frequent the bar to watch their backs."

"I'm sorry about that, sir," apologized Keough. "The story must have been leaked by someone Lewery interviewed. It didn't come out of the task force. We are looking into it to see who might have talked."

"I'm so glad. The owner of the *Night Dance* appears to think it is too late for those measures. He is suing the city and the department for loss of business. Apparently, he feels that this story could hurt his business."

"Bullshit," Mann said. "Every freak in the city will be out there hoping to dance with the Slasher."

"You may be right but the leak worries me. It highlights how easy things get out to these jackals. I don't want to see the killer's sign on the next television broadcast. I know that more people are being brought into the investigation every day but do your best to instill some sort of responsibility among the squad. Bottle things up. We can't afford anymore getting to the press. As it is, we have likely scared him away from the *Night Dance*."

Livermore grabbed the *Daily* and walked to the door of his office. He turned the knob and pulled the door open. "Just make sure this asshole and his paper don't get anything more."

Livermore turned and almost ran into three men crowded around his assistant's desk. She immediately stood and said, "Deputy Inspector, this is..."

"We've met," one of the men interrupted. "Bill Munro. I'm the asshole's boss."

"Bill? What are you doing here?" Livermore asked. "You know the channels."

"We need to discuss something and we need to do it right now," Munro said, his voice full of the urgency he felt. He had been working with legal for most of the night and only caught a couple hours sleep on the couch in his office. Already, they were working on promoting this thing for tomorrow's paper. He had to get this done and get back to the office.

"Maybe we can arrange something for this after..."

"You ever find McIntosh's ID, Stephen?" Munro interrupted. "You ever find her driver's license?"

Livermore glanced down at the large envelope Munro was carrying. "Oh no."

Livermore looked at Mann and Keough and then turned to his assistant. "Have coffee and some Danishes or whatever you can find sent to the conference room. Come on, Bill. You and the asshole follow us."

* * * * *

Lewery was sitting beside Mann, thoroughly enjoying himself. Munro had provided photocopies of the letter so all the members of this impromptu meeting had their own copies. The original and the driver's license were already on their way to the lab for fingerprint analysis. Mann had finished reading and was telling Lewery that he would have to be fingerprinted for elimination.

"No problem. The legal beagle over there already warned me about that. So how is Dani?"

Mann didn't miss a beat. "As beautiful as ever. She has something going in the financial district."

In the past, Lewery had let it slip out that he knew about Mann and the television reporter. He also made it clear that he wasn't using it as a bargaining chip. Instead, he had tried to use his knowledge as a peace offering, a bit of shared confidence as an ice-breaker. Mann didn't really dislike the reporter, as hard as he tried. He was always on the lookout for the next lurid headline but a straight shooter and more honest than most reporters. So they had an uneasy relationship, neither really giving the other much slack.

"If she ever gets tired of lugging that camera around, tell her the *Daily* would take her in a heartbeat. She's a hell of a reporter and I don't mean just for a Flashcam. She'd probably take my job."

"She can't type," Mann said with a grin.

Before Lewery could respond, Livermore started the negotiations. "I know what a civic minded individual you are, Bill. So what do you want?"

"Want?" Munro said, a hurt tone in his voice. "Hey, we want this guy caught. But, we also can't ignore the fact that he did pick us."

"Well, me, actually," Lewery interjected.

"Let's start with what you can't use," Livermore said, ignoring the reporter. "You can't use the mark. That is non-negotiable. We are withholding that and anyone who leaks it will have to get themselves arrested to ever see the inside of a police station again."

"Done," Munro said. "But when it is all over, we have the exclusive on it."

Lewery could have kissed Munro. The reporter could see the cover of his book already. The mark, carved in the back of a woman, dripping with blood. Perfect.

"If it is possible, it is yours," Livermore agreed. "How are you going to play this?"

"The advertising has already started. The letter will be front page tomorrow. We'll take the mark out so that nobody even knows it was there. I'll even black out the reference in the letter."

Livermore smiled. Without the reference, no other news agency would be sniffing around to discover what the mark was. And the black out would play well – a good visual. Win. Win.

"Are you going to try to set up communication with him?" Mann asked.

"Definitely going to try and set up some sort of a rapport," Lewery admitted. "But don't even think about tapping any of my phones."

"No taps. Unless he contacts you by phone and then all bets are off," Livermore said.

"I don't think he is going to be calling anytime soon," Munro said.

"Besides, you can't photograph telephone conversations," Keough added.

"Damn straight, Skippy," Munro smiled. "This ain't television."

Chapter 42

Thorman worked his shoulders, trying to ease some of the tension. They felt like rock. He had a pain running up from his right shoulder, through his neck and into his brain. The pounding was becoming almost unbearable.

Being in the office was beginning to wear on him and it was showing. Several of his colleagues had commented how tired he looked. How many times had he jumped when someone walked into his office? Every time the phone rang, his stomach turned and he could feel his bowels begin to loosen. He was so close. He just needed a little more time and he would have his revenge and more money than he could possibly need.

If he survived until this last deal happened, he would be set. He would have enough to be able to leave little pots of money buried in the banking systems around the world for Angelino to find. A multimillion dollar trail of bread crumbs to keep him off track and searching everywhere Thorman planned not to be.

If his brain didn't explode first, either from this headache or a bullet.

With that cheering thought fresh in his mind, Thorman stood and walked to the door of his office. He casually looked to his right toward the senior partner's big double doors. With nobody in sight, he stepped three steps to the left and quietly unlocked the fire exit door that went to the main hallway. Whenever possible, he used the washroom outside the office complex. Strangely, he felt the public washroom was more private.

He walked quickly to the washroom, hurrying inside when he heard the signal for the arriving elevator. Stepping quickly to one of the four stalls, he slipped inside and shut the door. He heard the main office door open and then shut. He hoped whoever had arrived wasn't there to see him.

When he realized that his heart was beating too rapidly, he tried to breathe and relax himself. Still leaning against the door, he made no attempt to take down his pants. Instead, he rested his forehead against the cool metal of the door and let it ease his headache.

The outer door opened. He didn't dare move. When the stranger's voice called his name, he began to wish he had pulled his pants down.

"Mr. Thorman?"

Silence filled the washroom and Thorman tried not to breathe.

"Mr. Thorman, you do not have time to jerk me around. I am here to save the life of you and your family."

When Thorman still didn't respond, he heard something hit the floor and slither under the stall. He watched as a photo slid across the floor and stopped at his foot. Another followed. And another.

He was looking at a picture of his daughter getting dropped off at her Day Care by his wife. He remembered seeing his daughter wearing the cute little blue jumper just this morning. Exactly what she was wearing when she kissed him goodbye at the breakfast table – a Cheerio stuck to her chin – looking sweet, adorable and so innocent.

The second picture was of his wife, looking so sexy, running in her tight yoga pants and crop top in the park. Trees and bushes lined the frighteningly empty path.

In the last shot, he saw himself, fast asleep in his bed, still in his clothes, obviously passed out from one of his late night drinking binges. His wife was asleep in the bed beside him, sheets pulled down, her nightgown in disarray, her left breast exposed. He felt violated, angry and frightened. But anger started to win out as he realized that this man had been in his house. He had stood over him and taken this disgusting picture. Thorman imagined this man touching his wife, who always slept so soundly.

But as a fourth picture slid under the stall door, all anger disappeared and fear returned. He felt his forehead slip against the metal door as sweat quickly beaded on his brow. There was his little girl, his sweetheart, his most treasured possession, asleep in her pink *Little Mermaid* bed. On her back, one arm wrapped around Mr. Froggie, the other with her thumb in her mouth. Her blonde hair, loose and framing her face on her pillow.

And pointed at her, held by the same man taking the picture, was a large gun, the ugly silencer pointing straight at his daughter's head.

Thorman didn't even hear himself moan.

"Are you ready to talk, Mr. Thorman?"

Thorman slowly opened the door and looked out at the man in front of him. He had expected a hardened killer with a gun. Instead, he was faced with an ordinary, boring mailman. And he was smiling a nice, reassuring, mailman smile. One that said, don't worry, I will be happy to deliver that letter to your grandmother.

"Sit down, Mr. Thorman."

Thorman just blinked at the mailman, looking at him as though he was speaking a foreign language.

"Truly, Mr. Thorman, don't waste my time. Sit down, pick up the pictures and hand them to me, please."

Thorman blinked twice more and did as he was told. He suddenly understood that it was all over and he could finally relax. This mailman was coming to end it all for him. No sense fighting, he could never win now. There was always another mailman on the next street. And all the mailmen knew where he lived.

"I am going to give it to you quick and fast, because we don't want to get interrupted," the mailman said, taking back the photos and putting them in his bag. "Angelino knows everything – except where the money is. Do you understand?"

Thorman nodded.

"Good. Do you still have all the money?"

Thorman nodded.

"Do you want your wife and daughter to live?"

Thorman nodded.

"Understand, you are already dead but I can save your wife and daughter from a very unpleasant death. Your wife would live a long time but she would be used, repeatedly. That fit, sexy body would become a play land for some very deviant, wealthy men. And all the time, she would know that your daughter was suffering a similar fate – all because of you. You understand what I am saying?"

Thorman nodded.

"Gather the money. I know you have it hidden all over. I want all the codes, I want everything you have. Hold anything back and I can't guarantee to save your wife and daughter. Give me everything and I can look after them. Will you do that?"

Thorman nodded.

"I need to hear the words."

"I will get you all the money to give back to Angelino."

"And the insurance you have? The disk you hoped to use against Angelino? You know it won't save your wife and daughter. I'll need the disk, too."

"I will give you the disk."

"Good. I'll contact you in two days. Don't think of running. We know about the passports. You are being watched. Your wife is being watched. Even your daughter is being watched. Look for the green sedan when you drive home tonight, that is one of your escorts."

"Green sedan," Thorman repeated.

"Don't arouse suspicion. Act normal but you must send your daughter to see your wife's parents. She needs to be away and safe right now. Do you understand?"

Thorman nodded. Some part of his mind wondered what would be on his headstone.

Chapter 43

Preston's fingers, already black from the newsprint, ran over the headline again as though he could feel the type. He had read the newspaper so many times; the long, front page story was committed to memory. The first part just rehashed the killings. Although being reminded of the details gave him an erection, it was the second half of the story that really excited him.

He felt Dale speaking directly to him, even if the words were not on the page. Dale, who always questioned the police, the biggest bullies going, had to be on his side. Dale was too smart to come right out and say that he supported Preston. Judging by all those letters to the editor, condemning his sacred mission, too many readers misunderstood his mission for Dale to publicly admit he was cheering him on to greater success. But Dale was a kindred spirit. Was he just so incredibly understanding or was he a fellow sufferer that would join him in his fight?

He watched as Dale exited the newspaper building and wandered down the street. How he longed to walk up and shake the newsman's hand. Thank him for his understanding. But it was too early. The police might be watching.

Soon enough, he would have his time with Dale. He already knew his home address. That had been easy. For now, he would just enjoy a closeness, a camaraderie he had rarely felt in his life.

He stood and followed Dale down the street, clutching the paper close to his chest.

Chapter 44

Men expect certain sounds when a woman dressed for a night out. Hangers shifting, shoes tossed aside, hair dryers. However, not when the woman getting ready was Danett Wood. Even before Mann wandered out of the bathroom of Dani's apartment, he could hear the rhythmic, rasping sound.

Dani was sitting on the bed. The special vest that held the batteries for her video camera lay beside her. But the vest carried more than batteries.

The sound was beginning to grate on him. "Do you have to do that?"

Dani looked up at Mann and smiled. She knew the cop in him didn't like her carrying the knife. However, it was as much a part of her as her camera and vest. The vest was her design because the heavy battery packs were too heavy to carry on the usual belt. The right shoulder also had special padding that helped cradle the camera and save her from incredibly sore muscles after a day of shooting.

The knife had been added later. She had been told to keep it sharp.

Commanded, was more like it. Major Jon Van der Meer, retired, was used to giving commands. Tall, blonde, and muscular, Jon was descended from South African stock. He had gone to England to study and joined the forces and then the SAS, although he would never actually admit it. He was the ideal of the SAS soldier – tall, muscular, fit, handsome. Not to mention an incredible lover.

Dani had met him when he was working as private security for traveling Englishmen. Their affair had lasted two months and in the rare moments they were out of bed, Jon had instructed her on the art of self-defense. Knowing some of the places she was heading, he had given her a knife and some rudimentary instruction on how to use it.

So far, the most she had done was keep it sharp. She was more than happy with that.

Dani checked the edge of the knife and ran it across the stone a couple more times. Van der Meer had kept his promise. Over their two months together, he had taught her the intricacies of blade fighting. She had learned to slash instead of stab. He had taught her how to protect her vital organs. How to take small slashes on her arm during a knife fight while searching for an opening. And, finally, the most lethal killing strikes.

She had not needed the lessons in Africa but by the time she left, she was very adept at defending herself with a blade. She took to carrying a knife in the battery vest as Van der Meer had suggested. She kept the knife in good repair. Van der Meer had shown her much and the very best hadn't involved a blade.

Dani could still remember the hot jungle nights with the Major. Often her fantasies ran back to that time in her life.

With a small sigh, she slipped the knife back into its disguised sheath in her vest. The vest had changed over the years. The basic design, now worn by most of the Flashcam operators, was the same but instead of canvas, Kevlar was used. The light weight, bullet proof material had saved more than one Flashcam in the Middle East, Bosnia and even the streets of DC.

Still thinking about Van der Meer, Dani wandered toward the closet to find something to wear.

* * * * *

Mann watched Dani move toward the closet. He was aware she had not answered him. He suspected who consumed her thoughts. He knew about the Major. The fact that she thought about her past lover occasionally didn't really bother him. He wasn't the jealous type.

He might be jealous that she had such good memories. His good memories were obscured by the bitterness he now harbored toward his ex. She had been his first great love. The boys had come early in their relationship. Rick even before they were married. Their life had seemed perfect until the arrests. At that time, he had privately had more supporters in the department than not. But there was no support from home.

His wife saw the department as a family and inclusion in something bigger than her. But that was no longer possible and Mann had been the cause. She soon resented him and then hated him. After that, she turned the boys against him and left.

"You ready? Brant and Ruby will be waiting."

Mann jumped up and grabbed his coat. He admired Dani in her cotton dress. A white belt was cinched around her narrow waist and neckline was just low enough to hint at things to come. In the car, she let him rest his hand on her bare thigh. Ex wives be damned. This was where the good life started.

Just down the street from Davis' house, Mann let the car coast to the curb.

Davis was as big and mean-looking as they got. At six foot six and 250 pounds, he dwarfed Mann's five foot ten. Now, the big man was playing a game of two on one with his sons in their driveway. Both would soon have the height of their father but for now were all lean muscle and explosive energy. Mann watched Davis use his extended reach to strip the ball away. And in the next instant, let the boys use their small size to slip under his guard and drive for the basket. Ruby stood at the side of the driveway, cheering the boys on and booing her husband when he took liberties with the rules.

The scene was all smiles, love and uninhibited joy. Everything Mann had been denied since his wife took his boys away. Jealousy often ate away at Mann during these moments and part of him almost hated Davis simply because he got to have what Mann knew he had lost. But how could you ever hate a father who loved his sons as much as Davis?

Mann felt an understanding squeeze of his hand from Dani. He slipped the car in gear and coasted up to the end of the driveway. "Did you beat the old man?" he called out to the boys.

"We slaughtered him," the eldest called out.

* * * * *

"So, when are you two getting married?"

Davis smiled at Mann and raised his eyebrows. He enjoyed the dig at Mann. Besides, it always got his wife going whenever he brought up the subject. Ruby was convinced that Dani should never marry Mann. She loved Mann like a brother but she thought she had nabbed the only worthwhile cop. A woman would be a fool to marry any other cop.

"Forget marriage. Dani has too much going for her. Things are perfect the way they are. The occasional good sex and a place of your own for escape when he is being an ass. You stay with your career, girl," Ruby advised. Ruby made a small motion with her fingers at Mann and smiled. "You go ahead and talk shop you two. Dani and I have plenty to discuss."

Mann was mildly surprised that Ruby had noticed his signal to Davis. Time to change it once again. The two women started talking about Ruby's most recent advertising account. Mann spooned more curry onto his plate and pushed a candle out of the way.

"Dani has heard a rumor about the department."

Davis nodded through a mouthful of food.

"It seems we have a high level snitch in the department working for Angelino."

Davis looked over at Dani. She and Ruby had stopped talking, both interested in the informant. "How good is the source? Is this Dominos?"

Dominos was what Dani called one of her most valuable informants in Angelino's organization. She had met him during a story she had done about Angelino allegedly baking some competitor in a pizza oven. He saw himself as a budding Henry Hill. He figured he would star in his own version of *Good Fellows* one day. As he moved up in the family, he had reached out to Dani, feeding her information on a regular basis with the idea of being a star. He already had an agent and a publicist lined up.

"No. He's been reliable in the past but this one is way out of his league. I'd want to check farther before I went to air."

"God, you aren't thinking about putting this on the air?"

"Not yet," Dani said, noncommittally. "I'd give you guys a chance at him first because Angelino would never let him get away. And from what my guy says, this cop has done some major damage."

"How high we talking, Boss?" Davis asked.

Mann shrugged and Dani answered. "Definitely above the rank of my boyfriend here. That's the only reason I figured I could trust him."

Mann could see that Davis was considering his nephew. "And to answer your question," Mann said, "I've been wondering if it's the same guy that screwed Degget."

"Any thoughts?" Davis asked Dani. "You got anything approaching a name?"

Dani shook her head. "The only thing I got was that Angelino call him 'My Tom Dick'."

Mann could hear Angelino, talking in his thick accent. "My Tom Dick," he repeated in a passable impersonation.

Ruby looked puzzled. "What does that mean?"

"Dunno. That's what my snitch said," Dani answered. "Maybe it is something to do with Dick Tracey."

"Or," Davis said, "maybe the guy is a detective."

"Nope," Dani said. "My source says he outranks a lieutenant, let alone a mere Detective."

"Maybe," Ruby said slowly, "he meant *tame* dick, not tom dick."

"Could be. My snitch definitely said 'Tom' but he might have heard it wrong. Tame Dick makes sense."

"If Angelino has a pipeline, someone really up there, we've got to plug the leak," Davis said.

"And, if he was high enough, we might be able to turn him. It would all depend on how it was handled. It would have to be handled very quietly. If his name ever hit the tube, he'd be dead meat," Mann said, looking hard at Dani.

"If it's the guy that turned in Cliff, then good riddance to him," Ruby said.

"I mean, someone that could put us into Angelino's organization?" Mann said, ignoring Ruby with a far away look on his face.

"We could do some damage of our own for a change," Davis agreed.

Mann looked at his friend, a gleam now in his eye. "Some major pay back."

"We have to get this guy, Gregg," Davis said, his eyes burning. "I need to do some looking."

Mann knew that Davis was going to be investigating right along with his nephew. "Just be careful and keep me in the loop," Mann said. "Force is going to hell."

Chapter 45

"Ladies and gentlemen, I give you Andrea Seymour, actress extraordinaire. The District beckons and future Tony awards are currently being engraved with her name."

The seven sitting around the table in the small restaurant applauded while Andrea stood and did an exaggerated bow. Her long blonde hair flopped forward onto the table and then snapped back as she straightened – a move she had practiced since she was eight. Andrea's face was glowing, her straight white teeth shining. She threw small kisses to her friends around the table and then pulled herself to her full height. Her nose high in the air, she addressed her adoring fans.

"Please, please, don't stop. The first thing a true *Star* learns is to talk over the applause. I want to thank all the little people for getting out of my way. I want to thank the director for his obvious wisdom and good taste. Finally, I want you all to know that, once I have my enormous mansion on the Bluffs, you are all welcome there. I'll need maids, butlers, a good chauffeur – feel free to leave your resume with the guard at the gate."

Andrea collapsed in her chair, laughing and breathless. Her friends applauded her again and a scattering of applause came from the other tables. She noticed several faces she knew from the endless auditions. Each of them could easily have been her. Every one of them had a life outside of the theatre and every one of them would toss it aside for the chance she was being given. All the usual professions were all represented here – servers, secretaries and dishwashers, and some less reputable and unusual ones. They all had the same dream. Tonight, she was the winner. Tomorrow, who knew?

Andrea settled farther into her chair. The excitement was finally hitting her. Today had been a whirlwind. Her friends, always ready to celebrate another's success no matter how depressing their own lives, talked and laughed, enjoying her moment. She pulled her chair back slightly from the table. Outside of the circle of revelry, she relaxed and caught her breath.

She could see out the window into the street. The sidewalk was beginning to fill as the theatres began to empty. Nice suits and fashionable dresses paraded by. There were no furs or truly expensive jewelry. No stretch limos, mostly sub compacts or mini-vans. Though physically close by, this was not The District. This was Leantown.

But tonight, for her, it was Broadway.

*   *   *   *   *

He had seen her flip her long, blonde hair – straight, combed and shiny. So much like bloody Sheila.

She didn't dress as well as she once had. In fact, Sheila wouldn't have been caught dead in those clothes when she was living on daddy's money.

He wondered if she still had the bright cherry red convertible with the sparkling white interior. The interior was so white it blinded you in direct sunlight.

That was Sheila. She lived to be clean. Not only were her clothes the best and her car the best, she had to be the best. She had to be perfectly groomed. Everything was scrubbed, pressed, combed, plucked and straightened. In all those years of High School, he had never seen her dirty.

She was obsessive about being clean. She was compulsive to the point that she needed mental help. But rich people were never considered strange or mentally unbalanced. Not like him. She was just neat.

The car was always as clean as she was. It was perfect. Cleaned every day by daddy's paid help. The driver's side door held the final insult. Her name was painted in white, flowing script. Everybody knew Sheila's car. Back then, he had recognized it as soon as he rounded the corner on his bike.

* * * * *

The car was at the side of the road and Sheila was grinding the engine. Over and over, she turned the key, trying to make the engine catch.

The day was already warm even though it was only eight thirty in the morning. The top was down and he could see two of her girlfriends in the back seat. They were the current *IN* crop – only the best in the school ever got to ride with Sheila.

For a moment, he considered making a fast turn and going a block out of his way. He was already late, very late. When he had left, he had known that he would have to ride like the wind to be there on time. If he took time to help them, he would be late for sure. He should just turn back. He would only loose a couple of seconds.

He couldn't, though. All the pain that Sheila and her friends had caused him and still he couldn't turn away. His mother had drilled her strong beliefs in him. They were heading for the same place and would be even later if they had to walk. You don't leave people in trouble. Even people who hate you.

He squeezed the brakes. The front wheel wobbled and he let off slightly. He was late and had been really moving. He got the bike under control and coasted to a stop next to the driver's side. He could see the flowing script and in his gut knew he had made a mistake.

Then, Sheila saw him and her whole face brightened. She gave him such a devastating smile that his doubts vanished.

"God, am I ever glad to see you. I'm going to be late. Could you help me?"

Her voice was so genuine. He could almost believe that she was glad to see him. He dragged his bike over to the boulevard. "Pop the hood and I'll see what I can do."

Hidden behind the hood, he glanced at his watch. He was going to be real late now. He could smell the strong stench of the gas. Sheila had flooded the engine. He took the air filter off and used his finger to pry up the butterfly. The fumes from the gas hit him and he felt himself swoon in the heat.

"Turn the key but don't step on the gas," he called.

It took a couple of seconds but the engine finally coughed to life. He quickly replaced the air filter and carefully closed the hood. He went around to talk to Sheila.

"There you go, all done," he said, hesitantly. "I was wondering, you know. I have to write the same exam as you. I'm really going to be late if I have to ride my bike. I was wondering if I could get a lift from you."

Sheila looked him up and down. The look she wore now said it all. The welcome smile was gone. She no longer needed him and there was not a chance in hell that he was going to get into *her* car. All she did was laugh in his face and floor the accelerator. As they pulled away, he could hear their laughter.

* * * * *

Andrea's joy seemed to be filling the enclosed space, forcing out the air. She needed to be outside. She needed to be alone for a moment to settle her thoughts and accept her good fortune.

She made her excuses and left the table. She accepted several congratulatory handshakes and pats on the way to the door. Finally, she escaped to the sidewalk.

The air was stifling but felt like a cold breeze. Andrea started along the sidewalk, fighting the urge to skip and sing. She understood John Travolta at the end of *Staying Alive*. She would have loved to go out and *strut*. Instead, she just walked along; enjoying the sense of freedom that success was giving her. True, she wasn't a household name, yet, but this play was the start. From here on, she was sure she was going to make it.

Tomorrow, she would telephone her sister! Janie had never questioned if she would make it. To Janie, it was only a matter of when. Now, with the income from the show coming in, Andrea could afford to bring Janie out for opening night.

Her mind on plans, Andrea did not see him until he was right beside her.

* * * * *

He could not believe his luck. Only an hour ago, he was consulting his small book, comparing the picture with the girl in the restaurant. Now, Sheila had left the restaurant alone and was walking down the street. She was in no hurry, just walking down the street as though she had no place to go.

He was beside her before she even noticed him. He held out his map to her and she stopped. She looked almost happy to see him. She obviously didn't recognize him. He was startled when she spoke to him first.

"Can I help you find something?"

He was momentarily at a loss for words. He suddenly wondered if this was a good idea. He had no plan. Why was he rushing? He was terribly exposed.

But you need this!

No, he could control the desire.

Not desire – need.

Was it becoming a need? He had a mission. The mission required him to kill – did he also need to kill? He was always prepared now. He always had a knife, cuff ties and duct tape. Just in case because it did feel so good. He felt himself get hard and the smile changed his face.

She's leaving.

He looked at her suddenly wary face. Quickly, he stepped close to Sheila.

"You see this knife?" He moved the map slightly to the side so she could see the gleam of the shiny blade. He sensed her starting to step away and moved closer. "Don't try to run. I'll cut you if you try to run. I'll cut your face. Just be calm."

* * * * *

Andrea looked into the man's eyes and knew he meant what he was saying. He had looked so harmless. Short, tubby. Nobody you would be afraid of. But his eyes weren't friendly. They were cold, so cold.

An older man and woman walked by. For three very rapid heart beats, they were close enough to touch. For half a second, she considered trying to run. He must have sensed her thoughts. He pressed the knife tight to her side.

"Don't," he warned.

She hesitated again.

Then, the couple was past and her chance was gone.

He took her into the alley beside a doll maker's store.

Up ahead was a dumpster. It had been left at a slight angle to the wall. Behind, a small set of steps led down to a delivery entrance. A small awning with a single light covered most of the stairwell. She glanced back at the street but could see nothing around the dumpster.

"I don't have any money."

"*I don't have any money,*" he mimicked. "What makes you think that I care about your money? That is all you ever thought impressed people, isn't it?"

She was at the top of the steps. He let her stand there for a moment longer. He wanted her to see the filth of the alley. He wanted her to know what she was going to die in before he broke the light and plunged her into his dark nightmare.

"I don't want your money, Sheila. Money doesn't mean anything to you. But I know what you need – your clean little world. Everything and everyone sanitized. Isn't that right, Sheila?"

He pressed the knife against her back so she would take a step down into the stairwell. "You don't want to get dirty, Sheila? It is time to learn how dirty the world is."

Andrea was confused and frightened. Her euphoric world was suddenly turned upside down and inside out. She could feel the knife against her back and involuntarily took a step down. She could not understand why this was happening to her. She had done nothing to deserve this. She tried to focus on his words. She heard the name.

Not her name.

The man was mistaken. He wasn't looking for her. It was all a mistake. He was making a mistake. All she had to do was tell him he had made a mistake.

Relief passed through her body. She stopped her step. All she had to do was tell him that she wasn't Sheila. She would go away and not tell anyone. That is what she had to tell him. She would just go away and call her sister to tell her the good news. None of this would every have happened.

As she was about to speak, she felt duct tape slap over her mouth.

In a sudden burst of clarity, she realized who this man was.

And Andrea tried to scream.

Chapter 46

Jill Thorman stopped and looked at the dolls in the window. She pointed one out to her husband but he didn't notice her. He was staring up the street. She shrugged and went back to the dolls in the window.

God, he was in a mood. Just like tonight, at the play. He barely paid attention. He had spent the evening fidgeting in his seat. Jill was sure that he hadn't heard a word of the play. Not that he missed much.

"Mr. Davidson, how are you tonight?"

Jill was startled by her husband's voice. She turned and looked at the back of the tall man that he was addressing. All she saw was the back. Had she known what would happen in the next five minutes, she would have made more of an effort to see his face. Instead, she played the dutiful and ignored wife and turned back to the window of dolls.

"Fine, thank you, Mr. Thorman. This is a fortunate accident running into you like this. Could I have a private word with you?"

"My wife?" Thorman asked.

"Will be just fine, I'm sure." Mr. Davidson replied.

"Of course," her husband replied. He turned to her, with what she would later describe as a forced smile. "I'll just be a second, dear. Why don't you go to the restaurant and I'll catch up?"

He turned away before she could answer. She shrugged and started down the street toward the restaurant. She glanced back in time to see her husband and the other man step into the alley.

* * * * *

"Did it work?" Thorman asked.

Hill heard the pleading in the accountant's voice and despised his weakness. "No, Angelino wants you dead and your wife and daughter brought to him."

Even in the darkness of the alley, Hill saw the blood drain from Thorman's face. He waited until the statement fully sank in and then spoke again.

Hill pulled an envelope from his pocket. "You were a bad boy. You kept some of the money."

Thorman nodded, realizing this man knew everything. "I wanted to make sure my wife and daughter were taken care of. Please, don't hurt my little girl."

"Shut up and listen. I don't do children and I won't help Angelino do anything to her if I can help it."

"But..."

"Shut up and listen. Take this," Hill said, thrusting the envelope at Thorman. I've sent your suitcase to the Courtyard Marriot by the airport. You are registered there under your new name. Your passports are in the envelope along with tickets to Paris leaving first thing in the morning."

"Why?"

"I told you, I don't do children," Hill said, reaching in his pocket. He enjoyed seeing the relief flood Thorman's face – from hope to despair to hope all in the space of a minute.

Hill thrust a large .45 automatic at Thorman who took it. "Take this just in case but get rid of it before the airport."

Thorman looked down at the gun and then back up at Hill, who now held another gun, pointed at his forehead.

* * * * *

Four stores down from the doll store, Jill stopped. She couldn't understand her husband. Normally, he was paranoid about her walking the streets alone. Muggings happen on the busiest streets in this city, he always said. Yet, he had told her to walk on alone. Then, he disappeared into an alley? Something wasn't right.

As Jill hurried back to the alley, she thought about her husband's employers. She knew that they weren't totally on the up and up. She wasn't sure exactly who they were but they were not *normal* businessmen. The more she thought about it, the faster she walked.

Rounding the corner of the alley, she saw the muzzle flash. She did not hear anything but she did see the small spark of light. She also saw her husband crumple into a small ball as he fell to the ground beside a dumpster. She screamed and the man turned toward her. She started to run to her husband but tripped. She landed sprawled out and dazed on the dirty, greasy pavement. She didn't notice the explosion of brick above her.

When she looked up again, the man was running down the alley and her husband was still on the ground.

Chapter 47

Dani's robe fell to the floor and she slid into the bed beside Mann for the first early evening they had been together in a long while. She let her long, red hair drape across his face, tickling him. He ran one hand along her side, feeling her soft skin and lightly brushing the swell of her breast. Dani lowered herself until their lips gently brushed.

The harsh ring of the telephone startled both of them. Mann sat up too quickly, hitting his mouth against Dani's chin. Cursing, he reached across Dani and grabbed up the receiver. Behind him, he heard Dani's cell phone go off. When she hurried into the living room to answer it, he was sure what the call would be about.

"Lieutenant, it's Greer. We got another."

"Where?"

"Leantown, East Humley between Fifth and Fourth."

"Call out the team. I want the area sealed."

"There's a complication."

"Let me know when I get there. I'll be fifteen minutes at the most."

Mann pulled on his pants. Dani was already back in the room. She had her clothes on, and was grabbing up her camera equipment. "I'll follow you," she said.

Mann was pushing the car as fast as he dared. His siren was blaring but, as usual, other drivers ignored him and didn't pull over. He laid on the horn and went through a red light. Dani slipped through in the gap that always followed in his wake. In his rearview mirror, he could see her headlights behind him and smiled. She was a good driver. After three years in Los Angeles and another year in both Rome and Mexico City, she had to be.

Mann was forced to ignore his rearview mirror as traffic suddenly snarled in front of him. He blasted the horn again. He wanted to be there before the scene got too old. God knew how long the body had been lying there as it was. And there was also the *complication*, whatever that was.

Leantown which was out of his official jurisdiction. Not that it mattered anymore. Under the new emergency policy, the task force could move anywhere in the city. Still, this was the first test run of the new system. Mann wanted all the various investigation units on the scene immediately. That was the only way they could hope to get anything.

Two blocks from the crime scene, Mann looked behind him. Dani's headlights had disappeared. As he made the right hand turn he realized what she had done and he hit the horn in frustration. A block back was a one way street. He had taken the longer route which took him a block out of his way. She had taken the shorter route – the wrong way on the one way.

Mann got out of his car and gave Dani a glowering look. She already had her camera out and was turning that annoying red light on him. "Lieutenant, what is going on here? There is a rumor that the Southside Slasher has struck again."

"As soon as I have any information, I will tell all of you what we have."

Dani smiled at his "all of you" comment. Except for a mobile radio unit that was still setting up and a single reporter with a pad, she was the only one the scene. "Any comment on the other victim?"

Mann stared at her and realized three things. One, Dani wasn't covering the Slasher case. Two, he should have let Greer tell him about the complication. Three, he was going to personally shoot Dani's contact when he figured out who it was.

Dani just smiled and lowered the camera, giving Mann an opportunity to turn away.

As he pushed his way through the crowd of onlookers, Mann opened his badge case and slipped it through the pocket of his T-shirt. The uniform guarding the perimeter of the crime scene lifted the yellow tape for him to slip under and made a note on his clipboard. Mann took a moment to survey the scene. The perimeter was good but there was still no sign of the coroner or CSU van. He glanced at his watch, already fifteen minutes since he got the call. Not good enough.

He followed the white tape on the ground. Each detective entering or exiting the scene would follow the same route.

When Mann reached the body beside the dumpster, he stooped down. The victim, wearing a dark suit, was laying on his side, curled in the fetal position. A small pool of blood ran from his head. Mann could clearly see the bullet hole in the forehead. He could make out the powder burns. Up close and personal. No exit wounds so a low caliber, maybe a .22? The victim was also holding a large caliber automatic.

As he straightened, he knew he had found Greer's complication. When he turned, Greer was standing over him.

"That's vic number two, Lou."

"Let's see the rest."

"Prepare thyself."

Mann followed Greer along the tape. As soon as the got past the dumpster with its distinctive odors, Mann could smell the foul stench being pushed ahead of the warm breeze coming down the alley. His stomach began to tighten when he reached the top of the steps. Greer handed him a flashlight. Mann paused a brief moment before turning it down the stairwell. In two seconds, he had seen enough to haunt him for a long time. He turned away and walked back to stand over the shooting victim. He could handle a simple shooting. What was in that stairwell was beyond normal comprehension.

"Tell me about it."

"That is Mr. Nickolas Thorman there," Greer began, pointing at the corpse in the suit. "We have him entering the alley with an unidentified male known to Mr. Thorman. The wife, who doesn't know the shooter, was with the husband until he went into the alley. Description of the shooter sucks. Mr. Everybody. Anyway, the wife was sent on ahead. She got suspicious and returned in time to see her husband shot."

Greer pointed at the corner of the building. "She panics and trips running into the alley. The shooter took a shot but missed when she went down. A patrol car was passing when she went down. They saw what was happening and the radioman got out of the car. He checked the woman and gave chase. The car went around the block but they both came up empty."

"So we have one cop running up the alley?"

"Oh, they trampled things up real good. He came back down the alley too. By the time he got back, the wife had her husband rolled over.

The Uniform got her away and tried to put the body back the way it was."

"What about the…?"

"It's a girl. At least, it was. Anyway, the uniform wants to secure the area. He starts to go down the stairwell to check the door. He figures to mark it so the detectives will know if anyone has used it to get into the area."

"He was starting to think."

"Maybe. Anyway, he made the smell as he approached. At first, he figured it was just a shitter for the street people. Almost didn't go down. He had his light on the steps so he wouldn't step in anything. He flicked his light down to see what he was getting into and saw her. Well, bits of her."

Greer flashed his light to a spot across the alley from the stairwell. The beam danced across some lumpy liquid and then darted away. "He lost it over there."

Mann stared off into space for a moment. He had seen enough for now and started back to the street. Greer followed him. Once under the lights but still inside the perimeter away from the crowds, Mann looked down the street. The CSU van had pulled up and the technicians were unloading their equipment. They would be setting up some lights which would make operating in the alley easier. Mann wasn't sure he wanted to see the girl under the better light.

He saw Dani behind the barricade and followed her gaze to the windows in the alley.

"Make sure they tent the stairwell right away before they put on any lights," Mann told Greer. "I don't want this out there for everybody with a camera phone. I want a cop on every window that over looks this alley. If I see a picture of the vic surface on the web, I'll have somebody's ass."

"Yes, sir," Greer said.

"You got anything more on the shooting vic?"

"He's an accountant with Curtis, Devine and Hayes."

"Oh this is too good," Mann said, his voice betraying his excitement. "That's one of Angelino's firms. I want to lock this one down. We are going to be taking point on this one if I can possibly swing it. I want a unit at this Thorman's house. Get on to Davis and see if we can work out jurisdiction. And…"

"Uh, sorry Lou," Greer said, pointing to the edge of the perimeter. Two plain clothes detectives, both in three piece suits, were flashing their badges at the uniform in charge of the line. "Looks like SOCU to me."

"Damn it," Mann said, recognizing the two detectives. "How did they get here so fast? OK, stay with the plan. I'll fight over this one and see if we can keep it."

Chapter 48

"Where is my freaking money?"

"That wasn't my problem," Hill reminded Angelino. "He saw those two idiots you had watching him and decided to make a run for it. Your words were, 'I want him brought to me, if possible. If not, take him.' I had no choice."

"So what was he doing in that alley with you?"

Hill had been expecting this. It was the one part of his otherwise tight story that had some wiggle in it. Hill had two ways to play it. The best defense...

"I was trying to save your money."

"Thought you said that wasn't your problem?"

"Not my problem but I'm not a bloody idiot. I'm the last resort guy, right?"

Hill waited, staring at Angelino until the big man was finally forced to nod.

"When have you ever told me to wait? I don't wait. I'm in, I'm out. The longer I'm in this city, the longer I'm exposed. I don't like being out there, especially in this city. But you needed me here because this guy isn't your usual mug. This guy was smart, right? He did you right up the ass and you had to prove you were smarter, right?"

Again, Hill waited.

"I underestimated him once," Angelino admitted. "I wasn't going to do it again."

"Good choice. He got a silenced .45 while your boys were all over him."

"They paid for their mistake. But you still haven't answered my question," Angelino said, his impatience showing. "What were you doing in that alley?"

"Ya, I did. I was trying to save your money."

"How?"

"By not having to take the guy out. Like I said," Hill said, pointing at himself, "not a bloody idiot. We're talking a lot of money, right? Normally, you plug the leak, you plug the guy and everybody else is scared shitless to screw you but not this time. You had to show you were smarter than him. You got a big ego."

Angelino's eyes tightened.

"Hey, not saying it isn't deserved but you blew it. You know it, that's really what you are pissed with, not me. I went above and beyond."

"How you figure?"

"I saw him take your guys out."

"You didn't stop him?"

"Again, not my problem. They screwed things up for me so screw them."

"You are a heartless bastard, you know that?"

"But I'm still alive, right? Guy sends his daughter out of town. Guy gets a silenced gun and takes out your guys. I'm thinking your plan isn't working. You should have just sweated the guy. Let some of your guys do his wife in front of him. He would have folded and you would have your money. That was plan B for me but I had to bring him in first."

"So why didn't you?"

"Because he drew down on me. I tried to keep him in public so we could talk but he walked into that alley. That little accountant was fast, you know? Desperate people will take chances and he thought he could take me. I guess he figured he had to take his shot, right?"

"So I should be thanking you?"

"The rest of the payment is more than sufficient. I am out of this town and I don't think I'll be coming back for a while."

"You might want to rethink your travel plans."

"Don't threaten me," Hill said, steel going into his voice. "I fulfilled your contract as per your specifications. I got no more responsibility here."

"What about the witness?"

"Thorman's wife wouldn't know me if I slapped her in the face."

"Not that witness. The other one."

Hill looked at Angelino, sizing him up, wondering what his game was.

"What the hell are you talking about?"

By the time Angelino had finished explaining, Hill knew he was stuck in the city for a while longer.

Chapter 49

Mann rolled his shoulders, trying to take the kinks out of his tired muscles. Taking another drink of Pepsi, he realized that he had never made it down to the gym with Blaak. He patted his stomach. Even without the workouts with Blaak, he was losing his gut. Not eating will do that. He leaned back in his chair and stared around his office.

Hart's connections, at least his boss's connections, had pressured the Mayor into expanding the task force. The Division muster room couldn't handle it anymore. The task force was relocated to an empty warehouse a few blocks from Southfield Division headquarters. Mann had brought his chair with him. Chairs were a cherished commodity in the force. When you found a chair you liked, you brought it with you if you could. More than stripes, bars, and clusters, chairs were the true gauge of rank in the force.

The small office he had been assigned used to belong to the accountant of the firm that owned the warehouse. Mann had dealt with the accountant when they had arrived at the empty building. The number cruncher had told Mann why he had put up with the cramped office for so many years when he rated a larger one. The peculiar shape of the alley next to the warehouse created a draft that went right in the window of this office and no other. Proximity to the lake brought in a fresh smelling breeze. The accountant had guarded that secret for years and was the only one that never sweltered in the summer.

Outside, in the open area of the warehouse, the telephones rang constantly. The task force had been assigned its own numbers that had been published in the papers and on TV. Tips now came directly into the task force. However, a complicated method of sorting still followed every tip. Mann knew that the tips would soon overwhelm the task force.

Stacks of paper littered the desk of each detective. Was the killer in those piles of paper somewhere? Or, was he just living out a normal life, taking only a night out every once in a while to strangle and hack a citizen to pieces, then going back to the dog and the family barbecue. Christ!

Mann got up and wandered into the open area. Last night had gone on forever. When things had finally settled down, he had gone home to sleep. He had tossed and turned for two hours. The vision of the girl kept intruding on his thoughts. The brutality and plain sickness was more than he had ever seen in his life.

The doctors said that this one proved that the killer was sliding farther into his sickness. There appeared to be less planning and control of the kill site and still no rape.

Mann tried to ignore the visions of the girl and looked instead at the large chart of times tracing the girl's movements immediately before her death.

With an effort, he shifted his mind, forcing himself to refer to her by her name. Normally, he made an effort to identify with the victim. This time was different. He had trouble reconciling that mass of human tissue as a living person or at least he didn't want to. Especially with what he had been doing while she was being killed.

But Andrea Seymour was her name and she was an actress. She had been celebrating her first big break. Then, she left her friends and was brutally, disgustingly, viscously murdered. The chart continued in sickening detail, estimating times for the various acts of the killer. Almost as disturbing was the chart beside showing the last moments of Thorman's life.

The times overlapped. Both killers must have been in the alley at the same time. And the cops had run right past him.

At least they still had a fighting chance at keeping Thorman's murder. Mann was working hard at that. If he was right, there could be some really interesting records in Thorman's possession that could be collected as part of the murder investigation quite legally and then used against Angelino.

If not, given the timing of the two killings, nailing the Slasher might get the shooter. And that would definitely lead to Angelino.

Chapter 50

SOUTHSIDE SLASHER KILLS FOURTH VICTIM
Dale Lewery reporting

Last night in a dark alley only steps away from a crowded downtown street teeming with unsuspecting theatre goers, the Southside Slasher brutally murdered his fourth victim in less than four weeks. In a dark stairwell, strewn with garbage and human waste, the body of 23 year old Andrea Seymour was found and quickly identified as victim number four of the Southside Slasher.

The actress, poised for the premier role of her short career, was killed in what Deputy Inspector Livermore described as "the most brutally sadistic murder" he has ever investigated.

Andrea Seymour had just left a celebration at a local restaurant in honor of her recently announced starring role in the upcoming play Ice And The Maiden Sister. Having spent the past 3 years in Kesle, struggling to land that breakthrough role, Andrea's hopes had finally been realized. At a time friends described as the pinnacle of her life, she was dragged down an alley and brutally murdered by a vicious, psychotic killer.

With everything to live for, her life was taken by a deranged killer who has the twisted mentality to call himself the "victim".

In a further twist in this increasingly bizarre murder investigation, sources in the police department confirmed to this reporter that officers literally ran past the killer in the middle of his horrendous crime.

Just feet from the scene of Andrea's slaying, Nikolas Thorman, an accountant, was gunned down in what police are calling a "gangland murder". (See Accountant, page A2). During the pursuit of the underworld *hit man, police ran directly past the Southside Slasher who undoubtedly had a front row seat to the shooting. In fact, police fear that the ensuing distraction provided by the second killing allowed the Southside Slasher to walk away from the grisly scene.*

As the city braces for more violence, the Mayor is promising to devote even more resources to the...

Preston folded the newspaper carefully. His rage was barely controlled and the slow deliberate movements helped to calm him. He looked across the street at the sidewalk café outside the Starbucks and his rage boiled up again. Closing his eyes, he breathed and felt the calm descend over him. When he thought he could look again, he slowly allowed his eyes to open.

It would be so easy. Just get in his car, a nice leisurely cruise down the street. At the last second, gun the engine and plow through the flimsy tables. Before the idiot could even begin to think, he would be under the wheels. Nothing would be simpler. But where would the satisfaction be in such an easy kill?

Once you have experienced the thrill of killing with your hands, nothing as impersonal as a car could ever really satisfy. Not after feeling the slick, warm blood flow over your hands and flutter of the heart as it slows and finally stops. The eyes, consumed with fear. The pleading, the begging, the promises...

He suddenly realized he was touching himself and he looked around but as usual he was invisible. People just didn't care about him. Nobody ever noticed him.

Lewery was still sitting at his regular table at Starbucks. Preston glanced at his watch and knew he had to get back to work soon. He took up his pad of paper and began drafting the letter he would type later.

As I sit watching you sip your double latte, I wonder at your abilities as an investigative reporter...

Chapter 51

Mann looked over at Greer's desk. The detective had been at it almost non-stop since he left the crime scene last night. First man on the scene, Greer had caught most of the paperwork. Between running the scene and filling out forms, Greer looked exhausted; Mann wandered over to his desk.

"Go home. You've been on it long enough."

Greer shrugged. "I've finished putting in most of the latest data. I was just taking a little break to clear the cobwebs."

"Clear them at home, that's a direct order. Keep going like you are and you'll be useless to us."

Greer nodded and stood. He pulled his coat on. "Yes, sir. I'll see you tomorrow morning then."

Mann nodded, distracted by an overweight, balding man in an Inspector's uniform going into the Livermore's office. Mann wandered over to Keough's office and knocked on the doorframe. Keough, busy on the phone, waved Mann to a seat. He slammed the phone down seconds later.

"I'm still trying to get those god-forsaken cots."

Several of the detectives had taken to sleeping in one corner of the warehouse rather than waste time with the commute home. Some had not seen their families for over a week. Marriages were going to break because of this case. Keough thought the men should at least be comfortable. Unfortunately, the unseen minions who looked after supply didn't agree.

"What's Flem doing here?"

"The Mayor has decided that the case now has official ties with SOCU."

"Thorman?"

"Thorman."

Mann swore. The SOCU was the Mayor's pride and joy. Standing for Special Organized Crime Unit, the SOCU investigated mob activities in the city. Tying Thorman with Angelino had been no difficult matter, at least for their purposes. Doing the same thing in a court of law would be much more difficult.

"You can't run both investigations, Gregg. It was clearly a hit so it had to go to them. It doesn't have anything to do with the Slasher and you have plenty on your plate with just that."

"I know but…" Mann said, even sounding like a whiny teenager to himself.

"Not even in your sandbox so I couldn't get it thrown to Davis. You'll get your shot at Angelino."

Mann shrugged, still looking sullen.

"What's the latest from Buchanan?" Keough asked, trying to change the subject.

"Nothing good," Mann said. "You already saw the preliminary shots of the mutilation. Buchanan confirmed our suspicions."

"The Slasher was there?"

"I'm afraid so. The signature was done but it was sloppy and obviously rushed. Buchanan said it looked like he had to do it, was compelled. However, he didn't have much time."

"What's your timeline?"

"She was already dead before Thorman got into the alley. He must have been working on her – slashing her. He had already taken her larynx. He likely heard the voices and panicked. He finished the sign and then got out. Given the speed that everything happened, it's likely he followed our guy right out of the crime scene. Mrs. Thorman was busy with her husband; the crowd hadn't really formed yet."

Keough sat back in his chair. Taking off his glasses, he rubbed the bridge of his nose. No amount of massaging was going to get rid of this headache.

"So, to recap," Keough said. "We have another dead woman – mutilated and covered in excrement and garbage. We have a dead Mob accountant, armed with an unregistered silenced Forty-five automatic –

undoubtedly a hit. He also had forged passports and airline tickets in his pocket for him and his whole family. We have a uniformed cop running right by the killer that an entire task force is searching for. And that same cop and his partner in a patrol car, likely distracted everyone so they didn't notice a psychopathic killer covered in blood strolling down the street. That about it?"

"Not quite," Mann admitted. "We have two dead men in a car parked down the street from Thorman's house. Shot with a large caliber weapon."

"What about ballistics?"

"Not yet, but I'm betting on a match with the gun in Thorman's hand."

"Is that it?"

Mann nodded. "That about covers it – except for the fact that our only witness to the hit is a psychopathic serial killer."

"And to add to the crucifixion we are going to get in the press, we now have Inspector WH Flem ready to camp out on our doorstep," Livermore said from the doorway.

Keough couldn't help but smile. "They did catch Hiz Honor's double chin, though."

There had been a Keystone Cop cartoon (featuring the Commissioner and the Mayor in the traditional paddy wagon) in one of the editorial pages.

"Is Flem really here for good?" Mann asked.

Flem was a lousy cop but he was perfect for the PR work. He loved to give interviews. He was on the news at least once a week and always wore his uniform. As far as Mann knew, the man didn't even own a civilian suit.

"Do we need that glory hound around here?"

"He smells the media and is already preparing his sound bite," Keough said.

"Watch yourself," Livermore warned. "That particular jerk off has the Mayor's personal emergency cell phone number – for the phone His Honor keeps hidden up his ass. And I don't even want to know what he has on the Commissioner. Something made James back off when the Mayor picked Flem. No secret that he's being groomed to replace James, and you better believe James knows it. And that will happen pronto if we don't solve this case very soon. Come on, it is time to meet the great Flem."

* * * * *

Mann had disliked Flem the moment he met him. The man had risen by the political route rather than by any great police work. It was true enough that early in his career, he had done some good things with organized crime. From the beginning, the mob had been his focus. He had even made some key busts. Since then, he had been just sitting on the political fence turning SOCU from an investigative unit into a political juggernaut. Now, the task force had to put up with him. Mann was determined to put the Inspector through his paces and spared no details of the killings. He even brought in some of the better stills.

"Is that, uh...?" Flem said, pointing at one of the pictures.

"It is. The shrinks figure the killer wanted the victim to be dirty. Hart was beaten, as though the killer wanted to inflict injury on the victim. For whatever reasons, and the shrinks have a handful of reasons, they figure that the killer wanted to punish this latest victim by making her dirty."

Flem shook his head. "It's all beyond me. Still, you figure that the killer might have seen the shooter?"

"If our timing is right, there's no doubt. He would have had a front row seat for the actual killing. They were standing in full view of the stairwell. ME is also of the opinion he was interrupted and did not complete his tasks. We think the hit was the interruption. My guess, he saw the shooter up close and personal."

"Perfect. The only good witness I have is a psycho. I'll need an office and a line plus a desk for one of my squad," Flem demanded.

"You could have mine, sir," Mann offered quickly. "It's quite small, though."

Livermore spoke up. "We've got a larger office toward the back. It would give you more privacy, sir."

Flem stood and shook hands with Livermore. "That will do nicely. I'll be moved in by the end of the day. Thank you, Captain. Lieutenant, I'll have more questions for you later."

Flem left with an air of dismissal. Mann fought the urge to flick him the finger.

"Art got some blood in the feces. Same blood type as the Yeck kill," Mann said once Flem was gone.

"Art has sent it up to Lifecode Corp for a DNA match. At least once we find him, we'll have enough to hang him."

"But we still have to find him," Livermore said.

Chapter 52

Dear Mr. Lewery,

As I sit watching you sip your double latte, I wonder at your abilities as an investigative reporter. In fact, I wonder how you fooled me all these years into thinking you have any intelligence at all.

I admit I am doing a dirty job but it is necessary for the survival of the human race. We must rid society of these bullies and tyrants. A person does a good turn for someone and what does he get in return? Shunned, laughed at, ridiculed, spurned, despised, lied to, and beaten. We try to make the world a better place because it is the right thing to do and what is the result? "Nice guys finish last." Or sometimes the nice guys don't even get to play. Ignored, never chosen.

But now the game is mine. I make the rules. I choose the players. I choose the winner. And I choose me. Now is my time. Time for the dodge ball champions to duck because I have the ball and I don't miss. For every welt that seared my skin, I make a cut. And believe me, the first cut isn't the deepest, it is just the beginning of the pain.

So I continue. Not as the mad psycho that you portray but as a true knight, prepared to do what is necessary to save the kingdom. Salute me or become my enemy.

Sit and sip your double latte and consider your position. Understand who the real victim is, lest you become a victim yourself.

Yours sincerely,

A suspicious friend and victim who has refused to take it anymore...from anyone. The time of vengeance is at hand.

PS: I thought about sending you a finger to help you type or an ear so you could learn to listen but I figured a momma's boy like you would prefer a nipple.

"Can you believe that?" Lewery asked. "The little coward has been following me! Following ME!"

Munro watched Lewery. Full of bluster that might fool the others in the room, Munro could see the edge of fear that tinged all that bravado. And the round, desiccated bit of skin had given the reporter a definite greenish tinge.

"I think we should put some men on Dale just to cover our bases. If he is following him..."

"No way," Lewery interrupted Mann. "No chance I am going to have a couple of your guys following me around all the time. I got a right to some privacy."

Mann looked at Lewery and saw some actual fear in his eyes that wasn't there when the serial killer was threatening him. Mann wondered what Lewery was worried might get exposed. Mann flashed again on the idea that Lewery could be the killer. It wasn't unusual, especially for showier killers to interject themselves into the investigation. And, what better way to get close than to be the sole contact with the killer? Mann had even entertained the idea that Lewery was doing the killing to increase his readership. More readers could earn him a lucrative book deal. But Lewery had been quietly checked out and the detectives had found easily confirmed alibis for two of the killings.

But was he meeting with the killer in secret? Did he have more contact than they thought? Was it all a ruse to build his writing credentials? A threatened reporter would certainly sell more copies when the inevitable book was written.

Mann knew that he could easily make a case for making Lewery a person of interest but the Mayor's office would have a fit if they found out. Still he had to put him under surveillance of some sort. It was too good an opportunity to miss.

"So, you're going to print?"

"Damn right," Dale said. "And he truly is nuts if he expects me to roll over. This guy needs me way more than I need him."

Mann wasn't too sure about that.

Chapter 53

He patiently removed all the pictures from the small binder and spread them around the floor of the living room. Finished, he sat cross legged on the floor and stared down at the array of pictures.

Several moments passed before he was satisfied with the arrangement. He picked out four of the computer simulated pictures and set them across the top of the arrangement.

He picked up a wide, black Magic Marker, ready to draw an X through each of these four pictures.

But they are still out there, aren't they?

Preston paused, the cap in one hand and the marker poised over the first picture.

They are still out there.

He felt a delicious hardening in his groin as he realized he might have the opportunity to kill them all over again. He carefully put the cap back on the marker and set it aside.

Taking a deep breath, he slipped on gloves and checked his equipment.

He had been busy modifying several of his sport coats. They had ridiculed him for his sewing skills. Now, he was using those same skills against them. He needed to have all his tools with him at all times. Sheila had taught him that.

You almost let her get away.

He showed her, though.

You cut her up good. But you still didn't do the slut.

I couldn't when she was covered in shit.

You should have done her first. They are going to call you a fag again. They'll say you can't get it up with a woman.

I just forgot. Besides, there was no time with that other guy getting shot.

But they won't be calling me a masturbator after I take care of Millership. Finally, the truth will come out.

He pulled up both pant legs of his special outfit for tonight and slipped a knife into each of the sheaths strapped to his calves. The knives were hidden, difficult to retrieve but they weren't for emergencies. They were for later.

A length of nylon cord with some sort of plastic coating was coiled tight and put in an inside pocket. It was very fine rope but unbelievably strong. Technology made his job so easy. A loop at each end made it even easier.

He had added two special additions for this time. He had sown a thin pocket into the lining of his overalls. An ice pick slid easily into the pocket and disappeared from sight. It was instantly available for him though. Last, he put a small box of pins into his pocket.

He had been waiting patiently, prepared to go at a moment's notice. Tonight was supposed to be the night.

* * * * *

Dear Mr. Lewery,

Although you continue to ignore my warnings, I still want to have some faith in you.

You will find out soon that not everyone is as innocent as you think. My next target is a liar and pervert whose sickness touches everyone he knows. I alone know the truth of his crimes but soon the world will know. YOU will know. Soon, my latest target will know that he cannot hide from me. He cannot hide from the world. His perversions will finally be known and I will be vindicated. You will have proof of what he is.

They think themselves invincible, untouchable. Nothing could be farther from the truth. The guilty will pay and I am the collection officer.

Don't miss my message. Make sure you print it. Tell the world the truth and it will set you free.

The alternative is to join them. And my enemies pay with their lives. Don't be my enemy, Dale. I don't want to be your enemy because I make war on my enemies. And this is a war you cannot win.

Yours sincerely,
A still-suspicious friend and victim who has refused to take it anymore...from anyone.

PS: I know the police will read my letter so I add this for them. Can those bullies protect their own and stop me in time? Warm and wet he will come forth but a missing pair of hands might let him fall. While he makes the bald man cry, I will bring his secret to the world. Save him if you can so the young will not fall.

"You've got to be kidding me," Dale said, putting the letter down. "Now he's challenging us with riddles? This is almost too perfect but what does it mean?"

"Warm and wet," Munro said. "How does the guy get warm and wet? Blood maybe? But it sounds more like the guy is going to be warm and wet before the murder."

"A swimmer!" Dale said, snapping his fingers. "The next victim is a swimmer! He's going to kill a swimmer."

"Are there any competitions in the city right now?" Munro asked, picking up the phone. He dialed an extension and tapped his pencil impatiently as he waited for the line to be answered. "It's Munro on the City Desk. Are there any swimming competitions going on right now?"

Munro listened and made a couple notes. "Thanks," he said, hanging up.

"Well?" asked Dale.

"There's a meet at the University. It's got something to do with Olympic trials or something."

"But what about the hands thing? Swimmers don't fall, they drown."

"I don't know but it's the best I can think of right now. Maybe a coach? Maybe Mann's guys will come up with something more."

Chapter 54

The smoke swirled past the lights and hovered in the air like the English countryside in an old black and white movie. The movement of the tall waitress or an open door twisted it into small whirlwinds. Then quickly settled in the heavy air until the next disturbance sent them dancing across the room. Tobacco smoke was not allowed but the customers ended up coughing up a lung just so the lights looked cool.

The waitress stopped at his table, bringing a burst of perfume. He let her scent settle over him before he shook his head. She shrugged and moved off. He watched her ass move under the tight jeans. He had been watching her move around the room for over two hours. Two hours of putting up with this God awful band and watching his next target.

Targets, they were targets. The newspapers and television called them victims but that was bullshit. They were anything but victims. They preyed on the victims. They created the victims.

They were scum that deserved to be eliminated. Lewery had better get with the program or he was going to learn first hand what these *victims* had endured.

Deliberately, he released his hand from around his glass. Every time he thought about the media, he got angry. He had tried to make them understand. He needed them to know the truth. Why had Lewery turned against him?

When he looked up again, he panicked. Where had he gone? He wasn't at the same table, eating his wings and watching the band. Then, he saw him. He was standing at the end of the bar. He was getting his credit card back from the bartender.

"This it, George?" asked the bartender.

"Doctor says so. Guess I'd better get on my horse."

"Did you get the hospital room changed over?" the bartender asked.

"No, thank you very much. Here, give this to Suzanne," Logan said, motioning to the lead singer. "I might as well make her night and let her know that the company is going to represent the band."

"Oh, man. She is going to go nuts. Thanks George."

He watched him leave the bar. He didn't hurry after him. They did that in the movies. One man leaves and then someone rushes after him. Everyone remembers. And memorable people get caught. Besides, he knew exactly where Logan was going. He had plenty of time. He would finish his drink and then casually leave. Nobody would remember him. Nobody ever did.

Chapter 55

Degget shoved the hanger over so he could look at the next suit. Arnie might be right about these SOCU guys all wearing three piece suits but their taste was for shit. And they weren't selling out cops for money to buy clothes. Everything was cheap fabric, off the rack crap. Nothing tailored. A few nice things that were likely presents but definitely no big money on clothes.

He moved over to the wife's side and saw the same thing. A bit better quality but none of the clothing was above the pay grade. No furs. No expensive jewelry unless they keep it locked up somewhere else and nothing on fingers or ears that amounted to squat.

Degget checked his watch. He figured he had at least another hour but wanted to finish up in twenty minutes to be sure. He moved downstairs to the den and rifled through files. Things were organized better than the last one he had gone through but it still didn't give him anything. He was halfway through the squad with nothing to show for it.

If you look at anyone hard enough, you would find something bent. Downloading bootleg movies, some kinky sex, drinking, drugs, affairs and gambling but nothing that made Degget suspicious of any of the squad. Everybody had the same bills, pretty much the same outstanding amounts on their credit cards. No cars, boats or big toys that he couldn't find sales slips for that didn't have corresponding debt attached to it. No big cash outlays.

He opened the laptop on the desk and tapped a key with his gloved hands. The screen slowly glowed to life and Degget looked at the list of programs. He opened up the banking program. He shook his head when the program loaded without asking for a password. God, cops were stupid when it came to computer crime. He looked over the register, seeing nothing. He clicked on the credit card entries, glad to see they downloaded their statements every month. All the cards ran below the limit but they never paid them off. And most of the charges were for groceries, gas, movies, meals out – everything that a guy would spend unreported cash on.

He spent another five minutes going over the laptop, checking emails, browser history and any picture files that might show some hidden cottage or boat. All the vacations were just your basic family trips and few and far between.

Wandering through the house, he inventoried everything he could see. Big screen TV but everybody had one of those nowadays. They had the usual spoiled kids with lots of toys but nothing out of line.

Once again, all he found was lots and lots of nothing. Seven suspects down and six more to go. He thought he should feel dirty going through the personal lives of fellow cops. But he was still convinced that one of them had almost killed him. He just had to prove which one and that made everybody a suspect and fair game. Glancing at his watch again, he decided it was time to go.

Moving toward the back of the house, Degget took one last look around to be sure that he had everything back in place. At the door, he slipped his little booties off his shoes. Breaking in had been disgustingly easy. You would have thought cops would be more careful. Only one of them had an alarm system on their home – although two had stickers on the windows but no actual service – something that fooled only the amateurs.

Mentally he crossed another of the detectives off his list. He was quickly running out of suspects.

Chapter 56

George Logan stretched his tired shoulders and yawned. He leaned forward and looked down the hallway. The clock on the wall said it was ten past three. There was a clock in each hallway. He wished he had the contract to sell clocks to hospitals. Whoever did was making a fortune.

He took off his glasses and rubbed his eyes. His mind was ricocheting from one inane subject to another. He should have been exhausted and yet he was wide awake. He considered going home and dismissed that thought immediately. He would just wander around the apartment until daybreak when he would return to the hospital.

He should be with his wife. But his cheap company's insurance only covers a quad room. He was being silly but those curtains gave no privacy. And the first night he spent with his new son should be private. He didn't want to share those quiet first night time moments and words with anyone but his new family.

He had tried to make a change in the room assignments. He had complained about it to everyone who would listen, including hospital staff, his boss, the guys at the bar and anybody in the waiting room. But no amount of complaining got anything changed. Besides, he had a lifetime of nights with his family. He could wait one more night to make a really special night.

He stood and left the small waiting area, beginning the same circuit he had taken three times already. He desperately needed to find a john because the closest one was under repair.

It was even quieter than his last walk. He hadn't met a single person so far. With no distractions, his mind wandered back to his new family.

His wife had been so good. After the weeks in the hospital, the baby had just popped out with no problem at all. He was going to be a big one, just like his father. His *Father*. God, he was a dad.

They had planned the child. Brenda had gone off the patch and got pregnant three months later. Were they fertile or what? His brother had been trying for years now. His brother might have a bigger house and a BMW and a Lexus, but who had the better swimmers? The first grandchild, a son at that, has to count for more than a lousy trip to Hawaii once a year, right Mom?

Now, they had a baby boy that desperately needed a name. Randy was the best bet, named after his grandfather. Jesus, his folks were going to spoil the kid rotten. But, like they say, that's what grandparents were for.

George smiled at the man mopping the floors and edged past the wet area. George had seen the same janitor twice that night. The guy must do the entire hospital. The washroom was ahead on the right. Without looking back, George pushed through the door.

* * * * *

Preston had arrived at the hospital well after his quarry. Millership had hurried while he had taken his time. Of course, he knew exactly where Millership would be. It was all about preparation and planning. They didn't stand a chance against his intellect.

His disguises were getting cleverer. Who would suspect a lowly janitor? He knew the layout of the hospital what with all those vending machines to audit. He knew every washroom, every exit, and every nurse's station. More importantly, he knew where every security camera was. They would have virtually nothing and what they might get would be all wrong.

He had found Jane Degenfeld here. He hadn't needed a disguise then while he kept watch on the little slut. But this time needed a bit more planning and some luck. Still, it was all so easy. Anyone could walk in and get the necessary supplies. And, the overalls were perfect for his purposes. When he was finished, he could just strip them off and walk away.

All he had to do was keep busy.

For over three hours, he had been working his tail off. And, the floors never looked better. For hours, he had waited while that baby took its sweet time. But eventually, Millership would be out here. Preston knew Millership wasn't staying with his wife. As always, he knew everything because he was always there, listening, planning, preparing. He should have done this ten months ago and there would have been one less of them to reproduce.

He might even have to kill Millership's kid. It would be best not to allow the line to continue. The gene pool was already polluted enough.

When the washroom door swung shut, he leaned the mop against the wall and rolled the bucket out of the way. He reached in the secret pocket of the overall and brought out the ice pick.

Without further preparation, he headed for the washroom. He broke out in an instant cold sweat as he realized the similarities between here and the school.

* * * * *

The hall had been better lit and lockers had lined the walls. He hated having to ask the teacher to go to the bathroom. It was so embarrassing to have all the girls know where you were going. He held it as long as he could but now he had to go bad.

He opened the bathroom door quietly. He always did. He hated to announce that he was entering. He hated using public washrooms almost as much he hated asking to use them. If he had pushed the door open like the other guys did, he would never have had the problem.

Somebody else was in one of the cubicles. As quietly as possible, he moved to one of the urinals. If he hurried, he would be done before whoever even knew he was there. But, first he had trouble with his fly. The harder he fought the more it stuck. He barely got it out of his pants before he started peeing.

Then, he heard the noises.

At first, he thought the guy was just laying a big one. The grunts weren't ones of pain, though. Then, he saw the stuff splash on the floor. Every guy recognizes that when it hits the floor. That was the precise moment that he knew he was in trouble.

He tried to hurry but he just couldn't stop. He did everything but squeeze it to stop. He heard the door open behind him just as he stuffed himself back into his pants.

"What are you doing in here?"

Jason Millership was a big, mean kid. A football player and a wrestler – you didn't go up against him. Nobody did. And there he was jerking off in the john during school just like the perv that he was.

It was funny but Preston didn't smile.

"I didn't see anything."

"Didn't see what? Huh? What didn't you see, you little geek?"

All he could do was stand there and quiver. He backed into a corner as Millership started toward him. Then, the big boy just stopped. He stopped and smiled.

"You aren't going to say anything, are you?"

All he could do was shake his head. Millership took one more step towards him and he cringed farther into wall. Millership only laughed and left him alone in the washroom.

He should have known something was wrong but he was too relieved to think. His intellect failed him as relief flooded his body. Having just escaped a severe beating, he didn't consider what was going through Millership's mind. He didn't credit the cretin with enough intelligence to come up with any plan that didn't involve his fists. After wiping the sweat off his face, he returned to his class. By lunch, he knew what the smile had meant.

Not relying on threats for something as important as this, Millership had immediately started spreading the word. Turning the story around, Millership had told everyone that it had been Preston jerking off in the bathroom. Before long, the entire school knew the story.

The rumor and teasing chased him for the rest of the school year.

"He gives a new meaning to the name JERK!"

Boxes of Kleenex and hand softener were left on his desk.

"Don't play tennis with the geek. His grip is too good."

Razor blades and instructions for shaving your palms were shoved into his locker.

"How is PP different from Dr. Pepper? Dr. Pepper comes in bottles but PP comes in his hand."

The last day of the school year, he found a hand exerciser on his desk. The attached note said it was to improve his grip.

Now, he was finally getting even with Millership and the truth would come out.

He wasn't quiet opening the door this time. He wanted Millership to know he was there. In fact, it was important that Millership not be surprised. He did not need surprise. He was going to use human nature.

He went around the corner of the washroom and into the main area. Five urinals, like upright bathtubs, lined one wall. A bank of sinks and mirrors lined the opposite wall. Along the back wall were four stalls.

As expected, Millership was standing at one of the urinals.

You can't deny nature. Nature always took charge eventually. Eventually, Millership would have to use the washroom. All he had to do was stay close and wait. An out of order sign on the bathroom closest to the delivery area took care of leading him to this bathroom. There were too many cameras in and around the delivery area. They had to watch out for those stolen babies. But this hallway didn't have any cameras so he didn't even have to worry about video tape. It was hard to look nonchalant if you are keeping your head down to avoid cameras.

He walked up behind Millership as though he was going to use one of the other urinals. Millership did not look around.

Human nature…at least male human nature. That was the rule.

Men ignore other men in the washrooms.

If you are going to whip your pecker out among strangers, you have to be sure that nobody is going to be staring at you. You might look at the ceiling or your shoes or the cake of deodorant in the drain but you never looked at the other pissers. You look at someone and they either expect a blow job or they are going to beat the crap out of you.

The ice pick was ready.

An intelligent man knows his own limitations and uses them to his advantage. He knew he was no muscleman. Pride might get him killed. Millership was too big for him to try to strangle, satisfying as it might be. As with Kraemer, he used his brains. Millership had to die fast.

Before Millership could even think another thought in that muscle clogged brain, the ice pick went through the soft spot in the back of his skull. The sharp point entered the brain and that was the end.

Millership slumped into his arms taking him to the ground. Squirming out from under him, Preston got his hands under Millership's arms and started to drag him to one of the stalls.

Looking down, he was happy to see that he might not need the pins after all.

Chapter 57

The *Daily* was on Livermore's desk again. The headline, in red letters said everything.

MIRACLE OF BIRTH SHATTERED BY VIOLENT DEATH –
SOUTHSIDE SLASHER STRIKES AGAIN

"What about the description of the killer?"

Mann opened the file folder in his hand although he had the description memorized. "Not much. We found a large pair of bloody overalls in the john with the victim. Two nurses remember seeing a janitor they didn't recognize. Maintenance is contracted out so they are always getting different people. And who notices a janitor anyway. One says medium height, light brown hair, mustache. She really didn't notice him. The other doesn't remember the mustache. Both say he was tubby."

"What about video? Surely to God the hospital has cameras?"

"We grabbed all the tape and we are looking. Don't count on much. So far, we've got one shot but he is wearing a baseball cap and knew exactly where the camera was. There was virtually nothing of his face visible. He has to know the hospital well."

"That is two from the hospital," Keough said. "Is that his hunting ground?"

"We keep coming back to doctors," Livermore added.

"We're making a list," Mann confirmed, "concentrating on all doctors with surgical skills that have privileges at the hospital. But it is a big list. We have eliminated some because of a conference during the Hart killing. It makes me wonder though. He disguises himself as a janitor. Pretty gutsy. A doctor might easily get recognized."

"Maybe," Livermore said, "but then who would tie the two together. You see the overalls first and the face would just look familiar to your mind. Your mind doesn't like contradictions and tends to ignore them. Keep at it; it seems to be our best lead."

"More like your only lead," Buchanan said from the doorway, carrying several copies of the postmortem report on George Logan. "Gentlemen, I'm ready if you are."

Livermore stood and shook hands with Buchanan. "Thanks for coming, Alf."

"Oh, by the way, you know that bar owner?" Keough said, as Alf took his seat.

"The *Night Dance*, the one suing us?" Mann asked.

"He isn't suing anymore. His lawyers informed us that he dropped the suit."

"Why? I figured he had a good case."

"He did. Then, he started to advertise to try and get business going again. But it was a Twitter thing that got it humming. One of the bartenders, I'm guessing the same one that talked to the papers, sent out this message about the bar being a favorite of the Southside Slasher. Business has tripled and the lines go up and down the block every night. Kind of blew his case."

Mann sometimes wished that human nature would surprise him.

"What do you have for us, Alf?" Livermore asked.

"He really used pins to hold the guy's pecker in his hand once it was cut off?" Keough asked, looking at some of the pictures.

"Yes, but he didn't have to," Alf said. "Cadaveric spasm would have taken care of that for him. Obviously, he either didn't know how long it would last or just wanted to be sure. He might have thought he was dealing with rigor."

"Rigor takes hours."

"We know that but maybe he doesn't. He might not be as knowledgeable as we first thought. That would definitely eliminate a doctor."

"Is this guy gay?" Keough asked.

Alf shrugged and looked over at Mann who said, "We are getting ahead of ourselves. Tell us how it happened, step by step."

"Cause of death was a sharp instrument shoved into the brain through the back of the head. My guess would be an ice pick," Alf said, opening his file folder. "The killer stood behind Logan at the urinals. Blood trail to the toilet where all the other injuries happened. I can't give you an exact order but based on overlay of blood evidence, I would say that the penis was cut off first and pinned to the right hand. Then the eyes were stabbed repeatedly. There are interesting wounds on the left hand like the palm was sliced off."

"And then he lost control," Mann interrupted.

"Big time," Alf agreed. "The shirt was torn open and then the victim was stabbed over fifty times. They were so hard, the hilt of the knife caused post-mortem bruising. We were even able to identify the type of hunting knife used from the distinctive marks. Then we have the usual sign carved into the victim's forehead and the larynx is missing."

"So, what does it all mean?" Keough asked

"I talked to a couple shrinks," Alf continued. "They don't agree or really know if the killer may be homosexual but they did figure out what the killer was saying. They recognized the bit in the letter about making the bald man cry. It's slang for masturbation. That points at this victim's secret being masturbation listing all the old wives tales about masturbation – hairy palms and going blind. Our killer made sure that we caught Logan masturbating."

"Jesus. No details to the press about the mutilation. I don't want anybody else figuring this out or we'll be neck deep in lawsuits from the victim's family."

Chapter 58

The psychological experts consulted by this reporter indicate that crime shows obvious homosexual tendencies.

"Homosexual tendencies?" Preston asked aloud. He glanced around but, as usual, nobody was paying the least bit of attention to him. It wasn't fair. He had been called a fag all his life when all he ever wanted was some pussy.

He took another sip of his Coke and pushed the paper aside.

Dale, Dale, Dale, he thought to himself. How can you listen to them? How can you be so blind?

Maybe it is you that is blind. Ever think of that?

But he has always seemed so balanced in his reporting.

Balanced? Look where he buys his coffee. Look at his car. Look at his house.

He thought back. He did have a fancy sports car. And it was a big house for someone who lived alone. And Starbucks?

We know the type that buys their coffee at Starbucks.

"Oh my God," he said in barely a whisper.

Oh my God is right. Feeling a bit foolish? You ordered that Taser for a reason. Do you think it is time for the warehouse?

The warehouse. He had almost forgotten that he'd gone to the warehouse.

Just another inventory check. He used to hate his job until he discovered how useful it was. Now he could get in. And, he had even found his weapon. He didn't have to bring it with him this time. Good thing too, it was damned heavy.

The Taser would be here in a day.

Time for one last letter?

* * * * *

The news was on and the *Slasher Update* was the lead story. The night before, he had even made it to the national news. Katie Couric had talked about him! Cute perky Katie. Luckily, he had TIVOed it so he could watch over and over while she described his successes.

His smile faded slightly when they showed a shot of the newborn baby.

"His father," the newscaster said, with a phony crack in his voice, "was taken after seeing the boy only once. He wasn't even granted the opportunity to know his new son's name. The newborn's mother was left to decide that on her own."

That report hit him hard. He still felt enormous guilt.

He had failed the world.

He should have killed Millership *before* he had a chance to reproduce.

He hit the mute on the remote to deaden the drivel.

The child would be better off without *that* father. Millership would have just turned his son into another of the scum of the world. Maybe now, he would escape the curse of the deviant genes of his father.

Christ, Millership masturbated so much, it was a wonder he had any sperm left to make the little bastard. Maybe that was the answer! Maybe his wife had got a little on the side and the brat wasn't even Millership's. Wouldn't that be a hoot?

She would have no trouble finding a new father for the child.

She deserved better and now she would have the opportunity. Now, she could get what she truly deserved. She was so beautiful, so obviously caring, such an addition to the world. She would flourish without Millership.

Possibly, he should marry her himself. He would be an excellent, loving, caring husband. He was more the type she deserved in life. She deserved someone like him, someone who thought of others and the good of the world.

Then, once he was close to the child, the ideal of the perfect father, he could kill the little bastard. No use risking that Millership was the father. The father's genes might be dominant. Bullies usually breed true.

His own seed would give the world the child it needed.

Was that the way it was to be? Were Tina and a child to be his reward for his holy task?

He couldn't contact her yet. It was too early. People might consider it gauche. Bad form, so soon after Millership's death. He would wait for a time.

After all, even if she proved herself unworthy and rejected him, he could still just kill her and the brat.

Preston needed a new messenger.

Lewery had seemed so promising, the perfect man to get his story out. But that was not to be. Lewery had proven himself unworthy. He would pay for that in just a few hours.

Who else could deliver his story? He would have to find someone to contact. Maybe the newspapers were too small time, not immediate enough. He needed television. Maybe it should be the idiot on the screen right now.

Was he still thinking too small with this local talking head? Maybe he should contact Katie? He could imagine telling her his story. Just the two of them, intimate and quiet.

He felt himself harden and slipped his hand inside his pants. No, he couldn't waste it. He had use for his seed tonight.

✳ ✳ ✳ ✳ ✳

How can someone spend his life writing about crime and not have an alarm? Lewery obviously thought himself impervious. Crime would never touch him. He was about to feel the touch. Very hard.

He heard the key in the front door and braced himself. He took a deep breath and held it.

Lewery came through the door and locked it again. After looking at the layout of the house, Preston expected Lewery to either go straight to the kitchen or veer left to his office. He couldn't be sure which so he thought hiding behind the short wall separating the front foyer from the living room was the wisest. He prepared to step out and shoot him with the Taser in the back.

Instead, a hard briefcase hit him in the shins and he grunted. Lewery looked down to see what was blocking the case and immediately looked up at the sound. Before surprise could even register on Lewery's face, Preston pulled the trigger and the twin contacts shot into the reporter's chest. With a cry of pain, the reporter instantly went stiff and toppled to the floor, twitching.

After several seconds of watching him dance, he released the trigger. Lewery moved slightly and he triggered the Taser again. Lewery cried out and was forced back onto the floor. Lewery had been too close and the Taser leads only inches apart. The manual had warned that it wasn't as effective if the leads were too close. He hoped the battery would last.

"Geez, that looks like it really hurts, Dale. Does it hurt as much as the brochure said? You ready to do as you're told? Personally, I would rather you didn't cooperate right away. But, if you would rather avoid the pain, just roll on your stomach right now and put your hands behind your back. I'm going to give you until three. One…"

"Don't, please," Lewery begged, his voice slurred. "I'll do it. It hurts. It really hurts."

Lewery tried to roll on his back. His body would not respond and he was kicked over. He felt his hands pulled together behind his back. Before he could clear his head enough to consider some form of escape, a plastic strap was pulled tight around his wrists. With his face pressed against the hardwood, he couldn't see his attacker. Confused and unable to focus, his brain was as sluggish as his body.

"Here's how this works," he heard his attacker saying. "We're going to walk out your back door to the alley. Don't cooperate, and you get another taste of the Taser. Try to run, Taser. Call out – *this* gets a taste of *you*."

Suddenly a huge hunting knife was buried into the floor so close to his eyes, it almost cut his brow.

"OK, time to go," the voice said as the knife was yanked out of the floor.

Dale struggled to his feet, his body still not responding. He could still see the wires hanging from his chest. Even without the threat of the Taser, Dale didn't think he could run. His legs didn't want to work. Staggering, he allowed his attacker to push him through the house and out into the yard.

He hoped that one of his neighbors would see something and call the police. He tried to walk slower, hoping to give more time to be spotted. But what if they came out? He could feel the point of the knife prodding him along. He sped up and walked through the back gate. He allowed himself to be put in the back seat of a stupid little car. He barely fit and hit his head on the doorframe.

"Watch your head, Dale," his captor laughed.

Lewery was on his back and saw his chance to kick his attacker. He started to quickly pull his legs back but they moved in slow motion. His attacker casually stepped back. Holding the Taser up for Lewery to see, he triggered the power and Lewery cried out again.

Preston reached down and grabbed a canister with a gas mask attached to it. Without waiting for Lewery to recover anymore, he slipped it over the newspaperman's ugly face. He opened the valve on the canister a bit and watched Lewery's face through the mask.

"Ever hear of Nitrous Oxide, Dale? Course you have. Ever take a suck of it at the dentist? You know what else they use it for? Whipped cream. Cool, huh? But it also whips your brain up just right. You soon won't even care that I'm going to kill your sorry ass. You do know who I am, don't you?"

Lewery stared up through the mask.

"Just a little addled, are we? You named me, for Christ sake. Are you that dense or have I actually scrambled the old grey cells? I'm the Southside Slasher, you sorry little turd. Nice catchy name, by the way."

Dale was slowly beginning to slip back into the world. He could see he was lying in the back seat of a car. Small car from the way he was all squished up. He could hear strange grunting noises coming from the front seat. They finally ended with a long moan.

There was a rustling and he heard a zipper and the clink of a belt. But he really didn't care enough to wonder what he was hearing.

Suddenly a fat face loomed in front of him.

"Know what happens when someone is abducted and killed, Dale?" the face asked him, as it pulled off the mask.

Dale felt his head lifted by his hair but it only felt vaguely uncomfortable.

"Here, drink this. You'll feel better."

Dale felt the cup against his lips and coughed as the warm liquid poured into his mouth. His mouth and nose were covered. "No spitting, Dale. You have to swallow. It would be a few minutes before I could get anymore for you and we are on a schedule here."

Dale swallowed and gagged.

"So you didn't answer my question," the voice said, as the mask was replaced over his face. "Do you know what happens after the victim's body is found?"

Dale made some incomprehensible sound.

"Well, they do an autopsy, of course. They want to trace your movements. So they analyze your stomach contents. Got to know when you last ate and maybe even where. Guess what they're going to find?"

Dale just stared blankly into the face above him.

"Well, Dale, my friend," the voice said, laughing so hard he was spitting on the mask. "Guess who is going to be the fagboy now? They are going to think you stopped off for a quickie with your boyfriend on your way home. Think about that one. Your permanent record will forever say that the last thing you did before you died was suck off some guy. You will be officially listed as a homo forever!"

* * * * *

Lewery came fully conscious and screamed.

He lifted his head as far as he could. He was tied spread eagle on a hard cement floor. A man was sitting on his stomach carving something into his chest with a large knife. He screamed again and realized he wasn't really making any noise and couldn't open his mouth.

"Oh Dale," said the man sitting on him, "suck it up and be a man. After all, you do want them to know you were killed by the Southside Slasher. This will be a great scene in the book. You were planning on writing a book about me, weren't you? Of course, you'll just be a chapter in it now, instead of the author."

As the knife made one final deep cut, Lewery lost consciousness again.

"Wake up, Dale."

Lewery sputtered and spat as a pail of water splashed on his face. The pain in his chest returned in a rush, threatening to make him pass out again.

"No, no, Dale. Stay with me for a bit. We just have one more paragraph in this little story. Look up, Dale."

Lewery looked up and saw the great roll of paper suspended over him.

"You ever take a tour of your own newspaper, Dale? Did you know that is the beginning of that rag you call a newspaper? Once it stops being a tree, anyway. Before you sully it with your spurious words, all that paper, weighs over eighteen hundred pounds and has seven miles of paper on a roll. That's a lot of your bullshit on a single roll. Actually, I imagined the rolls even bigger – big enough to squish you. Now, I'm not sure if your head will pop off."

Peterson caressed the roll. "Enough chit chat. I just wanted you to know that for all the good, innocent people like me that you stomped on, we're getting even. Goodbye, Mr. Lewery."

Still looking into the panicked eyes of the reporter, he triggered the fast release on the chain lift. The roll plummeted to the floor.

Guess I win.

He looked at the blood splattered for several feet in each direction. "Bummer," he said quietly, as he mopped up the blood with a small paint brush, "I really wanted his head to pop off."

Chapter 59

"Mr. Munro?"

Munro looked at the mailroom kid in the doorway. "Ya, what have you got?"

"Sir, I think we have another one."

Munro looked down at the young man's hands and noticed he was holding an envelope by a pair of tweezers.

Munro motioned him forward and cleared a spot in the middle of the desk. "Get Lewery."

"We can't find Mr. Lewery anywhere. I've tried his house and his cell but I'm not getting any answer. This was couriered and the label says that I'm to give it to Lewery's replacement. Has Mr. Lewery quit?"

"Oh Christ. Stay right there while I open this thing."

Munro carefully slit the envelope open using the tweezers and a letter opener. Tipping up the envelope, a small card slipped out, falling face down on the desk. Munro flipped the card over and swore. Even upside down he could read the three word message and recognized the sign immediately.

Mr. Lewery – RIP

"Jesus Christ on a bagel with lox. Keep trying Lewery. Send someone over to his house but tell them to just wait on the street. Don't go near the house. Send someone with a photographer. Whoever is closest goes. You got that?"

"Yes, sir," the young man said, racing from the office.

"Make sure they have a phone," Munro shouted as he picked up his own phone. "Get Mann at the Slasher Task Force. Tell him that it's urgent. Don't take any bullshit."

He slammed down his phone saw someone running toward his office through the newsroom. Breathless, he slid through the doorway as the phone rang. Munro picked it up. "Hang on."

"Boss, we got a dead body at the paper warehouse. It's a mess. Looks like someone got squished by one of the paper rolls. Boss, they said that Lewery's ID is on the floor by the body."

Munro could hear Mann shouting into the phone. "Mann? We got another letter. You got to get someone over to Dale's house right now. And you better get some guys over to our warehouse on Eastern down by the Harbor. I think the Slasher just killed Dale."

* * * * *

With the death of one of their own, the newspapers reported Slasher updates on the front page of every edition. Television shows highlighted the frustrated efforts of the police. Since it was public knowledge that Dale had been threatened, the story was leaked that he had refused a protective detail. However, it was also discovered that Kesle PD had still put Lewery under surveillance. An unmarked car with two detectives had been parked out front when Lewery was abducted.

As only television can do, every "expert" imaginable was trotted in front of the camera to give an opinion of the Slasher. Hour after hour, the same dozen pictures or two minute video loop ran on the screen while voices droned on. With little new to report about the Slasher, special broadcasts described, often in revolting detail, the past exploits of other infamous serial killers.

The weather continued to heat up. Spring fever had passed and expectations for summer vacations flared. With the warmer weather came long walks at night, open windows and tempers. It all added up to one inescapable conclusion...paranoia.

The city was poised on the Slasher's knife edge.

The Southside Slasher was due to strike again. The only thing all the experts would agree on was that he was not finished. Everyone knew he was going to kill again. The police had even given up denying that inevitable fact. If had been replaced by when, where, and, most importantly, who.

Who would be the next victim was on everyone's mind.

Every psychologist, psychiatrist, sociologist and varied other "ist" with a book to sell was paraded in front of the public. Their *expert* opinions predicted who was at greatest risk. The dozens of conflicting opinions reinforced that everyone was at risk.

And along with newspaper sales, television revenue and expert witnesses, others prospered.

Sales of handguns and ammunition were up a staggering percentage. Extra shipments were being brought into the city as though war had been declared. Rifles and shotguns sold especially well since the licensing and waiting period was less strict. Local NRA chapters began holding special instruction classes seven nights a week.

The emergency rooms saw the next increase in business.

In three nights, as many husbands, all returning from late shifts, were shot by anxious wives with new guns. Two women were shot while practicing with their new guns. The first had misunderstood how to use the safety and shot the second in the leg. Enraged, the second had shot and killed the first. Finally, the father of a ten year old girl was shot while coming home from work. He was carrying a skipping rope for his daughter and his fifty year old neighbor panicked, seeing him walking up their shared driveway and thinking he was about to strangle her.

Alarm companies were deluged with calls after it became known that Lewery's killer had been inside waiting for him. An advertisement, which implied that an alarm would have saved Lewery, began to appear a few days after the reporter's death. The company pulled the ad after two days, supposedly out of respect for the late Lewery's memory. In truth, they couldn't handle the volume of calls.

Less lethal self defense courses also benefited from the windfall of the Slasher. Overweight couples suddenly found themselves tossing each other around gymnasiums. Heart attacks and strokes followed as people practiced their newly learned skills in the humid ninety plus heat.

One clever inventor created a strangulation-proof device to be worn around the neck. Thousands were sold before the hot weather defeated the idea.

Then, the vigilantes appeared.

Groups of weapon totting vigilantes began patrolling neighborhoods.

Anyone found alone was harassed and often searched. Ideally, suspicious individuals were turned over to the police. The ideal was seldom met.

Slasher fear was used as an excuse for racial violence, harassment of gays, and any other cause celeb. Three black youths discovered by one neighborhood patrol were severely beaten. Two escaped with broken bones and scars that would last their lifetimes. The third died from internal bleeding on the way to hospital. They had been in the neighborhood to visit a clergyman who had been instrumental in getting them admitted to college. All had finished their first year in the top ten of the respective classes.

Gays demanded protection from the police after one member of their community was found naked with forty seven gunshot wounds. The investigation of the shooting revealed a frightening story.

The shooting victim, a known homosexual, was walking home in the late evening when he came upon a neighborhood patrol. They demanded that he submit to a search. When he refused, he was taken forcibly between two houses and strip searched. He fought his captors and a rifle discharged. One of the patrollers was shot in the foot. Seeing his opportunity, the victim tried to run. He was shot down before he had gone three feet.

"We just shot," recounted one member of the patrol. "It was just reflex. We just kept pumping shots into him. Every time a shot hit him, it looked like he was jumping up. So, we hit him again."

When asked why they had finally stopped, the vigilante answered, "I suppose, we just ran out of bullets."

Rumors about the Slasher spread through word of mouth, the media and especially the Internet.

New Facebook pages appeared daily. Each had its own take on the investigation. Some posted pictures and video from the news. Others had maps and predictions on where the next murder would take place. Others linked to sites selling memorabilia of other serial killers or DVDs of real crime scene photos. Most traded stories and gossip about the Slasher. Still other groups ran pools on who would be the next victim. Accurate guesses of the next victim's age, gender, hair color, etc. promised big prizes.

Tweets burned up band width as each latest new Slasher "fact" was reported. Rumors took on a life of their own, quickly moving from speculation to accepted fact.

One such rumor had the Slasher driving a red Chevy. Police never learned how that rumor began but the city began to watch for the red Chevy. On a crowded downtown street during the afternoon rush hour, they found it.

The owner of a Chevy had parked illegally to run into the drug store to pick up medicine for a sick child. When he returned to his car, a mounted policeman was giving him a ticket. Worried about his son, the man started to argue with the officer.

Witnesses said that the rest started with one shout.

A pedestrian noticed the argument between the driver and the policeman. He recognized the red Chevy and pushed through the crowded sidewalk. He wanted to see the arrest of the Southside Slasher; his cell phone was already out to capture it all for YouTube. At the same time, he couldn't resist telling people as he pushed past.

"The Slasher. They got the Slasher!"

In a city the size of Kesle, it takes a lot to make anyone take notice. That was enough. The man immediately attracted those within earshot. There was a silence around him and he sensed that he had become the centre of attention. He pointed toward the red car. "There! The Slasher!"

The mounted policeman, fought to control his mount as the crowd surged forward. Hearing the shouts, he started looking for the Slasher. The driver, ticket in hand, started to get back in his car, his thoughts still on his ill son.

The crowd surged forward as one and traffic crunched to a halt.

Thinking the driver was trying to escape, a large man yanked him back out of his car, clamping him in a bear hug. Another man swung at the driver but his legs were kicked out from under him. As the crowd moved in closer, the horse and policeman were pressed back.

With the driver still clutched against him, the burly man was rammed against the car. He had to release his prisoner in order to keep his balance. The driver went down on the ground.

Sanity was restored in five minutes. By then, the driver was dead, kicked to death by the angry mob.

Chapter 60

There she was, just waiting for him at the bus stop.

Preston barely had time to get to the stop before the bus came. He slipped on behind and carefully chose his seat with a clear view of her. While they rode to whatever destination fate had decreed, he took out his small book. He compared her picture. As usual, his memory was flawless.

She was the perfect target to show the liars the truth. He would prove that all those stories were false. He would show them what a real man he was. He would show them he was not some faggot.

And, who better to prove it with! The years had not dulled the pain she had caused.

It wouldn't happen tonight. He wanted to be sure that he would have plenty of time with this one.

Chapter 61

"You have nothing!" Mayor Dalton stormed around his office. "Seven bodies and you have nothing!"

Keough could not make the meeting. His daughter was getting married and Mann had to sit in for him. Mann had tried to talk Livermore into going alone but he wasn't having any of it. So, Mann had to follow Livermore to The Hill.

"We have some suspects," Livermore said, soothingly. He nodded encouragingly to Mann.

"We do have suspects," Mann agreed. "But, none of them have any substantial backing."

"What the hell does that mean? Either you have suspects or you don't. Do either of you have any idea what the press is doing to me?"

Mann and Livermore knew exactly what the press was doing. Besides making their job extremely difficult, they were all over the Mayor. With Lewery getting killed, the case had become very personal to the media. If the case dragged on, the Slasher would become an election issue.

"I need to tell the press that we have come up with something."

Mann shook his head. "We don't have anything solid. We cut the doctor loose. He was being watched during the next killing."

"That isn't good enough. What about all the tips that are coming in? Surely something must have come of that."

Mann looked over at Livermore. What did they expect? Did they just want him to pull a suspect out of the pile? "We have got one person that is a possibility," Livermore said.

"But," Mann rushed to add, "the investigation has just started. We can't definitively place him at any of the crimes."

"But haven't been able to eliminate him either," Livermore continued.

Dalton stopped his pacing and sat down in his seat. "So, you do have something."

"Not much. We have some circumstantial evidence and some of the information jived with past offenses. It's possible. We have to take it slow. We want to build a proper case against him. We are considering bringing him in for a DNA test."

"What's the name?"

Warning bells were ringing in Mann's head.

"Drabick, Stephen Drabick," Livermore said.

The Mayor suddenly stood and reached out his hand to Livermore. "Keep us informed, Deputy Inspector."

Mann and Livermore rode the elevator to the lobby. They were surrounded immediately by the press. Questions were shouted. Livermore cleared his throat. "We just gave an update to the Commissioner and the Mayor."

"What about suspects?"

"At the moment…"

"Deputy Inspector Livermore has informed us that they have a suspect in the case. Naturally, no names can be given."

Mann and Livermore swung around. Mayor Dalton and Commissioner James stood at the elevator doors. Mann knew they had been had. The entire meeting was a setup. The Mayor had everything planned and timed well in advance. All he needed was a confirmation that there *was* a suspect. Now, if they didn't make an arrest shortly, the Mayor could dump Livermore and put in someone else. The buck would be successfully passed and blame would not fall on the Mayor, at least for now.

Mann slipped around the back of the crowd of reporters. He winced as he heard the Mayor talking about an imminent arrest. Disgusted, he went out to the car to wait for Livermore.

❈ ❈ ❈ ❈ ❈

The next morning, Mann sat bent over his desk reading from a folder spread out in front of him. He checked to see how many pages were left. He was relieved to see he was on the last page. To the left of the current file, a stack of similar folders were piled haphazardly. One file was set by itself to the right.

Mann shut the last file and set it on the top of the large pile. He looked at his watch and yawned. Grabbing an empty Pepsi can, he went out into the main office. Greer was just coming in carrying two racks of donuts from the shop down the street.

"You're in early, Lou." Greer took another look at Mann's unshaven face and rumpled clothes. "Didn't you go home last night?"

Mann shook his head. He tossed the empty can in the recycle container and opened the fridge. Two cases of Pepsi were waiting for him. The cleaning crew must have restocked the pop before they left. Bless them. He popped a can and took a long drink. "I was going over the files."

"Still not a believer?"

"Hardly."

Greer set the donuts down. Mann looked at his watch again. "Aren't you a bit early yourself?"

"I was up anyway. It's so damned hot. I figured what the hell, so I walked in. It's just a couple blocks."

Greer was pouring himself a cup of coffee. He didn't look particularly good himself. He was looking exhausted. Working too hard and spending too many hours at the warehouse or out on the street chasing down leads. They all were. Cops were going to destroy their marriages and their health because of this case.

After returning from the meeting with the Commissioner and Mayor, Livermore had called in each of the detectives heading major areas of investigation. They each brought in their top suspects. Nobody had anyone that they were overly hot on, just dead end leads and questionable tips. From that, Mann and Livermore had narrowed the list down to the pile on Mann's desk. Drabick was still the best name and he was a long shot at best.

Drabick had come to their attention through the regular check of traffic violations in the areas of the killings. The Task Force regularly checked all parking violations for a ten block radius around the murder sights for eight hours either way. More if the ME was not confident of time of death.

Mann supported the practice but didn't put much stock in Drabick's tickets.

"Drabick's got over a hundred tickets. I don't think he parks unless it is illegally," Mann argued.

"We know that the Slasher is not just picking his targets at random. The other tickets could be from his touring times while he is looking for a victim."

"They got Son of Sam through a parking ticket," another Detective pointed out.

Mann looked at Livermore who nodded. Even the Deputy Inspector was being affected. Mann had feared exactly this as soon as the Mayor announced the suspect to the press. Mann had experienced it before. When a case is at a stand still, especially one as emotional as this one, detectives will cling to anything positive. Unfortunately, too often the evidence was molded to the suspect rather than the other way around. What fit the suspect was amplified, what didn't was altered or ignored.

Livermore was concerned about the Mayor's spies. Unless they played along with the brass to a certain extent, they risked a clean sweep of personnel by the increasingly panicked Mayor. And that would set the investigation back days or even weeks as a new team got up to speed.

Stephen Drabick had a long history of criminal assault as well as two convictions for rape. In both cases, he had used a knife in the rapes. One of the women had been cut in the struggle. Drabick did not fit the profile as far as Mann was concerned. Drabick was an opportunistic rapist who used brute force rather than intelligence. However, word had spread through the Task Force and the detectives had begun to believe that Drabick was the best suspect. Some had even given up their own favorite suspects.

"If you are convinced that Drabick isn't our guy, what do you suggest?"

Mann looked at Livermore. "Put a team on Drabick. We have enough for that. We'll put someone on him round the clock."

"And wait?"

"We don't have enough for an arrest. We've questioned him twice. He has refused a DNA test."

"Is there anything from his other convictions?"

Mann shook his head. "It was eye witness identification and fingerprints that got him. He wore condoms. No DNA samples from back then."

Livermore and Mann had discussed the course of action. Both hated to pull the manpower away from the other promising leads but had no choice. The Mayor aside, there was the *chance* that Drabick was the killer.

Livermore turned to Mann. "Get a team together to watch Drabick. I want the first team over there within the hour. If we can get anything on him, we will pull him in again. I'll inform Flem about Drabick and the stakeout. If we want this to get back to the Mayor, Flem is the person to tell him."

* * * * *

"Nobody knows where he might be, Lou. The manager hasn't seen him since yesterday. Do you think we spooked him with the second interview?"

"Keep on him," Mann said, ignoring the question. "As soon as you pick Drabick up, stay with him."

Mann swore and banged the phone down. He would have to send teams out to Drabick's known hangouts. More manpower chasing air.

Mann had a feeling churning in the pit of his stomach. With Drabick in the wind, he prayed there wouldn't be another killing.

Chapter 62

Tonight was the night.

He was becoming impatient with just following her. The rage was growing and so was the dissatisfaction. He missed the rush, the feel of the warm blood running over his hands. Crouching in the shadows, watching, waiting, the anticipation was sweet but frustrating.

He wished she would break her routine and let the dog out early but knew she wouldn't. He would wait. He was safe here in the dark, where he always belonged. Safe, hidden as he always was. But now he was starting to come out. And soon they would know the truth about beautiful, little Tracy and the mystery of all those years would be settled.

✻ ✻ ✻ ✻ ✻

She finally let her little mutt out so he could "do his business". The stupid dog had barked at him the first night. The second night, the dog barked but he had brought meat and the dog loved him. The third night, the dog only whined the whole time.

Tonight, the dog hadn't made a sound. Well, there had been that satisfying little crunch but otherwise he was very quiet now. Such a delicate little doggie skull under his heavy work boot.

He turned up his wrist and looked at his watch. The luminous dial showed eleven twenty five. She would soon bring the dog in or at least try.

She always came out each night at eleven-thirty.

She would stand in the doorway and call the dog. She stayed in the doorway so that the light shone through the short nightie she wore. Not that she wore it to bed. He knew she would be naked in bed. Sluts like her always slept naked.

She only wore the nightgown so he would be tempted. She let the light shine through to tease him. She always liked to flaunt herself. She had always flaunted her body to him. She had not changed at all.

* * * * *

Tracey Mitchell was the best looking girl in the school. Every guy dreamed of her – masturbated to fantasies of her naked body. She had long golden hair and a curving body that screamed to be touched and caressed. Every boy wanted to find out if she was a natural blonde.

"Do you think Tracey has a golden pussy?" was *the question* during tenth grade.

Plenty of boys got close to the answer. Very close but Tracey foiled their attempts. But not because she didn't let them in her pants.

Tracey was a slut. She loved sex and she loved what the boys would do in order to have their time with her. And she took all they had to give. And she gave them all what they wanted, except the one answer they craved.

She knew what the guys all wanted to know. She knew about the bets. So, she had only done guys in the dark. That way, no guy could ever boast that he had got her. He would never be believed if he didn't have the definitive report on her pussy. They all said they had her, and everybody knew they had, but nobody could give the word.

She worked through the boys in the school before the real surprise happened. Her parents were going out of town and she invited him to her house. She wanted *him*. He was supposed to show up at nine o'clock. It would be dark by then.

But, he wasn't stupid. He wouldn't fall for her tricks. He wasn't one of the dumb jocks that she normally tricked. He told her it would have to be earlier. He would be there before dark. She would not be able to hide her golden hair from him. He was too smart for her.

By seven thirty, he was in her bedroom.

"Take off your clothes," she said to him. "I want to see your naked body. Get naked and I will put something really sexy on."

He couldn't get out of his clothes fast enough. He already had his shirt off as she was leaving the room. He stripped off his pants and underwear. He was already hard as he lay back on the bed.

When the door opened, he was ready. Leaning back against the headboard, his arms open wide and his stomach sucked in as far as it would go.

He hadn't heard them. They must have been giggling before they got to the door but the radio was on. Now, they were laughing. All her friends, boys and girls, stood in the doorway. One of them had a Polaroid and snapped his picture. They laughed at him and pointed as he got small. Tracey was laughing the hardest.

The bigger boys from the football team grabbed his clothes and wouldn't give them back. They chased him to the front door and threw him out on the front lawn. He had to run all the way home covered only with a tarp from a neighbor's wood pile.

* * * * *

"Benji! Here boy." Tracey came out on the porch, blonde hair gleaming. He could see right through her little gown. Her narrow hips and big breasts showed through. She called for the dog but he didn't come – the only one who wasn't going to come tonight.

She looked out into the back yard but couldn't see anything in the light coming from the house. She stepped off the porch onto the lawn and thought of the gate.

He knew she would think of the gate. She would check to see if the gate was closed. She would walk away from the light. They were all so predictable. His superior intelligence would always make it so.

She never heard him. She didn't even sense him. No scary music, no sudden sixth sense. She didn't know anything was wrong until she felt the rope around her neck.

Using the rope, he dragged her back to the door. She didn't put up much of a struggle. Maybe, she had read that if you don't struggle, you won't get hurt. Thank God for books.

Inside the door, he turned off the light. The kitchen was in darkness. There was plenty of time to decide if she was a natural blonde or not.

He tightened the rope around her neck. She finally started to struggle against him. It was too late.

She was pressed against him and he could feel her flimsy nightgown shifting up around her waist. He felt himself harden.

He could see her laughing at him and pointing. She had said something about how small he was. She had said he was hardly a man.

She would know his manliness before she dies. She would know what she missed that day.

She had gone limp, supported only by the rope around her neck. He let go of the rope and she fell to the floor. She was unconscious but gasped in a deep breath. She regained consciousness as he bound her hands and gagged her. He stood up and started to undo his pants. Then, he remembered her legs.

Girls like to kick.

He tied one foot to one of the table legs. He then pulled her other ankle over to the next table leg. He tied it quickly because she was starting to make noise.

He turned on the light in the oven. He could see her eyes were open. She stared up at him.

He liked the fear.

Her nightgown ripped easily. He used the knife on her panties.

He smiled. "I knew it!"

Chapter 63

"He kept this one alive for a long time," Buchanan said. "Most of what he has done to his previous victims has been post mortem. Not this time."

Mann looked over at the naked body of Kelly Bronson. Thirty-four, unmarried, blonde, five foot five, slim, pretty and a legal secretary, she was lying back in a recliner with her throat cut. Her upper torso from the belly button up had been mutilated, many of her organs ripped from her and tossed around the room. Her throat had been slashed so deeply it was almost severed to the spine. Her larynx was missing.

"Run it down for me," Mann asked Shane, who had been on the scene for the past two hours. Most of that time, Mann had been dealing with the media and trying to organize the rest of the task force. As they still couldn't find Drabick, he was a suspect in this killing.

"He knew her movements well enough to know when to kill the dog. He got her by the back gate and dragged her into the house. She has grass stains on her heels where he dragged her. Ligature marks on her ankles and the rope in the kitchen suggest she was tied to the table, legs apart."

"He raped her in the kitchen?" Mann asked.

"Yes. The table was handy and high enough for him to get under. I think he wants us to know he did it. Lots of ejaculate all over the floor. She had to have been alive at that point. Buchanan has no doubt she died in this chair."

"Why the kitchen?"

"I've already been on the phone describing the scene to the shrinks,"

Greer said, interrupting Shane. "They seem to think he is reacting to the homosexual inferences in the newspapers. They think he wants us to know what a stud he is. According to them, he's saying 'look at me, can't even wait to get in the door'. And he wanted us to know she was alive when he did it."

"Wonderful," Mann said. "He wasn't psycho enough; we had to make him worse."

Shane continued. "He did most of his worst in here."

"What the hell is with that?" Mann asked, pointing at the victim's abdomen.

"He used that bucket and cloth to wash her down," Buchanan answered, taking up the story. "Post mortem, he cleaned up the blood on her abdomen and pubic area. He was careful not to clean up the evidence of the rape though."

"But…" Mann said. "What does it mean?"

Written in permanent marker, with an arrow pointing to the dark patch of pubic hair, was

FRAUD

Chapter 64

Mann massaged his temples. The city was getting into a greater panic and this latest kill had done nothing to ease the tensions. Livermore was down at The Hill trying to ease the agonies of the Mayor while trying to keep his job with the Task Force.

"We need something solid," Mann said to himself.

Like an answer from the Gods, Alf Buchanan walked into the office.

"Talking to yourself? Bad sign, Gregg."

"So are bleeding gums and a stomach to match. Tell me you have some good news."

Buchanan perched his thin frame on the edge of the chair and handed a file across the desk. Mann, recognizing the look in Buchanan's eyes, didn't bother opening the folder.

"Our boy is five foot five to five foot seven."

"You sure?"

Buchanan shrugged. "Best guess, I have to admit. The girl was killed sitting down in the easy chair. The killer had his back to the wall. He slit her throat. Blood spurted from carotid. The first splatter shows him at about five feet. The second shows him at five five to five-seven. Good silhouette."

"When he cut her, he was bending over. The blood sprays; he steps back and straightens to get as far away as possible. Backs right against the wall. The next heartbeat gets that picture."

"That is how CSU reads it. I tend to agree. He did try to wipe down the wall, though."

"So, he knew what he was doing?"

Buchanan shrugged. "The wall was porous, a plaster. Once the wall was treated, the darker spots show the original splatter pattern. He also moved the furniture to further confuse the issue. Indentations on the rug gave him away. He knew what he was trying to do, though."

"A cop?"

Buchanan shrugged. "Or he just watches TV. Either way, the guy is intelligent. And cool. He just banged the girl and then cut her up something awful and still has his balls together enough to try and screw us over."

"The video from the hospital puts him at five foot nine or ten."

"He wore lifts, I suspect," Alf said. "He took too much time trying to disguise the splatter."

"He knew we'd get him on video even if we didn't get his face so he disguised himself. So we can't rely on the weight either. He could have been wearing a body suit. What about the shower?"

"We cleaned out the drain but it's going to be hard to get much. We're matching everything we come up with. We have his DNA so if we match a hair, we will have color. It is going to take time."

"The one thing we don't have. He's working faster."

Livermore walked into the office. Mann noticed how haggard he looked. "How are things at The Hill?"

"A zoo. You get anything, Alf?"

"We got a height. Five five to seven."

"Which clears Drabick," Mann added.

"Drabick is five nine," Buchanan said. "I don't want to eliminate anyone too quickly just based on this. It could still be him, stooped over. But if you want my opinion, it isn't him."

Chapter 65

Degget listened to the two detectives in the next booth bullshit each other about their waitress and who was going to leave with her. Nursing his third beer, Degget was depressed. These were the last two detectives on the SOCU squad for him to clear. And they were already all but cleared. He had found no evidence of any major amounts of cash, unexplained spending or anything that might lead to blackmail. Arnie had been right, nobody was totally clean but there was nothing to suggest any of these guys were in so deep that they would roll over on another cop.

That only left Flem and Degget had already cleared him in his mind, regardless of how he felt about him personally.

Inspector Flem had been the one that his Captain had met with regarding Degget's deep cover operation. However, Flem was on the short list to replace Commissioner James and was tight with the Mayor. He had to have IA crawling all over him to vet him for this position. No way somebody gets that high and hasn't been cleared right back to when they were still getting their ass wiped.

Suddenly Degget's attention was brought back to the two detectives.

"Flem was totally pissed and was making noises like he would fire Beverly for getting the assignments all screwed up," one of the detectives was saying. "We missed a couple surveillance opportunities. Flem made it sound like it was a big deal."

Degget stopped listening as he suddenly realized his mistake.

Beverly was Flem's assistant, a civilian who Degget had all but ignored. A position that close to Flem would offer some really useful information and the opportunity for a savvy person with good computer skills to find out even more. He had been so focused on the possibilities of a bad cop, he forgot that there were increasing numbers of civilians working on the Kesle force.

Feeling better at the prospect that it wasn't another cop that had turned on him, Degget downed his beer. He quickly left to get some more information on Flem's assistant.

Chapter 66

"Go Rams!"

Although Mann barely heard the shout, the ensuing commotion caught his attention and he looked through the door into the outer office. A janitor was backed up against the wall just outside the picture room. Blaak, imposing as always, was talking to the man. Suddenly, Blaak was pushing past the janitor and shouting.

"LT, come here. We got something!"

Mann hurried across the warehouse. The janitor was looking confused and frightened at all the activity. He immediately started to apologize to Mann.

"I sorry, Lieutenant," the janitor said in heavily accented English. "I new. They send me from Division. Regular guy sick. I not know I not supposed to go into room. Door open so I clean. I no mean harm."

"Gregg, he recognizes the sign," Blaak said, ignoring the apologies of the janitor.

Mann wheeled on the janitor who cringed farther. Mann smiled reassuringly and the man relaxed. "You know what that is?"

The janitor looked at Mann and Blaak as though they were crazy. Other detectives had come up behind him. Nervously, he nodded.

"What is it? You said something about the Rams. The football team, LA?"

"No. What is LA? No this High School. My son. He go Freemont. They called Rams. That on shirts. Circle with curve. Horns. Rams."

"Where's Freemont?"

"No there no more. Big fire ten years. Two girls. No study and start fire. No rebuild. No more Rams. Too bad. Good football."

Mann looked at his watch but it was too late to get in touch with the School Board at the offices. He sat the janitor down at the nearest desk. "Somebody get this man a cup of coffee and a sandwich. Then, get working on Freemont."

Mann started back to his office. "Blaak, get the team assembled. Then, get me someone on the School Board. Somebody that has been on for a while. Ten years would be good. Send a wake-up call and a car. I don't care what it takes. Call the flipping Mayor if you have to. Just get a trustee down here."

Feeling the pall lift, he walked back into his office as his cell phone rang.

* * * * *

"I've heard from another source."

Distracted, Mann took a second to recognize the voice. "About?" he asked.

"Uh-huh. He confirms. It's solid, Mann. Real solid."

"Where are you?" Mann asked.

"At a bar," Dani replied. "It's uptown along Banker's Boulevard. *Short Sell.*"

"Isn't that a clever name," Mann said. "You still working on that piece?"

"Should come together for next week or so. I'll tell you about it tomorrow night?"

Mann pretended to think about it for a while. "I guess so."

"What are you doing tonight?"

Mann looked at his watch. It would be at least an hour before anyone arrived from the school board. There was time to take care of a little side business.

"I think I'll find Degget and have some wings."

"How coincidental."

"OK. I'll see you tomorrow. I may be late," he added, nonchalantly.

"I may not be there to notice," she shot back.

Mann put the phone down and wandered into the main office. Even at eleven o'clock at night, all the desks were filled. Degget wasn't there so he wandered over to The List. Everyone on the Task Force, like everyone on the force, had to leave a contact number for after hours. The List, since they often contained numbers other than a spouse's, was sacrosanct.

Mann dialed Degget's number. When he got voice mail, he left a message. By the time he had grabbed a can of Pepsi and wandered back into his office, his desk phone was ringing.

"Mann."

"Lou, you called?" Degget sounded relaxed but his voice was pitched low.

"Ya, would you like to get some wings?"

"Uh, I'm sort of in the middle of something here."

"Sure, I understand," Mann said. "I just got some information about an old case you were interested in."

Degget played it calm but understood Mann's message. "Well, it's not like I'm doing anything important. Just let me finish up here and I'll meet you. How's fifteen, twenty minutes?"

"Know Harley's?"

"Sure. I'm not far. See you then."

* * * * *

Harley's was a cliché cop bar in Southfield Division. It was all dark wood, a long bar, private booths along two walls and tables in the center. No cops were in uniform but two minutes in the place and you could tell you were surrounded with cops. Girlfriends were not encouraged and spouses were virtually outlawed. Still a sexist, closed lot, most of the brotherhood still felt uncomfortable with female members of the force. Most of the women knew they weren't exactly welcome but found a way to put up with the bullshit and give as good as they got. It was a work in progress.

Degget arrived as Mann was talking with some Southfield detectives who weren't on the task force. They walked to a back table that cleared when word passed that Mann was in the bar. At the table, they had barely sat down when Linda bounced to their table, braless breasts prominent under a white T shirt. "Hi, Lou. What'll it be?"

"Give us a pile and a pitcher."

She nodded and walked away. They watched her ample ass, barely contained in a pair of shorts. "I don't know if we'll get one glass or two. I'm not sure she even noticed me," Degget complained.

"When you grow up and get to be a lieutenant, you'll get noticed."

Mann brought Degget up to speed on the latest break in the Slasher case while they waited for the food. Linda was back in a couple minutes with a pitcher and a large plate of wings. Degget pointed at the pitcher. "What kind of beer is that?"

Linda laughed. "The Pepsi kind."

"Shit," Degget said, the disgust clear in his voice. "Can I get a Bud Light?"

As Linda left, Mann told Degget about Dani's snitch. "She says it's solid. Whoever is working this for Angelino is high up."

"Doesn't track with what I'm working on," Degget replied.

"Which is?"

"It is early yet. Give me a bit more time. I'm feeling stupid enough as it is that I missed it."

"SOCU?"

"Gotta be SOCU. I was burned two days after the meeting. No way that's a coincidence. Coincidences just don't happen. Not after two years. It had to be someone in SOCU. I've narrowed it down and I think I have my guy."

"So you think we are looking for two guys?"

"It figures. Angelino probably has ten guys. But I'll make you a deal. You can have in on my guy if I get in on your guy."

"To be honest, I was hoping my guy was your guy. Davis has been looking at it and has come up with nothing. You were our best lead."

"Sorry. Tell you what. After I finish taking care of my problem, I'll be more than happy to solve yours for you," Degget offered. "I'm sure a younger mind would help you *seasoned* detectives."

Chapter 67

Hill worried the pick back and forth in the lock. His practiced fingers sensed the proper alignment and twisted the fine pieces of metal. The lock opened and he turned the door knob. Picking up the briefcase, he eased the door open. One minute and twenty two seconds after he started working on the three locks, he was standing in the front hall of the apartment.

A quick search of the apartment turned up an extra set of keys and about three hundred dollars. He took the keys but left the money. He went into the kitchen through the swinging door and saw what he needed. Setting the briefcase down, he began pulling several pieces of equipment out. He laid them on the floor and crouched behind the door.

Using a special epoxy, he attached a piece of flint to the bottom of the swinging door. Then, he carefully eased the door open until it was about half way – what he calculated as the point of maximum thrust. He laid a piece of metal on the floor so it was in line with the flint. He secured this to the floor. He stood up and nodded with satisfaction.

After waiting for the epoxy to dry, he tried the door. Pulling it open, the flint struck the metal. The piece of metal broke away from the floor but not before giving a large spark. Satisfied, he re-glued the piece of metal to the same spot on the floor and left the kitchen.

He sat down on the couch in the living room and opened his briefcase again. He removed a thermos of coffee.

Thank God for Angelino's pipeline into the police. If not for that information, he would not have been able to clear up this loose end so easily. Between Angelino's rat and his own network, finding his man had been a simple task. Hard to believe the lowlife was the Slasher but if the police thought so, who was he to argue?

He felt his phone vibrate in his chest pocket and then go still.

Taking the phone out, he glanced at the text message.

10, was all it said. He had ten minutes until he arrived.

Hill returned to the kitchen and went to the stove. He dowsed the pilot light and turned on the elements. He could instantly smell the gas. He eased out the kitchen door, making sure the flint did not make contact.

Picking up his briefcase, he casually left the apartment. Using the extra set of keys, he relocked the door. He left the apartment building but lingered in the neighborhood. Finally, his prey turned up. He didn't look all that strange. Sure didn't look like a crazy killer.

But Hill didn't look like a hit man either.

❉ ❉ ❉ ❉ ❉

Drabick came in the apartment and set the pile of mail down on the sideboard. He took off his jacket and tossed it over a chair.

The pile of mail was large but most of it was junk and bills. A quick look through showed him only two interesting pieces. He placed them at the top of the stack and went for a beer.

He could smell the gas before he even got to the kitchen.

Instinctively, he hurried into the kitchen, shoving the door open hard.

❉ ❉ ❉ ❉ ❉

"They said to wait for SWAT," the patrolman behind the wheel cautioned after they saw Drabick walk into his apartment building. "They don't want to lose this guy. Think one of us should check the back?"

His partner never answered. The explosion from the second story window cut off his words. They both instinctively ducked down as bits of building showered down on the car.

Seeing which apartment had exploded, the driver responded first and reached up for the radio mike. "Omega watch three to Omega central.

Omega watch three to Omega central."

"Omega central, go ahead."

"We have an explosion at fifteen thirty Water Street. Request fire and ambulance. Plain clothes detectives on scene."

"Roger."

"Central? Get me a secure to Lieutenant Mann, immediately."

While he waited for the patch, his partner got out of the car. He leaned back in through the open door. "Mann's gonna shit."

"Maybe the tax payers just saved a whole lot of money on a trial."

"As long as Drabick was the Slasher."

Chapter 68

Leonard Beverly.

Degget began to think of himself as a closet sexist. He hadn't really expected Flem's assistant to be a man. But here he was following a man in his late twenties out of SOCU headquarters.

Unfortunately, because Beverly did have a good alarm system in his home, getting any information that way was out. But although Degget's own alarm system was sounding loud and clear, he just didn't know if he could trust his intuition anymore.

Two years spent with nothing but bad guys made you very suspicious of everyone's motive. It hadn't been so much as if a guy was guilty; it was *what* he was guilty of. Besides, he wanted someone to be bent. He needed to find the person that had handed him to Angelino. That person needed to pay and so Degget was suspecting guilt where it might not exist. Still, Beverly just seemed wrong.

First, there was the car, a Lexus IS 250. Great car, not an SC 450, but still way too rich for Beverly's position. Degget had run the plates and couldn't find anything against it. DMV revealed that it wasn't a lease so how did Beverly afford it on his wage? Especially along with the rather nice condo that he also owned – apparently free and clear from what Degget could find out. There was too much money flowing unless he had won a lottery or inherited a lot of money.

And then there was the fact that Beverly didn't like to be followed.

Three nights running, Beverly had lost Degget by parking his car and getting lost either in pedestrian traffic, once in a mall or by taking a passing cab. The first two times, Degget blamed himself because he just hadn't expected the moves. The third time was just bad luck that he couldn't get a cab to follow Beverly. Getting back to his car in time was impossible so Degget had given up and again waited for Beverly to show up at his car. The first two nights, Beverly returned to his car sometime well past midnight. The third night, he hadn't come back to pick up his car until eight the next morning.

Degget would have sworn he hadn't been made. Beverly just seemed to want to disappear. The real question was why and what was he doing that required such behavior. Although determined to find out what that reason was, Degget was finding his additional investigations difficult. With things really heating up on the Slasher case, Degget's coverage of Beverly was spotty at best. Nevertheless, he was sure that he had his mole.

Chapter 69

"Yes, sir. Can I help you? Excuse me, I didn't mean to startle you."

"No problem," Preston said, hoping he didn't look guilty. "I'm looking for a bathing suit."

"Of course. Let's see what we can find."

The saleslady turned to the rack of swimsuits and started to shuffle through them. "Was there a particular suit you had in mind? A style or a color?"

He shrugged and smiled. "To be honest, I'm not really sure. I've never bought anything like this before. I, well, you know how it is."

Della smiled in return. She had seen many men come in wanting to buy a gift but not really knowing the first thing about what they were buying. Still, at least they would come in and make the attempt. Her own husband wouldn't even come in the store to pick her up.

"No need to be embarrassed, sir. I'm sure that we can find something she will like."

"Thank you, you're very kind."

He smiled again and she smiled back. Such a courteous man, she thought to herself. Nervous, but that was understandable. "What size is she? A larger girl?"

"She takes a size six dress."

She averted her eyes and blushed.

"Yes, of course," she said, angry at herself for assuming he would be with a large woman. "Sounds like you know her size quite well. That helps. The suits aren't returnable, you see, for sanitary reasons."

"Certainly. The size is no problem," he chuckled. "I've been snooping."

She nodded knowingly and he relaxed. He'd had to guess at the size but that wasn't important. Not like she was going to wear it forever – just the rest of her life.

"One piece or bikini?"

"A one piece. Something sexy but not too revealing. Tastefully enticing. Sporty."

Del nodded. "I have just the suit. Down the rack this way."

Del showed him several suits before he decided on one. She was impressed with the care he took in choosing. As she packaged the suit and took his cash, she made small talk. "Is it a birthday present?"

"No, just because she is who she is."

"Isn't that sweet."

* * * * *

Preston's legs ached as he crouched in the bushes. According to the luminous dial on his watch, he had about fifteen minutes before she got home. She was prompt; he had to give her that.

As an after thought, he used his knife to cut the labels out of the suit. No sense having them trace it too easily.

The labels went into his pocket and he edged closer to the driveway. Her parent's car would block her approach. He would appear behind her like a wraith.

Then, he would strike. Like the wrath of God. A wrathful wraith – he liked that.

He checked his watch again. He was getting giddy. He was excited – mentally and physically. And, who wouldn't be? He could still picture little Miss Wendy Hoellstern in her swimsuit. Not a bikini like all the other girls. Wendy wore a one piece, a racing suit. It was tight, form fitting. Perfect for slicing through the water. It covered a lot of her body, not like the bikinis. It was sexier because it did cover so much and still revealed so much.

Once she was in the water, the suit clung to her. It outlined her every curve, from her ripe breasts to her pouty little twat. Wendy knew that. She took advantage of that.

Her body was so lean and muscular. She flaunted her tight, tanned body in those swimsuits and little summer things she loved to wear. Her body was always there – hidden but on display.

Offered to all – except him. For him, there was only ridicule.

He couldn't swim. He tried to learn but every time he got in the water, he'd go under and start to panic. He'd be dragged to the side – sputtering and gasping. She would just laugh and do an easy dive into the water.

She told him that she'd have him when he learned to swim or Hell froze over so he didn't have to learn. He still couldn't swim but that didn't matter anymore. Tonight, she would see what she had been missing.

Then, she could do a dead man's float all the way to Hell.

※　※　※　※　※

He listened to her walk up the driveway, just as he had listened to her on the previous nights. She was full of confidence and so sure of herself. She didn't hesitate, she didn't pause.

He sprang and wrapped his arm around her, covering her mouth. "I've got a knife."

He jabbed the end of the knife through her top, just nicking her side to make the point. She didn't struggle.

"I'll kill you if you scream. Throw your bag in the bushes."

He watched it land. It slid straight down and disappeared into the darkness. It might be seen in the daylight but that would be too late.

He had the tape ready. It hung from his jacket like a party steamer. And what a party it was going to be. One piece went on her mouth. He grabbed her hair and pulled her head back. She let out a muffled cry. "No noise. Put your hands together in front of you."

The next piece of tape went around and around her wrists. He slipped the rope around her neck and pulled it snug. "Go ahead. Along the garage. Make a noise and I'll kill you."

He led his captive to the back fence. His heart was beating as they covered the open ground. He forced her over the waist high, chain link fence. He had to half lift her and enjoyed the feel of her tight ass in his hands. She fell in a heap on the other side.

The rope caught on the fence and he could hear her choking. He took his time struggling over and untangling the rope.

They crouched on the ground for a moment while she tried to breathe through her nose. She had started to cry so it was hard for her. Poor baby.

When she was breathing again, they continued along the yard and cut across the back of the neighbor's house. He opened the gate and went through.

The night before, WD 40 had taken care of the unholy squeak that the lazy owner hadn't bothered with.

At the next neighbor's house, he pushed open the garage door that he had popped earlier with a crow bar. He shoved her through the door and she sprawled out on the garage floor.

Chapter 70

Degget smiled as he watched Beverly walk into Club 9.

That was one mystery solved. He was beginning to understand why Beverly took such pains to get lost in the crowd before he headed here.

Degget walked through the door into the dark interior. He could hear the singer even before he paid the cover and walked past the bouncers. Degget gave the bouncers a once over and approved of the professional stance. They were relaxed, non-threatening and smiling but with enough muscle to make anyone think twice about making trouble.

Degget took in the bar while he searched for Beverly. There were many couples on the dance floor dancing to the Melissa Etheridge song. The singer was doing a decent job of the pounding guitar beat. Degget just wasn't sure if she really was a she. The bar was pretty crowded and the two male bartenders, shirtless and in tight jeans, were kept busy. Beverly was already standing with his back pressed up against the bar with a drink in his hand. Too fast for him to have had to order, he obviously was a regular at the bar.

Moving to the other end of the bar, Degget waited to be noticed by one of the bartenders and settled in to watch Beverly. The singer switched to another Etheridge song, 'Nowhere To Go'. The men on the dance floor stepped closer, enjoying the slow beat. Degget decided that if it wasn't a she, he was definitely on his way to becoming one. He certainly captured Melissa's raw, sensual voice and Degget found himself almost swaying to the sound.

Degget ordered a Manhattan and took a small sip when it came. The bartender waited a brief moment. When Degget nodded and smiled, the bartender returned a satisfied smile and moved on to the next customer.

Good music and a good Manhattan – as undercover assignments went, this wasn't too bad. Degget settled back and watched Beverly scope out the men around him. Carefully cataloging the man's reaction to each new face and body, Degget created a profile for his next visit to the bar.

Chapter 71

"Barky, Barky, Barky!" the little boy called to the yapping dog. "Shut up, dipstick. Mom will make us come in and unpack."

The small dog ran a circle around his tail and bounded toward the young boy. It jumped up and put its paws on the boy's shoulders. He scored one lick before being pushed away. The boy didn't notice the long bloody paw prints on his shoulders. By then, he had seen what the dog was barking at.

He ran up to the side of the pool and stooped down to peer at the lump under the solar blanket. "I'll be damned," he said, mimicking his grandfather. "Hey, you can't swim in our pool. You're gettin' the water all dirty. My daddy is going to be pissed at you. Hey!"

"William, get in here and help me with your suitcase."

Five year old Billy turned to where his mother was standing in the sliding doors. Before he could get a word out, his mother was running toward him. "William! Did Barky do that to your shoulders?"

"Huh?" He wiped at the blood on his shoulders. "I guess so. But, Mom, somebody is swimming in our pool."

Billy's mother was way ahead of him. She had already seen the body floating under the blanket. She screamed for her husband and scooped Billy into her arms. That set Barky off again.

By the time Billy's father ran out back, Billy's mother was collapsed in one of the lawn chairs, sobbing. Billy was running back and forth from his mother to the pool with Barky in close pursuit.

* * * * *

Mann stepped out of the hot sun into the bit of shade under the roof. Shane Kydd joined him, her notebook open. Alf Buchanan slipped in beside her, juggling three cups.

"I hope that's something cool."

"Lemonade."

"Thank God." Mann looked into the cup at the pink lemonade and swallowed the bile rising in his throat. The liquid in the cup resembled the water of the pool, pinkish with bits of... He drank the entire cupful down and waited to see if it was going to come back up. When it didn't, he asked Alf what he had.

"The girl's name is Linda Forrest. You can just see the roof of her house over there. She lives there with her parents."

"Did they know she was missing?"

"Reported her three days ago," Shane cut in. "She was very prompt and they got concerned when she didn't show up after her night class at the University."

"What happened to the report?"

"Filed and forgotten. Missing person's reports are up almost three hundred percent since the Slasher started his little games."

"Three days?"

"Goes with what my prelim shows," the Medical Examiner said. "It's a tough one to call though with this heat and the chemicals. The owners were away and the auto chlorinator was working really well. She's in pretty bad shape."

Mann didn't need to be reminded.

"What did you get from the parents?"

"We haven't shown them the suit but they're sure it isn't hers. She only owned bikinis."

Mann looked at Shane. "I'll want a complete work-up on her timetable on the last night she was seen. And then back for two weeks. I want to know when that psycho got to her and where. Canvass the neighborhood and talk to everyone. Anyone that doesn't want to cooperate, I want to see at the warehouse."

"Her parent's already found her knapsack beside their garage. I think we can start the walk from there."

"Do you think he's a local?"

"No, but somebody had to have seen something. He was here a long time. What about the people looking after the house?"

"They didn't see anything. They did a half ass job. They just came in the front and out the front. Assuming they came in at all. They didn't even notice the jimmied door on the garage. Everything is automatic with the pool. The people have a pool of their own so they didn't use this one."

"All right," he said to Shane. "Get on the canvass. Oversee it yourself. Talk to everyone and get a list of names of anyone visiting over the past six days. Check all the usual, deliveries, power, phone, cable, the works. Track them all back to a work order. I want this neighborhood covered. He didn't find all this by accident in the dark. He has spent time here before she was taken."

"Yes, sir."

"Love that girl's voice," Buchanan said, after Shane had hurried away.

"How can you pull something like that from the water and then think about Kydd's voice?"

"What makes you think I could pull something like that from the water without thinking about Kydd's voice?"

Mann nodded. He had a point.

"At least this clears Drabick," Buchanan said.

What was left of Drabick would provide a DNA sample but he was in little crispy pieces when Linda Forrest was killed.

* * * * *

Mann looked at the detectives scattered around the room that the workmen had created only three days before. A thick wall separated the main room, with all its distracting telephones and comings and goings, from this meeting room. Comparing notes was important and so was just general bullshitting of ideas back and forth.

"Kydd, tell us about Linda Forrest."

"Nice girl. Well liked. Good grades. She had gone back to school to get her MBA after spending time in Rwanda, for God's sake. Not the usual save the world type but she did want to do something before she went into the business world and spent two years in that hell hole."

"Was she into the market at all?"

"No, not yet. She had few contacts but nothing substantial. She started in January and was barely in the program. We don't see any connection with Hart. He didn't go to the same schools. We know that much for sure. I'm looking for any connection, though."

"What about that night?"

"She had written an exam in the afternoon. She had another regular class that night. She attended that until the end. As far as anyone knows, she got on her usual bus, then subway, then bus. Her backpack was found in the bushes beside her garage."

"When?"

"Two days before the body was found. The parents tried to get the police involved. A uniform did an initial interview, filed the sheet, but that was as far as it got."

"Did the parent's search the neighborhood?"

"After they found the backpack but they didn't see the body in the pool. We play it like this. She was taken across her back yard and to the neighbor's garage. At the house she was found."

"What about a car?"

"No. We found rope fibers in the fence behind her place. Doc, you might be able to fill in more here."

"Not much. She was tied and gagged. He used tape again. He obviously does not trust his knots for anything but the noose or, more likely, the tape is easier. She was raped."

As Buchanan paused, each of the detectives pictured the scene in his own mind. Naked and alone in a dark garage with oil and gasoline stinking in her nostrils, overpowered by the stench of the sweating body of her attacker

"After the rape, he started to cut. He wasn't as neat as before. She was," Alf wiped his lips. "She was still alive when he started cutting. He just started to cut her. CSU found clear evidence in the blood smears that she was thrashing around in her own blood."

Alf sat heavily in one of the chairs. "He cut her real good but didn't take any organs. Then, he put the bathing suit on her. He cut his signature in her back and tossed her in the pool. She drowned or bled out. Then he took her larynx while she was in the pool. He just left her there for that little boy to find."

"All right. We've lost time on this one but we can make it up. Continue the canvas. Someone saw him – find that someone. Get a sketch of the suit to the media and hit the streets. Find out where it was sold. Right now, those are our best bets."

Chapter 72

Propped up on one elbow, Leonard Beverly ran his hand over Degget's chest and muscled abs. "When I saw you at the bar, I thought you were a piece of heaven. I was so right."

Degget smiled. After watching Beverly at the bar for a couple hours, Degget knew exactly what the man was looking for. A shopping trip for some different clothes, three nights of waiting for Beverly to show at the bar again and a few drinks was all it had taken to get invited back to the man's condo. Unfortunately, Degget wasn't able to get the code to the alarm. Beverly was very careful about that. But there were other ways to get information.

Relaxing under the other man's caress, Degget looked around the large bedroom. "From the looks of this place, I'm afraid I might not be in your class. What do you do for a living?"

"Don't let this place fool you," Beverly laughed. "I didn't buy this."

"Is it just a lease?"

"No," Beverly answered, a sadness creeping into his eyes. "I own it. I just didn't buy it as such. I was in a relationship for a couple years. I thought he was the one, you know. We had even been talking about marriage, the whole bit. He was a doctor. Nip and tucker. I'm sure you have seen plenty of his work but you'd never know it, if you know what I mean. We lived here."

"Did he die?"

"No, not that I don't sometimes wish it. Oh, that sounds awful doesn't it? But the bitch went back to his wife. I mean, he just says one day that he doesn't think he is really gay. Two years of some of the best sex I have ever had and he suddenly thinks he's straight? I hope his wife leaves him for one of his bimbo breast jobs. Serve him right."

"And what, he just gave you the condo?"

"Ain't guilt a wonderful thing? I got the condo and a sweet little ride – a hot red Lexus IS 250 – all free and clear. He even paid the taxes and the insurance for a year. He broke my heart but I'm getting over it," Beverly said with a smirk. "And you are just what the doctor ordered."

An hour later, a very satisfied Beverly was laying next Degget. Degget had decided that Beverly wasn't the leak. All that extra spending had been accounted for. Blackmail? Maybe but it didn't seem likely. Beverly was too easy taking Degget home. A victim of blackmail would be a little more gun shy than this. "You never said what you did for a living," Degget said.

"I work for the cops," Beverly said sleepily.

"You're a cop?"

"No, I'm the personal assistant for Inspector Flem with the SOCU. The Special Organized Crime Unit."

"Wow," Degget said, sounding very excited. He started to caress Beverly's inner thigh, who reacted despite the past hour's activities. "That must be so exciting. I've seen Flem on the news. He's like Elliot Ness. I heard he might even be the next Commissioner."

"Trust me, he's no Elliot Ness. He's a bloated egotistical jerk who has no personal skills but is a hell of a political player."

"You don't like him?"

"Not in the least but the job pays and it's pretty easy for the most. Except for the exulted one, nobody really bothers me. Actually they treat me pretty well because they know that I grease the wheels. Not to mention a few of them look pretty good, for cops anyway."

"You don't like cops?"

"They're OK to look at but pretty boring between the sheets."

Degget massaged higher on Beverly's thigh, adding pressure, eliciting a moan from Beverly.

"And you don't like Flem? The Mayor makes him sound like a one man police force."

"The Mayor is only interested in votes," Beverly said, sucking in his breath when Degget hit a tender spot. "Flem knows politics. Just look at the convictions. You'll see the pattern."

Degget started running his tongue over Beverly's chest in circles that promised to move lower on the man's body. "Patterns?"

"Who gets arrested and when," Beverly explained dreamily. "Even before SOCU, Flem played the game and brought in the big, flashy arrests. Flem always knew how to make sure his arrests got noticed."

"But hasn't he sworn to get Angelino? I saw that on the news."

"Oh sure, he talks a lot but I think he doesn't really want to arrest him. If he arrests his arch nemesis, where will he go from there? I swear he has pulled guys away from investigations just to keep the game going. The other week, he went up onside of me and down the other because he said I screwed up some assignments. I had to just sit there and take it but he was the one that messed it all up. And the one that got missed was a move against one of Angelino's operations. Maybe it's just my imagination 'cause the guy really is an obnoxious bore. Or maybe he is just saving the big bust for right before he gets named Commissioner."

Degget almost stopped his ministrations on Beverly as he thought about what the man was saying. Arrest records, patterns, of course. Excited, his mind whirling with the possibilities, he bit down hard. Beverly moaned and arched his back, his legs sliding over against Degget.

"Hmmm, you feel like you are getting excited yourself. God I might have to take the day off tomorrow if you keep this up."

Chapter 73

As he dealt with the client on the phone, Bert Haynes kept glancing back at the front page of The *Daily*. He normally ignored the Slasher. The case revolted him and he just wasn't interested. Most days, he just skimmed the articles, often not even the entire article, and continued on to the sports page.

Today was different.

Haynes stared hard at the picture of the latest victim, Linda Forrest. As he looked at the picture, he played the name over in his mind. No matter how he tried to associate the name, he couldn't recognize it. Still, there was something about the girl's face. There was a memory, tantalizingly close but elusive.

The picture in the newspaper was a studio shot. Maybe the photographer was a client? But that didn't feel right. He had never been near the University. He had often been asked to guest lecture in the computer classes but his stutter always got in the way. The classes weren't long enough for a lecture from him. So, if not the University, where?

He read the article for the tenth time. He didn't recognize the girl's address. Her father was a plumber. Being handy, he had never needed a plumber. Her mother was a housewife. Not likely he would know her. None of them were customers, he had checked.

Why did her face bother him so?

His phone rang again and he set the paper aside. While he tried to concentrate on the telephone call, his eyes kept straying to the picture.

Sports? Maybe she was an athlete? Something nagged at the back of his brain. Sports. Basketball, track, something. He followed the University sports scene but more the men's teams.

"I don't s...s...see why not," Haynes said. He wished this idiot would just get to the point and ring off. Everyday he hated the phone more and more. If only he could rid himself of his stutter, he could knock an hour a day off his phone time. "Just let me check my calendar."

Haynes spun in his chair and looked at his computer screen. Family pictures flashed across the screen saver and he saw his daughter's graduation photo. As he stared, open mouthed, at the screen, he didn't even hear the customer on the telephone. He had difficulty breathing and goose bumps broke out over his body. The phone almost slipped out of his hands when he slammed it down on the receiver – without saying another word to the puzzled customer.

"A...A...Anne, g...g...g, g...get in here!"

He looked from the screen to the newspaper and back again. The picture changed to a scene from a family vacation. He swore, barely conscious that the string of swear words didn't come out in a stutter.

When Anne entered the office, he was already bent over his computer console. Seeing his pale, sweaty face, she ran to his side. "Bert? Are you all right?"

"I...I....n...n...need..."

He stopped talking, frustrated by the stutter. He took a deep breath and tried again but the words tangled. Anne's face went from puzzled to concerned. Normally, he never stuttered around her. Finally, he picked up a pad of paper and began to write out his instructions.

Anne took the torn sheet from his hand and read it over. She looked at him again, worried and confused. "This is what you want? Customer records? You sure you're all right, Bert?"

Haynes nodded and pointed to the door. She shrugged and left the office. Stupidest thing she ever saw. Customer receipts from a couple months ago? He was acting like the end of the world.

Haynes bent over the computer again, his fingers flying over the keyboard. He loved his computer because he could type. He didn't stutter when he typed.

Except today.

Today, his hands were shaking as he tried to call up the correct pictures.

* * * * *

"I c...c...called s...s...six times but nobody ever c...c...came around to s...s...see me. I really need to talk to s...s...someone."

"If you could just have a seat, a detective will be with you as soon as possible," the uniformed cop said. Haynes recognized the look. The cop probably dealt with nut cases all day and here he stood, not even able to get a sentence out.

Resigned, Haynes sat down between two old women.

Haynes was angry, excited and frightened. A deadly combination when it came to his stutter. Today was a day for Cs and Ss. Every time he hit a hard C or an S, the stutter reared up and clobbered him.

He had tried the telephone. He had called as soon as the computer had spit out the pictures and he compared them online to back issues of the paper. Then, when he had received no reply, he called again several times for two days. Now, almost four days after he had made his discovery, he had decided to bring his story down in person.

He laid his briefcase across his knees and leaned forward. One of the women reached up and shoved him back in his chair. Unnoticed by him, the two women continued their discussion over top of him.

Both of them had the Slasher living next door to them. They both had the *proof* that was going to put him away.

Haynes looked around the large waiting room at the collection of people. He realized what a mammoth task the police had to try and cull through all the assorted weirdoes and nutcases to find the genuine tips from concerned, normal citizens. People like him.

People who stuttered every time they said a hard C or an S.

Haynes got up and wandered across the room to sit beside a man dressed in a three piece suit. All his speech teachers had drilled into him that he must not avoid conversations. If the stuttering got bad, he had to dive right in and try to overcome the difficult words. Concentrating, he addressed the businessman beside him.

"Lot's of people here. Guess everybody knows the murderer," Haynes said, choosing his words carefully.

"I'm here to turn myself in," the businessman said, smiling. He pulled his coat open to reveal a long butcher's knife. Haynes smiled back and got up to sit in one of the few isolated seats.

* * * * *

"Who's next?" the patrolman asked, stretching and working the kinks out of his neck. His "ticket" to a gold shield was to interview the assorted citizens, idiots and nutcases that came into the Task Force. At last estimate, the Task Force was receiving three hundred tips a day. Most, thank St. Michael, came in over the phone. The walk-ins were the worst. Most of them were nuts, some were just mistaken, and some might, just might, have a genuine clue that would break the case. He held out for them.

"There are two old broads who both say they live next to Slasher. The guy in the three piece suit wants to confess. The lady with the baby, she thinks it's her husband. They just got divorced and he's trying for custody of the kid. There are six who saw his car."

"Do we know what he drives?"

"Rumor is a red Chev. Least, I think it's a rumor."

"I'll check next time I'm in the room. What about the guy with the briefcase?"

"He says that the Slasher came to him to get pictures made of the victims."

"What the hell?"

"Hey, that's what the guy said. He's called us a couple times, apparently. He's real serious, that dude."

"I'll take that one. At least it is original."

"Got a stutter. Take you forever."

"Good, then I won't get the old broads. Ever notice how bad those old ones smell?"

"Suit yourself. Guy's name is Haynes."

The officer stepped around the desk. "Mr. Haynes? Could you come this way please?"

* * * * *

Blaak was lounging back in his chair listening to the rabble around him. He was finished for the day, a thirteen and a half hour day.

Letting his mind drift, he keyed on the man being interviewed by one of the uniforms at a nearby desk. He had caught a real winner this time. This witness sounded like an idiot. Blaak tried to catch his eye but the officer was focused on the stutterer. Blaak knew a feigned look of interest; this was serious.

Blaak let the rest of the din around him fade into background, a talent acquired from surveillance work, and focused on the stutterer. He was having a real time of it but Blaak soon realized that the man was coherent, even educated. Not that there weren't many educated nuts but...

The guy was talking about school pictures. Blaak listened intently, the mention of a school setting off warning flares. The guy had done something to school pictures. He was some kind of computer expert and could age photographs. He used a computer, using the same process they did for the missing kid photos.

Blaak stood up so quickly, he knocked his chair over.

Blaak knocked lightly on the door frame. "L-T?"

Mann looked up, setting his pen down and rubbed his eyes. "Ya, Blaak? What you got?"

"Would you be pissed if I brought you one from left field, sir? Like we are talking maybe way down by the third base foul line."

Mann caught the excitement in Blaak's voice. The big man was holding something back, trying to keep the edge out of his voice. Mann let Blaak play it the way he wanted. "You got something?"

"I think I do. Actually, one of the uniforms was kinda there first. I just jumped at it. An interview from a walk-in. Guy's name is Haynes, sir." Blaak lowered his voice. "This Haynes, he stutters like a worn out carb. Sounds like he's a bit shy of a load, know what I mean? He's not though. Just sounds like it. Guy's some computer genius. Anyhow, just thought I'd warn you, sir."

Mann nodded and Blaak went to fetch Haynes. A close friend of Mann's in school had been a stutterer. One of the best friends he had ever had until a move separated them. Once you got past the shyness, he could usually overcome the stutter and he bet this Haynes was the same. All he'd need would be some confidence.

Mann straightened his desk while the three men made their way to his office. He drank the last, warm, flat mouthful of his Pepsi and wished he had another. When they arrived in the office, he stood to shake hands.

"Lieutenant Mann, sir, this is Mr. Haynes," Blaak said.

"Mr. Haynes, thank you for coming in."

"Please, c...c...call me Bert, Lieutenant."

"And, you can drop the lieutenant. Name's Gregg. I won't waste your time because I think we've already given you the run around."

"I did have s...s...some trouble getting anyone to listen. I think what I have is important." Mann noticed Haynes' timidity. He was not snide or condescending. Mann could see that Haynes believed in the information he possessed. He just wasn't so sure he could convince others.

"From what my detectives tell me, it is," Mann said. "Of all the tips we get, I have had exactly one person brought in to see me this week. That's one person counting you."

It took a moment for Haynes to see Mann's point. Then, he smiled and his increased confidence was evident in that smile.

"I hate to take up more of your time but could you go over it once more for me. I am very interested in what you have. I understand you work with computers."

"Yes," Haynes said, "Computer art and graphics mostly. Retouching photographs, lots of model work, turning the incredibly beautiful into perfection. I also put something into a photo or take it out. I do movie work as well, getting into some video but I prefer stills. I have also done some reconstructive work. Putting a face on a skull to help identify a body. But some of our proudest work is with missing children. You might have seen some of the work we have done. The computer ages a picture so that a child who has been missing for a number of years can be more readily recognized. The computer does a lot of the work but there is an art to tweaking the filters."

Blaak looked at the patrolman who returned the puzzled glance. The stutter was gone and only reappeared occasionally as Haynes spoke to Mann.

"This one picture stuck in my mind because it was of a girl on the swim team, not a grad picture. To be honest, the girl was quite good looking. The picture he gave me was labeled 'Pool Princess'."

They were in the evidence room. Mann and the two detectives had been joined by any of the other ranking members of the Task force that were available. At first, Haynes had slipped back into his stutter as the room filled. Eventually, he calmed himself by speaking directly to Mann and ignoring the others.

"And those are the other pictures?"

"Yes, sir. I pulled them off the computer and printed copies. I can print more copies."

Haynes handed them over to Mann. Mann took them and mixed them up. He began looking through the stack of computer generated pictures. To him, they looked like a cross between grainy black and white photographs and drawings. He passed by the first two and stopped at the third.

Over the course of the investigation, Mann had spent hours looking at the various photographs of the victims. He had looked for some common thread, something that had triggered the killer into picking them. He knew their faces as well as he knew Dani's. Maybe better. He had no difficulty recognizing Lionel Hart. The nose was bigger, the chin slightly longer, but the likeness was there. No denying it. Not brothers but maybe cousins. This bit was wrong or that, but they were close enough.

Mann grabbed a magnet and used it to put the computer picture under Hart's.

The rest of the detectives crowded behind Mann to look at the resemblance. Murmurs rose as Mann pinned up the next photograph under Andrea Seymour's picture. He worked through the stack of pictures until he had a computer picture hanging under each of the photographs of the victims, except Gabel.

"Son of a bitch. We got him!"

✳ ✳ ✳ ✳ ✳

"Sorry Gregg, the building isn't there. Nothing by that number on the block."

Mann let his shoulders sag. Haynes had already told him as much but they had to check it out themselves.

"So, he used a false name and address. It was too easy."

"And, he paid cash," Haynes added. "I can tell you what he looked like."

"That is going to have to do, for now. You realize that you may have to testify?"

"I'd do it gladly. That guy used me. I get s...s...sick just thinking about him c...c...coming back to my shop. I mean I could have ended up like that poor newspaper reporter."

"All right. I want to take you down to our artist and get a sketch done." Mann lowered his voice. "I'd like you to keep this under your hat, right now. We don't want to spook the killer. I also don't want to put you in danger."

"Don't worry, you aren't going to s...s...see me on the news. S...s...should I be worried? I mean, is he going to c...c...come after me or my wife?"

"I doubt that very much," Mann said, not very convincingly. "Just in case, I'm going to assign you some protection. It will also give us the chance to stake out your business in case he comes back for more pictures."

"Thank you. Now, about the pictures? Naturally, I know you want them but would it be possible to get a receipt and a statement that they will remain my exclusive property with all rights?"

Mann stared at Haynes. He knew exactly what was going through the man's mind. The dollar signs floated to the floor every time the man blinked. Normally, Mann would be furious. But with their first break in weeks coming from the man, how upset could he get?

Chapter 74

Preston stood across the street from the bar. In some ways, it was foolish to return but he knew he would find a target here. Looking carefully both ways, he darted across the street and went into the entrance of the *Short Sell.*

He instantly remembered Kraemer and felt himself get hard. He could hear sound of the baseball bat on the bare skin and the crack and crunch of bone. The moaning sobs as he slid the flute up his ass. The tearing sound as he hammered it deep and blood gushed out the metal tube.

He stopped and took a deep breath. He had to calm down. He was rock hard and it wouldn't be the first time he had spontaneously orgasmed just thinking about the killings.

God, he needed another.

If only he knew then what he knew now.

Wendy had been so much fun. She had struggled and fought but, eventually, she had given in and realized what she had been missing all these years. She had tried to hide it but he knew she had several orgasms.

There was still the other one's wife. She and her new born child were waiting for him. He would not disappoint them.

As though waking from a dream, he suddenly looked around, not really sure where he was. He guiltily scanned the crowd to see if anyone had noticed him.

And that was when he saw the mop of red hair bob across the room.

Ellen Hutchison. Little, sweet, Ellen Hutchinson. Lousy, slutty, Ellen Hutchinson.

He remembered Ellen Hutchinson. He remembered her well. How could he forget that little stuck up snob?

He smiled a genuine smile at the bartender and ordered a draft. He had been right all along. Kraemer had not been one-time luck.

Close to the financial district with its leeches and cowards, the bar was perfect.

And, Ellen Hutchison was perfect.

God, how he had loved her.

Every boy wanted her but he truly loved her. Not just for her red hair and cute little figure. Not just because she lived in a big house. Not because her father was important. Not because she had a pool with a curvy slide that water ran down.

He loved her because of what she was – not who she was.

At least, what he thought she was.

He had been wrong.

Ellen was no different than all the rest and maybe even worse than the rest.

In the same class since kindergarten, he had seen her every day at school for years. Every summer, he would ride his bike past her house a hundred times, hoping to glimpse her behind the high, cedar hedge that surrounded the back yard of their big white mansion. That is what it looked like to him, a mansion with its two car garage and intercom system at the front door. Each fall, he would pray he would be in her class again. Hope that this would be the year he was invited to her house, invited to that all important pool party.

He had been to her mailbox so many times in the dark of night.

For years, he had been her secret admirer. He had written her letter upon letter, always typing them on his old manual typewriter. He had to make sure she was in love with him before he revealed himself. He kept the stream of letters pouring into her mailbox. Many times, he would include a poem. Some, he would copy out of books, some he wrote himself. His words were parts of him, sent to win her. He gave her a piece of his soul in every letter.

Finally, he sent her a box of Turtles on Valentine's Day. Not one of the little boxes. This box had cost him a week's pay from his paper route. This was to be the final step.

The next day, he was sure he would hear how she felt. Sure enough, she brought the box of chocolates to school with her. He was so proud. Then, she started passing them out. She gave away his present.

She didn't like Turtles, she said. She laughed at the note that had accompanied the candies. She told everyone that he must want to fatten her up so she was the same size as him. Only a fat cow could ever love a tub like him. All her friends laughed with her.

That was when he realized that she knew who he was. She had known all along and was laughing at him. They were all laughing at him.

But, he would have the final laugh. He would deliver the punch line and it would be a belly buster.

She was still here. She belonged with this crowd.

The stench of abused power surrounded them like flies on dog crap on a hot summer day. They insulated themselves with material things. They could not face the real world and expose their lack of morality. They wore their Armani suits like armor, protecting themselves from truth. Their daily trade was lies. The truth lost in a web of deceit and money.

They were pretenders. Killer instinct? They maimed, wounded and killed with a fountain pen. They destroyed lives but from a safe distance. They did not have his strength, his resolve, his drive. They might kill second hand but, cowards that they are, they could not face the truth of their actions. They could not accept the blood that is on their hands. Their money washed their hands clean every time.

He welcomed the blood and was proud of the sticky red stuff. Would wear it proudly, his clothes drenched in the copper smelling liquid of life and death.

He was the one with the killer instinct.

God help him but he hated them all. He wanted to wipe them all from the face of the earth and start all over.

When Ellen left, he waited for a moment before getting up to follow her home.

By the time he made it to the sidewalk, she was gone. Tail lights from a cab flared up the street as it made a right.

He had missed her. Not that it mattered. Not tonight.

Her time would come soon enough and the little redhead would learn of her foolishness.

Chapter 75

Mann was flipping through the pictures, looking at the faces, trying to memorize them. More and more, the faces had come to resemble the victims. Others had spent time looking through the rest of the pictures supplied by Haynes. They had played a game of seeing if the pictures resembled anyone they knew.

For several days, they had been tracking down leads at the school. So far, there was nothing. With no names to go with the pictures, they were still trying to identify the year they came from. The fire had destroyed all the year books that had been stored at the school. They were working on getting copies from other sources but it was slow going. They couldn't go public for fear of driving the killer underground.

Until they hit on a year, narrowing down a suspect from the school register was going to be next to impossible. All the same, the complete record of enrollment was being fed into the computer. It would pull names out of the list and compare them to the lists of suspects, run down criminal records, etc.

All that took time and there was no guarantee that the killer went to that school during those years. Haynes had not seen the book and had no idea what school the pictures came from. For all they knew, the killer could have picked up the year book at a garage sale.

But, Mann's gut told him they had the killer. He was right in their sights, just waiting to be picked up.

Mann thought about how the killer would pick his victims rather than why.

If he wanted to find these people, how would he go about it? These victims came off the streets. He chose these victims. Found them somehow. The hospital, Leantown, the University. No connections.

Mann laid the pictures out in front of him in their proper order. Then, he tried to think like a psychopath.

An hour later, Mann still had the pictures laid out in front of him.

He decided that if he was the killer, he would want to have the pictures with him at all times. There were too many pictures to hope to be able to remember what they all looked like. No matter how many times he looked at them, he would want it there instantly when he noticed a potential victim.

Mann could envision the killer carrying the pictures around like a family album and standing on street corners, sitting in bars, waiting and watching. Some progress. All they had to do was watch for someone consulting a book of pictures.

No problem.

He left the warehouse with the file folder of pictures under his arm. Picking a busy corner, he stood against the building. As people went by, he tried to see if he recognized any of the pictures. Constantly referring to them, he missed about seventy five percent of the people that went by.

He was jostled by a large man with a pizza box. The pictures slid out of the file folder and scattered on the sidewalk. Mann quickly stooped to gather them up before the hot wind took them. Cursing, he straightened and found a recessed doorway to stand in.

Before he was in the doorway for two minutes, someone bustled out and the pictures were creased.

The pictures were too large, too bulky. They would also have to be bound together. Bound in a way that would allow them to be flipped through easily but secure enough to prevent them from being dropped and scattered. A loose leaf binder would be ideal but still too bulky. The killer would stand out if he was constantly checking faces against a large binder. Someone would remember him and Mann knew this killer wanted to remain invisible.

Mann patted his pocket where his own notebook always rested. Yes, something that fit nicely in a suit pocket and where the pages could be removed.

The killer could use something like that. He could slip it out of his pocket and glance at the pictures. Except when it was being used, the pictures would be hidden from view. No large binder to explain to co workers or friends. The pictures could remain the killer's own secret.

At that moment, looking down at the file folder, it hit him and he hurried back to the warehouse.

* * * * *

"So, his pictures are the same size as the ones you provided us?"

"Yes, sir."

Haynes voice came through with a hollow echo over the speaker phone. The detectives sitting around the conference table all had puzzled looks on their faces. Mann had gathered them together while waiting for a call back from Haynes.

"And you didn't provide him with smaller versions?"

"We could have but we didn't."

"Thanks very much, Mr. Haynes. I'll be in touch if anything comes up." Mann pressed the disconnect button and sat back in his chair, a satisfied smile on his face.

"What gives?" asked Kydd, recognizing the look.

"I went out onto the street with the pictures. I was trying to work out how the killer operated. What I ended up with was a bunch of dropped and bent photographs. The things are too bulky to handle."

"You were hoping the killer had got smaller versions from Haynes?"

"No," interrupted Greer. "You were hoping he *didn't* get them from Haynes."

"Move to the head of the class."

"I don't get it."

"Where would you go to get a smaller version of these?" Mann asked, drumming his finger on the stack of pictures.

Ashdown snapped his finger. "I had a map of this reception hall for my parent's fortieth anniversary party. It was too big to fit in the invitations so we got it reduced. We used a printer to do it. Made them smaller and cut them for us and everything."

The implications began to sink in. Several swear words circled the table and everyone pulled their chairs closer to the table. The collective exhaustion was thrown off by the excitement of the new clue.

"I want every available man looking for printers, photocopy places, Kinko's, hotel business centers, the works. I'll get Buma compiling a list.

For now, we'll concentrate on an area around the first killings. I still think we have a geographic link for the first killings. If that doesn't work, we'll spread out farther. Get on it."

The detectives filed out and Mann remained seated. He was glad that none of them had voiced the most obvious problem with the theory. What if the killer worked in an office with the proper equipment?

Chapter 76

Degget had painstakingly compiled all of Flem's arrests for his career. The pattern was beginning to emerge and Degget couldn't believe what he was seeing. Bev was right. It was all in the numbers.

Assuming that the estimates were right and Angelino ran over sixty percent of the organized crime in the city, the arrests should follow the same basic statistics. Angelino ran a good operation but criminals are stupid, no getting around that. And stupid people get arrested. But Angelino's guys weren't getting arrested enough.

Sure, there were some big busts, some major drugs off the streets but nothing that really amounted to heavy damage.

Degget walked along the wall looking at the different organizational charts he had taped up of the various criminal families in Kesle over the past fifteen years. They detailed the arrests, deaths and murders of all the players. Most of the other families had arrests and plenty of deaths in the upper echelon. Since Angelino took over, his organization hadn't seen any of these types of reorganizations. Thorman was the most recent death and he was just a low level number cruncher. Something wasn't adding up.

Just maybe, he and Mann were looking for the same rat.

Degget started to sift through the data again when his computer signaled a new message.

Degget read the message. He read it a second time and picked up his cell phone, his investigation into Flem instantly forgotten. He was grabbing his badge and gun as he listened to the phone ring at the other end. He walked out the door when it was finally answered.

"Kydd, we got a hit. Ya, I'll meet you in twenty."

Chapter 77

"He was very impatient. That is what I remember most about him."

"You do the work in an hour, don't you?" Mann asked. Tetrault had brought in the owner of Monteith Printing when she remembered a job that matched the description.

"Normally," Sylvia Monteith replied. "The machine was down though and the service man took his sweet time getting there. Anyway, the guy kept calling and asking if the pictures were ready."

"And you think you can describe him?"

"I'll try," she said, hesitating. "It was a while ago. I do remember he was kinda tubby."

"That's all we can ask." Mann got up to leave as the sketch artist came in. "I'll leave you to it, then."

"Uh, Lieutenant?"

"Yes?"

"This guy, I mean, like, do you really think he's the Southside Slasher?"

"He is definitely one of our suspects, ma'am."

"The guy I saw didn't look like a crazy," she said as Mann left. "He didn't look like anything."

Mann wandered over to where the detectives were sorting through the records. "How's it going?"

Each of the detectives and uniformed officers looked up and mumbled something that Mann knew would be better left unheard. He turned to Greer who was slowly working through his pile. "What's the problem?"

"The problem is the lady's filing system. It doesn't exist," Greer answered. "She just lumps everything together. So far, we haven't come up with any easy way to sort through them. And for a place with so many copiers, she has never touched a computer for her accounting. Everything is hand written by a dyslexic chicken."

"How have you separated the piles?"

"I just divided them up," Tetrault said. Mann had forgotten that Tetrault had brought the information in and was therefore leading the investigation. "The lady does some kind of business. She must be doing two hundred jobs a day. We're working backwards."

"Not from the present?"

"No, sir. I didn't see the sense in that." Mann sensed the pride in Tetrault's voice at having been one step up on Mann. "I figured to cut the work down as much as possible. I started the search at the date of the Yeck kill."

Greer turned to Tetrault with the same look of disbelief that Mann wore. "From the Yeck kill?"

"Yes, sir," Tetrault said, becoming worried.

"Bloody hell! You mean we've wasted the last three hours?" Greer's big voice boomed.

"Tetrault," Mann said, barely keeping his anger in check, "get in my office. Greer, clear this out of the way and start at the right date. Work forward from there."

"Sure, Lou."

Tetrault was already standing in front of his desk when Mann slammed the door to his office. He took a deep breath to calm himself and leaned against the front of the desk.

"Do you read the updates?"

"Yes, sir."

"What makes the Yeck killing different from the rest?"

"Overall? The lack of planning."

"Very good. And, when did the killer approach Haynes for the pictures?"

"After the Yeck killing," Tetrault said slowly.

"Logically speaking, how would the killer get reductions made of pictures he does not have?"

"Sorry, Lou. I wasn't thinking."

"Some habits are hard to break. Go and get some sandwiches. When you get back, get real busy. I don't want to see you much for the rest of the afternoon."

"Yes, sir."

* * * * *

Greer's face said it all.

"OK, this is not good news, right?" Mann said to Greer.

"Nope. We did find the receipt. Bloody bookkeeping is a mess but we found a receipt that matches what Mr. Haynes said he gave him," Greer said, holding up a sheet of paper and reading off it. "Twenty-three reductions of 8x10 photos. Cash and the same address as what he gave Haynes."

"Damn it," Mann swore. "I really had hopes for this one."

Mann sat quietly for a moment and finally pushed away from his desk.

"I need a Pepsi and then I want everyone in the evidence room."

Mann walked to the fridge and grabbed a Pepsi, realized it was still warm and dug around until he found a cold one. He popped the top and stood drinking it while he thought about his next step. He watched Deputy Inspector Livermore shaking hands with a tall, lanky man in a three piece suit.

As the man left the warehouse, Livermore came over to Mann. "That was Dr. Arthur Baskin. He's in private practice but consults with the Donway Institute of Abnormal Psychology."

Baskin has stopped at the outer doorway and was looking back into the warehouse. Mann sized up the doctor. Clean shaven with short, wavy hair, Mann didn't think he looked like a shrink specializing in abnormal psychology. Mann always thought that those doctors should look slightly scattered, rumpled. More disturbed and confused by what they saw and heard from their patients. "What's he after?"

"He just got back from an extended tour of Europe. Lecturing about our American serial killers. He offered any help he could give."

"Keep his number," Mann said. "We might just need him."

Taking another drink, he realized the can was already empty. He tossed it in the recycle bin and took another can from the fridge as he briefed Livermore on the latest failure.

* * * * *

Mann walked to the front of the room and picked up a marker on the way. He stood in front of the large board at the front and blinked from the bright light of the projector. He looked at the detectives in front of him, noting that a few of the faces he expected to see weren't there. Degget, Kydd and Blaak were all missing but he saw the same look of disappointment on the rest of the faces. Greer's discovery of the bogus address had circulated around the room and everyone knew they were back to square one.

Well, not exactly square one, Mann thought.

Mann took the cap off the pen and turned toward the board.

"Lieutenant!" yelled someone at the back.

"Yes?" Mann asked, looking at the kid in the back. He had long hair pulled back in a pony tail, a beard and was wearing jeans and a black T-shirt with "Humans Suck" written across it.

"Uh, sir, that's the new Smart Board we just installed. You don't use those markers. Just use that pen there," he said, pointing to the tray at the bottom of the big white board.

Mann capped the pen and tossed it on a table. Picking up the black pen, he looked at the piece of plastic. It was a toy marker.

"Just pretend it's a marker, sir. It works the same."

Mann started writing and was amazed when the words seemed to appear on the screen. He wrote WHAT WE KNOW across the top.

"You've all seen the pictures that Mr. Haynes brought in. We all know we have our guy. At least, we know he is using these pictures to find his victims. But our efforts to trace him through the pictures haven't panned out. What we need is just one solid piece of this puzzle."

"And I think we have it, LT," Blaak said from the back of the room. "We got the year book!"

Blaak brought the book up to Mann who quickly opened it and began flipping through. He walked over to one of the boards with the pictures from Haynes. It only took him a moment to see that they did indeed have the correct book. All the other detectives and uniformed officers began to crowd around to see the book.

"Lieutenant?"

Mann looked over at the guy in the black T-shirt.

"Lieutenant, if you give me the book, I can put it up on the screen for you."

Mann looked doubtful but handed the book over to the young kid who walked across the room to a table. He laid the book under a device that looked like a desk lamp. Suddenly, the screen was filled with the image of the year book. The picture had barely focused when the kid pulled the book out from under the desk lamp, which Mann now realized was some sort of projector. "Wait, put that back up, that was perfect."

"Just give me a second, sir," the tech said patiently.

Page after page appeared and disappeared on the screen. In about 3 minutes, the tech shut the book and walked up to the screen. Using just his finger, he started to pull files up on the screen like a regular computer.

"We already digitized all the evidence," he said, as the pictures from Hayes were lined up along the top of the screen. The tech ignored his audience and began working on the yearbook. Nobody interrupted him, all too fascinated watching him manipulate the images. In less than five minutes, he had isolated and blown up each matching image from the year book.

"This is definitely the book that he used," the tech said. "You know anything about your killer?"

"I think we can assume he is a student, rather than a teacher," Mann said. The others in the room murmured their assent. "My guess is he is a member of the same class."

Again, the tech manipulated the images. On the screen, a five by six grid appeared. Pictures popped into the grid, filling all but two boxes. Each picture had a name beneath the image.

"There you go," the tech said. "If he was in that class, and not one of the aged photos, one of those guys is your killer."

Mann walked up to the screen and looked at each image, reading off the names. "All right," he said, slapping the tech on the shoulder. "I want everybody to take a name and start checking them out. Find out where they are now, who's still in the city. It has been what twenty-five years? Run them all down and do it now."

As everyone started forward, a voice cut through the general chaos.

"We can narrow that list down for you."

As one, everyone in the room turned to face the doorway. Degget and Kydd stood just inside the room, both wearing huge grins.

"What do you have?" Mann asked. "How many names can you eliminate?"

Degget strutted forward. "Just guessing, but I would say all but one."

This announcement was greeted with silence and then everyone started talking. By the time Degget and Kydd were at the front of the room, Mann got some order and the others in the room were drifting back to chairs or perching on the edge of tables.

"What have you got?" Mann asked.

"Preston Peterson," Degget said.

Mann looked back at the list and scanned through the names. He scanned through a second and third time but with only twenty-eight names, all in alphabetical order, it wasn't too hard to see it wasn't there.

"No Preston Peterson," Mann reported.

"No way!" Kydd exclaimed.

There was silence in the room and Mann looked at Degget. "What she said."

"He isn't there."

"He has to be there," Kydd said. "We have been all over him today and he fits."

"Who is Preston Peterson?" Livermore asked.

"The god damned, psycho Southside Slasher!" Kydd said.

"Relax, Shane," Mann said. "The rest of you guys, get on the phones and track these other guys down."

Mann motioned Degget and Kydd over to a table with Livermore. "Why this Peterson?"

"OK, I do a lot of shit on eBay," Degget said. Seeing Mann's puzzled look, he elaborated. "You know eBay, Mann? The auction thing on the Internet?"

"Ya, sure."

"OK, so we tried to track the flute with stores in and around the city, right? No luck because it hadn't been bought in the city. I was sitting on eBay one night and realized that was likely where the guy got the damn flute. It was perfect. So I started contacting some sellers. Some of them didn't want anything to do with me but a couple answered me. One guy gave me a name. It was delivered about three days before the Hart kill."

"I assume you have more than that," Mann said.

"This time, he used his own name and address. Harder to spoof things with eBay but he probably thought he was safe anyway. We checked him out today," Kydd said. "Went through DMV and the age was about right."

"We also found out that he works for Jackson Catering," Degget said.

"David Jackson's company," Livermore said. "He's a big donor to the Mayor's opponent."

"Not surprised you know the company," Degget said. "They have vending machines in most of the places in the city, including the hospital, the University and they even have some machines down in the warehouse where Dale Lewery's rather slimmed down corpse was found."

"They are also bonded," Kydd added. "That would explain why he was worried about prints. He is in the system for his background check with us!"

"And," Degget said, "he lives a mere three blocks from the Fillup where Gabel's body was found and four blocks from Jake's Tavern."

"Damn it. He does sound pretty good for it," Mann agreed. He glanced up at the board but the pictures were gone. The detectives had their assignments and the tech guy was fiddling with the screen again. Mann turned back to Degget and Kydd. "OK, stay on him and see where it might lead. Maybe...."

"Lieutenant!"

Mann turned back to the kid with the ponytail.

"Lieutenant, he didn't have his picture taken," the tech shouted.

"I know," Mann said. "We are still going to investigate him."

"No, I mean, he didn't get his picture taken *that* day."

The tech ran his finger in a circle on the board and the screen magnified and filled with the words:

ABSENT: Preston Peterson

* * * * *

Mann looked up at the clock. Four forty. The surveillance team was in place. It was just a matter of time. They had already sent a pizza to his apartment but there was no answer. Same with the phone call – voice mail. Mann was worried but it was early. He might be on his way home from work.

"The surveillance should be reporting in soon," Livermore said, quietly. "I want this tight."

"When he gets back, we'll cover him, don't worry. Are you sure you don't want to take him?"

"The Mayor doesn't," Flem said. "And neither does the Commissioner. We are in strict watch and learn mode."

Mann nodded. He had seen Flem on his little cell phone just after

Degget burst into the warehouse with the news. Damn Mayor running the investigation was bullshit. First, they are falling over themselves to arrest an innocent man. Then, they can't distance themselves enough when they have something solid. If this Preston kills again while he was under investigation, there will be hell to pay. At least Drabick's name had never been connected to the Slasher case in the press.

"We should move on him," Mann said.

"The consensus," Flem said, "is that we don't have enough. Detective Degget should have matched a serial number or something on the flute. You need something to actually tie this Peterson to the crime scene. Mr. Haynes may recognize him but none of the pictures were left at the crime scenes. We have been ordered to find him and bottle him up until we have something solid. We want an air-tight case against this psycho. I want pressure on him so that I can use him on the Thorman hit."

"We all do, Inspector," Livermore said. "Mann, I want you there when we do move in. Full SWAT takedown. I want this done right and sooner than later."

"It will be. They will let me know the minute he gets back and then we will be set to move. You just have to give me the word."

Flem stood up and went to the door. "If you'll excuse me, waiting on things like this always gives me indigestion. Let me know what you come up with."

Chapter 78

As Preston passed the corner, he glanced up at the building that housed the Securities and Exchange Commission. It read four forty five. He confirmed the time with his own wrist watch. The SEC's clock was one of the few street clocks in the city that could be relied upon.

The temperature briefly replaced the time. Thank God it had dropped below ninety, he thought. Keeping vigil on the street was hell in this heat. Of course, the beer tasted all the better. He thought he would have time for at least one beer tonight.

Tonight, Little Miss Red was going to meet Mister Enjoyment. He would wait at the *Short Sell* until she showed up. He could risk being in there that long. Then, once she showed, he would casually leave. He would be ready so he didn't lose her this time.

She wouldn't spend a long time in the bar. None of the sluts like her did. Anyway, by the time she came out, nobody would remember the stranger's face. He would be forgotten, as he always was, and free to complete his appointed task.

Thinking of the thrill the night held for him, he went through the heavy doors and sat at the bar stool.

Chapter 79

"Haynes ID'd his DMV photo," Mann said to the Commissioner over the speaker phone. "That doesn't give us much. We haven't tied him to the bathing suit."

"Why not?"

"The sales lady is on some kind of retreat with some group of leaf eaters doing a spiritual cleanse," Mann said. "No phones, no cells. Just a bunch of canoes. We have the local Sherriff trying to track her down."

Mann still wanted to pull the suspect in as soon as he appeared at the apartment. The Commissioner had overruled him, albeit reluctantly. He wanted to hold off until the case was more solid. His words sounded hollow, as though he was following orders.

"We have enough to go for an arrest and a search warrant."

Warrants for the task force seemed to be easier to obtain as more bodies were found. They had been issued on much less than they had now.

"We've got him tight," Livermore said, agreeing with Mann but needing to play his political role. "He isn't getting out of the building. Let's sit on him tonight and see what more we can come up with. We can do a lot of digging in the next ten to twelve hours."

"I agree," added the Commissioner. "I don't really want to test the new warrant powers in the courts. The city already faces several wrongful arrest suits because of this thing. If the other warrants don't hold up, and they won't, we're screwed. It could taint this case and our guy could walk.

There is no way this guy walks."

"We have the physical evidence," Mann said. "We bring him in and nail him with the DNA."

"The DNA evidence is useless if the arrest warrants fall apart. I can't have that."

"This is the guy!"

"Then get me more than a year book," the Commissioner said. "I have faith in you gentlemen. Right now, I'm going to get out of here. I haven't been home on time all week."

Livermore stood up and pressed the disconnect button. Neither Mann nor Livermore mentioned that they hadn't even been home in a week.

Chapter 80

After an hour and three beers dumped in the plant, she arrived.

He left his seat on the bar stool and moved across the room in pursuit of the red hair. As casually as possible, he moved up behind her and edged around to get a glimpse of her face. She turned suddenly and their eyes momentarily locked before she looked away.

Every instinct told him to run.

It was the wrong redhead.

Worse, he recognized this one. He knew her. Would she know him? Would she remember him, later?

The panic ebbed away as he realized he knew her from the television. She was a reporter or something.

He circled to get a closer look, wondering if this might be his new contact. Ellen was forgotten for the time being. He was a mere three feet from her, intending to pass by her on the way to the door, when all hell broke loose.

The men in the dark blue suits surrounded three other men standing about five feet from his prey. He was in the middle of what had become the centre of attention for the entire bar.

The guys in the suits were showing official identification and one guy said he was from the FBI.

Preston backed up and almost tripped over a table. He caught himself but attracted the eye of the Fed. He got the once over and was ignored.

The most important man in the city and he was ignored. On the front page of papers across the country and they just looked right through him.

The FBI was helping the SEC arrest some twat in a designer suit – likely for insider trading – and letting the Southside Slasher get away! Their brains had been in their foreskin; lopped off at birth.

He backed away, blending into the crowd. That was the way – money before lives. Like gawkers at a car accident, everyone in the bar was staring at the small knot of men. As they started to leave, the television broad shoved past with her camera so he beat a hasty retreat. Outside the bar, he grabbed the first bus that went by, not even caring that it wasn't heading toward his home.

* * * * *

William Hill hated improvising. Improvisation was for ill-prepared amateurs who had to rely on luck because of their poor planning. Hill prided himself on his careful plans.

However, time was against him. The call from Angelino's cutout came only minutes before. The message had been clear. They had identified the Southside Slasher and an arrest was imminent. If Hill was going to eliminate the threat, he had to move quickly.

Unfortunately, unlike Drabick, this mark was not under Angelino's control whatsoever. He was a totally unknown citizen. They had no track on him, didn't know his location, couldn't say when he was going to return home and were unsure when he was going to be arrested. The good money was on the morning but Hill couldn't count on having that kind of time. He had to act now with the small bit of information he had.

He had the mark's name and address, as well as an undetectable way into the apartment building so he wouldn't be seen by the watching police. Now, he just had to get at the psycho in the kill zone, assuming the very definite possibility that he might be in his apartment by the time Hill arrived.

Hill watched the street from the doorway he had been standing in as the brown truck drove slowly along the street and stopped, double parking.

His ride had arrived.

The brown uniformed UPS driver bounded out of his truck and went into the store. As he went in, he snatched the UPS envelope from the front window – his indication that there was a pickup. Hill had walked the downtown streets for half an hour, looking for just such a sign. Hill lucked out that the driver was male and an approximate size match.

The driver came out of the store and Hill matched him step for step. As usual, the driver went immediately into the back of the truck. Hill followed him in and clubbed him with his sap before he even knew he was there. As the driver fell forward, Hill grabbed his cap and put it on his own head. Sufficiently disguised for now, he slid behind the steering wheel and pulled down the street to a parking lot at a convenience store.

Shutting both doors and locking them, he went into the back and unbuttoned the unconscious driver's uniform shirt. Working quickly and efficiently, he was as adept with his latex gloves on as any heart surgeon. If he'd had more time, he would have bought a uniform at a costume store over the Internet. Instead, he had to wear this guy's sweaty stinking clothes. Once the guy was stripped down to his little red bikini briefs – some people really should wear boxers – he started to come around. His eye flickered open briefly and looked at Hill before sliding back into unconsciousness.

Hill made a small sound of regret and propped the driver up against a large box and pulled out his silenced .45 – a match to the one he had given to Thorman. Hill preferred using a .22 since there was better penetration control and less chance of collateral damage that might draw undo attention. However, the hollow points should solve that problem and Hill wasn't sure what he might face. He might need the stopping power that the .45 offered.

However, contrary to what the movies showed, even quality silencers quickly wear out and loose their effectiveness. Putting the gun away, he considered other options. He reached over and grabbed the roll of packing tape. Taking a strip, he put it across the driver's mouth and then flipped him on his stomach. He taped his hands behind his back and then taped his ankles together. Finally, sure that the man wasn't going anywhere, Hill pulled out a knife. Lifting the driver's head by his hair, he slit his throat, making sure to stay clear of the arterial spray.

While the man bled out in the back, Hill returned to the driver's seat and started the truck again. At the exit of the plaza, he waited for an opening in traffic, cursing the drivers.

God, he hated this city. He couldn't get out soon enough and he would only come back once. And that trip would be strictly pleasure…to put a bullet into Angelino's thick Italian skull.

* * * * *

Safety.

Preston needed the safety of his apartment. Being so close to the arrest and the camera had frightened him. On the bus, he was sure people were staring.

He was sweating as he trotted across the park behind his apartment building and stumbled over the curb at his parking lot. He felt his heart pounding against his ribs, threatening to burst. The sweat soaked through his shirt and molded it to his back and chest.

He tasted blood in his mouth as his lungs ached for air.

He collapsed just inside the back door of his apartment building.

He coughed and coughed until he thought he would vomit. He knew he would be coughing for the rest of the night.

He was too close to his goal to get caught. He just needed the safety of his apartment to continue his plan. On the long bus ride, fighting his fear, he had planned his next move. His mission was going too slowly. He was too exposed as he sought out his old classmates. And killing them was too limited. They had already done their damage. Killing them was cleansing, liberating but did nothing to help the world. He had to broaden his scope. Diversify. He had to cleanse the world before they perfected their bullying techniques, while they were still in school.

Now, he knew he was going to be recognized for his feats.

Tina would marry him and they would raise a son.

All he had to do was start work on his explosives before the big football tournament in two weeks. A truck full of explosives parked under the stands.

Glorious.

With his confidence returning, he dragged himself up the stairwell to his apartment on the second floor.

* * * * *

"Lou, our bird has come home to roost."

"Save that for the radio, Ed," Mann said.

"Sorry. Anyway, they got a light on and movement. Somebody pulled the drapes."

"Anybody see him?"

"They caught sight of a man that matches the suspect's description entering the back just before the lights went on."

"Okay. Now that we have him, I want to keep it tight. Have another team standing by in case they need help."

"One more thing."

Mann felt his stomach flip. He didn't like the tone on Buma's voice.

"The guys watching the back said that the perp arrived out of breath. They said he had been running across the park behind the apartment like the devil himself was on his ass."

* * * * *

"I can hardly hear you," Mann said into the phone. He reached across his desk to shut the door.

"I'm in the car," said Dani. "Damn headset is low on juice. I've been on the phone a lot tonight."

"I thought you'd still be at the bar."

"Damn SEC jumped the gun on me. They arrested my damn snitch. My story is dead."

"They hit your guy?"

"Ya, with the Feebs. Blew the doors off the place arresting the guy early. Wait till next time. If they think I'll sit on another story for them they are so mistaken. Screw it, I got something better."

"I got something for you too but not on the phone."

"Mine shouldn't be either but I don't have time. You know Drabick?"

"I do but how do you?"

"Screw that, no time. This comes straight from Dominos."

Dominos was truly beginning to deliver if he had that kind of information. "What about him?"

"He says Drabick wasn't an accident. It was a hit."

Greer waved and started to leave. Mann snapped his fingers and waved him back. "What do you mean?"

"The same guy that hit that accountant..."

"Thorman?"

"Ya, him. Dominos says the guy that whacked Thorman, hit Drabick. Someone is afraid of getting ID'd. Angelino is very worried and so is the hitter."

Mann could hear the tone of Dani's voice. She was holding back, stalling. "What else?"

"Your latest suspect?"

"You DO NOT know about him!"

"He's next."

"How good is this information?"

"You tell me. I think your Great Aunt figures into it."

Mann paused for a moment, trying to remember his Aunt's name. Blanche. And the suspect lived on Blanchette Street.

For the briefest moment, he considered pulling the team off of the apartment complex. Let the psycho get his ass blown to hell. The thought passed as quickly as it came. "Don't go near the place," Mann said, as he slammed down the phone.

Mann was already explaining Dani's call to Greer as he ran from his office. After a quick look around the warehouse, staffed tonight by rookies while almost every other detective was running down anything they had on Peterson, he decided that he had nobody there that he would trust to back him up. Jogging to the front desk, he was glad to see Ed Buma still there. In as few a words as possible, he described the situation to the sergeant.

"Warn the guys at the apartment. Nobody is to move but everybody is to watch their backs."

"Sure Lou. What about backup?"

Greer was checking the load in his gun. "He's covered."

Mann looked at Greer. "What about the hand?"

"Time I got back on the street. Yes, Mother, my hand is fine."

Smiling, they sprinted for Mann's car. Mann slid behind the wheel. Greer popped the glove compartment and pulled out the red dome. The siren screaming, they screeched away from the curb, the back end swerving dangerously. A block away, the radio crackled.

"Task Force Central to Lieutenant Mann."

"Go Central," Greer said into the mike.

"Both teams responding. All quiet."

"Central, instruct teams to remain outside on doors. No further action and no one, absolutely no one, is to enter the premises. That includes team members unless a clear emergency exists. Dispatch SWAT and ambulances to the scene. Got that?"

"Roger. They're rolling. Central out."

Chapter 81

Hill walked up to the second floor from the basement of the apartment building, taking the steps two at a time. A short walk down the hallway, he stopped in front of apartment 202. He heard the television. It sounded like the nightly news. Listening, he could hear the announcer talking about the Southside Slasher and the lack of progress in the investigation. Hill smiled despite that fact that he would have preferred an empty apartment.

Hill shifted the box and signature tablet to his left hand. Making sure the open end of the box was hidden, he knocked on the door with his right.

The television almost instantly muted.

Hill waited another three seconds and knocked again.

He could hear the jingle of a belt buckle and the sound of a zipper before footsteps came toward the door. As he had hoped, he saw the light change through the peephole. He shifted the box slightly, his right hand ready to disappear into the box.

"Yes?" came the voice from inside the apartment.

"UPS. I have a delivery for Preston Peterson. I just need a signature."

"I didn't order anything," Preston said, sounding unsure and suspicious. "Who is it from?"

Hill glanced down at the tablet. "Brickhouse Corporation," he said. "If you don't want it, I still need a signature refusing it."

"I don't want it. I didn't order anything."

Hill glanced at the deadbolt lock and reached into the box. "Hey buddy, give me a break. I'm just trying to do my job. If you don't sign that you don't want it, they'll just make me bring it back tomorrow."

There was a pause and then Hill heard the dead bolt turn. As soon as the door knob turned and the door edge past the jamb, Hill hit it with his left shoulder as he let the box fall away from the gun. He felt Peterson move backwards and he pushed harder as the door suddenly had no weight.

Peterson was turned and running down the short hallway. Hill put two quick shots into the fleeing man's back. The force of the shots shoved the big man forward. He ran fast first into the side of a wall unit and bounced back. His legs crumpled beneath him and he landed on his back, his head toward Hill. Hill shut the door behind him, took four steps and stood looking down at tubby man bleeding on the floor.

Peterson's mouth was moving, trying to speak, like some fat fish gasping for air. Hill didn't try to make out the words, he just took in the round, pathetic face, thick glasses, and chubby physique. He looked even less likely to be the Slasher than Drabick. Without another thought, Hill put two more shots into Peterson's head. Time was short and he wanted to make sure he had the Slasher this time. God knows, he couldn't rely on the police to get it right.

He started to search the apartment.

* * * * *

Mann jammed the accelerator down and nearly bottomed out in a pot hole. Approaching the apartments, Mann slowed and swerved around a double parked UPS truck. Greer called out numbers as they drove past three identical three storey walkups.

Mann pulled beside one of the surveillance vehicles. Greer rolled down his window and Mann leaned across. "Other than the suspect, who has entered the building in the last half hour?"

The mark sheet was consulted. "Only the suspect and one woman."

"No other men?"

"No, sir. Just the woman carrying something in a large green garbage bag. Just before we got the call to stop anyone entering. Nobody exited."

Mann looked down the street and saw Dani's Jeep. "A redhead, brown vest?"

"Ya. Great ass. You know her?"

Mann ignored the question. "Keep the other team on the exit. Greer and I are going in. Nobody else goes in. Detain anyone leaving. Consider everyone armed and dangerous. SWAT is on the way. Got that?"

"Yes, sir."

Mann looked at Greer and took a deep breath. "Ready?"

"No. But, let's go."

* * * * *

Dani set her camera down in a small recess in the hallway on the second floor. Now that she was here, she wasn't exactly sure what her next move might be. Between fighting traffic and her call to Mann, she had spent all her time trying to get here. All she could think was that the story was too good to pass up. She stood, trying to decide how she was going to handle this.

While she was still deciding what to do with her camera, a UPS driver came out of an apartment just up the hallway.

In a flash, she took in the UPS cap, brown shirt and brown shorts. In the next blink, she noticed the black outline highlighted against the brown of the shorts. Held tight against his thigh, the UPS driver had a gun.

The man stared at her. And then she saw that same look she had seen so many times. That searching puzzled expression that suddenly changed as someone recognized her. Dani saw the recognition come into his eyes just as the gun started to rise.

At that instant, Dani could hear someone running up the steps. She knew it was Mann and she started to turn to the stairwell door.

The UPS man was suddenly in motion. He ran toward her and fired a single shot. A large hole appeared in the wall beside her and she froze. She felt herself grabbed and dragged away from the stairwell and down the hall. She tried to fight and she felt the gun jammed into her stomach hard enough to knock some of the air out of her.

"I'd prefer a hostage but I will just kill you if you slow me down."

* * * * *

Mann and Greer both had their guns drawn as they ran up the central stairwell. Just before the reached the top, the wall near the door to the second floor exploded. Both men slammed themselves against the wall and pointed their guns up. Mann took a fast look and saw nobody on the second floor landing. Slowly, they moved up the stairwell and eased open the door to the hallway. Mann ducked his head out the door and pulled it back immediately. For a split second, he let his brain register what he had seen in the hallway.

Nodding to Greer, they slipped through and took cover in an alcove by the stairs. Mann could see Dani's camera at his feet, still in the garbage bag. With an effort, he pushed aside the knowledge that Dani never left her camera and concentrated on the hallway.

Mann pointed down the hall at the spill of light coming from an open door. Greer counted doorways and held up two fingers. Mann nodded. Two-oh-two. Peterson's apartment.

With his head, Mann motioned for them to continue.

At the open door, Mann ducked by and came up on the other side. He motioned Greer down low and they kicked the door open full and moved in.

Mann looked at the mess on the floor. The ruined face and blood pooled under the man's back. Obviously no threat, he ignored him for now, quickly searching the small apartment. Confident it was empty except for the body, they went back into the hallway where Mann stationed Greer at the entrance. "Nobody goes in. I want to be sure we have him, this time."

"Were those what I think they were in the jars?" Greer asked.

Mann ignored his question and looked at the door. "He wasn't waiting inside; Peterson was shot running from the door."

"Ya, so?"

"That is a fresh kill. That means Peterson beat him here. So, how did he get past our guys?"

Mann suddenly took off for the far stairwell, shouting to Greer. "Stay here, nobody gets in until I get back."

Mann grew up in Kesle and had learned many of its legends and history from his father, a city worker who loved Kesle trivia. Somewhere in the back of his mind, Mann remembered that the five apartment buildings were built by the same landlord years before when rents were collected weekly in person. All these apartments had basements that connected so the landlord wouldn't be on the street in bad weather or with the large sums of cash.

Mann headed down the stairs in a dead run.

At the basement, he slowed and began to move more quietly. The door came open easily and Mann moved into the lit hallway. Hurrying as fast as silence would allow, he almost ran into Dani and a UPS driver when he rounded the corner at the end of the hall.

"Put the gun down."

Mann kept the gun level, aimed just below the UPS cap. "I think that should be my line. Just let the lady go and we can talk."

UPS shook his head. He had one arm, the hand with the gun, wrapped around Dani. The silenced barrel of the gun rested firmly against her jaw bone. The other hand was on the connecting door behind him.

Mann sighted on the killer's head and knew he could take the shot but was afraid of what the gunman might do. Even dying, he could pull the trigger and blow Dani's face off. This was not the little .22 that had killed Thorman.

Mann saw it in the killer's eyes – he knew Mann wouldn't take the shot.

The door opened and the hit man started to back out, pulling Dani by the hair. As they were about to clear the door, he lowered the gun. Mann saw the motion and dove behind a pile of furniture. He landed hard on a low table. The bullet blew a fist-sized hole in the wall behind him. Mann waited a beat and peeked over the couch. The connecting door was closed.

Mann considered following, calculating how many men he would need to cover the three remaining apartments. Before he could make a decision, he heard a thud; something hard landed against the connecting door. He brought up his gun and moved closer, fearing the worst.

"Mann, I'm coming out."

The door opened and Dani stepped into the basement. The front of her vest was drenched in blood. Mann rushed to her but his eyes were drawn behind her.

The hit man was crumpled on the ground, blood leaking out of the wound in his throat. Driven in deep, only the hilt of Dani's knife showed.

"Bastard pulled my hair."

Chapter 82

Blame slides down The Hill but success sticks like glue to the top.

In front of the bank of television cameras and radio microphones, the Mayor took most of the credit for the end of the Southside Slasher's reign. In the glare of the hot lights, the Mayor's smile was blinding. He carefully spread the praise, allowing the Commissioner, Deputy Inspector Livermore, and even Mann, to be photographed with his arm around them. Naturally, Inspector Flem was present, promising to trace the hit man back to his Mafia source. Still, the Mayor kept the true accolades for himself and his administration's tough stance on all crime, highlighting both the Slasher's demise and especially SOCU's successes.

Mann slipped from the stage as quickly as possible, nauseated with the entire proceeding. In his mind, he still saw all the victims' photographs pinned up on the board at the warehouse.

All for revenge on people who had supposedly done Peterson wrong in the past – bullies who had terrorized him during his youth. What a waste of innocent lives.

Confucius was right. When you set out on revenge, dig two graves. This time, there were even more graves. But at least two of them were filled with the right bodies.

Regardless of the Mayor's posturing, the Commissioner had given Mann his due. James had given Mann an open invitation.

Meanwhile, the press was running full tilt with the death of the Slasher. The Slasher had made twenty-three pictures and Haynes had made a lucrative deal with the *Daily*. Rumor had it that the rag had paid three hundred thousand dollars for the exclusive rights to the pictures. Haynes, Mann discovered, had donated all the money to the fund for the Lucas child.

The paper's advertising campaign had already started. Every day, they were going to run a picture with a screaming headline:

COULD YOU HAVE BEEN NEXT?

Shoving the paper off the table in his living room, Mann popped the caps on three more beers and another Pepsi. He passed the beers to Davis, Degget and Dani. "You know I'm right," Degget said.

"It has to be Flem," Davis agreed. "Who else had access in both occasions?"

"With the man power on the Task Force? Any number of people," Mann replied. "There is no guarantee it's the same person."

"My snitch seems to think so. Angelino got everything about the Slasher from his *Tom Dick*."

"All he had to do was make a phone call," Degget said.

They were silent for a time, sipping their drinks. Finally, Dani spoke up. "What about…"

"Son of a bitch!" Mann yelled as he jumped up.

"What the hell?" Degget swore. "You made me spill my beer."

"Son of a bitch!" Mann repeated. "I knew something was gnawing at my brain. When you brought in the address for the flute, Flem made a call almost right away. I figured he was calling the Mayor."

"But you figure he was calling Angelino?"

"Maybe, I don't know," Mann said. "That isn't it. It was the phone. He has a BlackBerry. Nice shiny red one. He's always on the damn thing."

"You just hate cell phones," Dani said. "And anything you can get email on is just plain beyond your Neanderthal mind."

"Ya, ya. No, you don't get it. He wasn't on his BlackBerry. I knew something was bothering me. He was on some little silver thing."

"He has a throw away?" Degget said.

"I'm betting. He's using it so there is nothing to trace."

"Then," Dani said, "we have to get that phone or at least the SIM card."

"What do we want with the SIM card?" asked Mann.

"You thinking cloning?" Degget asked, ignoring Mann's question.

"It doesn't take much. I have a cloner. I picked it up a couple years back from your beloved eBay. I've used it a couple times. Comes in handy."

"I'll bet," Davis said.

"What are you talking about?" Mann asked.

"You will have to excuse Mann. He isn't exactly up on the latest technology. He tries but, you know."

"Ya, screw you too."

"What Dani is proposing is copying the SIM card from Flem's phone," Davis said. "Then, we can possibly get the numbers he has called."

"No possibly about it," Dani said.

"Let me guess," Degget said. "You got a guy?"

"Oh ya, do I have a guy."

"No. No way," Mann said, shaking his head. "Not that paranoid freak. I still think he put a bug in our bedroom last time he was around. I don't want him around here."

"Now who's paranoid? You know he won't let anyone near his place. It has to be here."

Mann was still shaking his head but continued. "So, let me get this straight. All we have to do is get Flem's phone, clone the card, get the phone back so he isn't suspicious, get the clone to the Freak, and maybe trace what calls he has made?"

"Basically."

"Why do I think I know how you are going to get the phone?" Mann asked.

"Because you are brilliant when it comes to strategy. A regular Hannibal."

"The General or the Colonel from the A Team?" asked Davis.

"You can screw off too," Mann said to Davis, without taking his eyes off Dani. He didn't like the way her eyes were dancing. "You want to use the Dickerson boys, don't you? It's going to take two or he'll be suspicious. How long are you going to need for the cloning?"

"Five minutes tops. I could do it right in front of Flem and he wouldn't know what I was doing. Jason can get the card out before he even hands it to me. He should have been a surgeon, with those wonderful hands," Dani added, a wicked gleam in her eyes.

"Oh please," Mann said, rolling his eyes.

Mann turned to Degget, trying to gauge him. Mann knew where he stood with Dani. Degget was obviously all in. From Degget, Mann turned to Davis. For Davis, it was simple. Degget was family and family always came first.

Making his decision, Mann said, "OK, now we are in the dark place. We aren't talking about getting a search warrant and putting this guy on trial. I don't know where we are going to go if we have proof."

"I have an idea about that," Dani said. "First things first. Let me call the boys and get the SIM. We just need the opportunity."

Davis was smiling. "When is that big reception at the warehouse?"

"Oh God," Mann moaned.

Chapter 83

"You know, being dressed like this could get me tossed out of the bad guy union," Jason Dickerson said to Mann, flicking an imaginary fleck of lint off the blue arm of his uniform jacket.

"Oh, God," Mann moaned, looking at the younger of the Dickerson boys, dressed in full dress blues. "Dani is going to be the death of me."

"Relax or you're going to give us away. Is Degget ready?"

Mann looked around the warehouse at the rest of the reception guests. Everyone that had been connected with the Task Force had been invited. The Mayor was looking for votes and support among the department while delivering an important message. He was holding court at the front with Flem at his side. The Commissioner, Livermore and Keough were relegated to a secondary position. The message was clear to the rank and file – time to get on board the new train.

The Mayor needed someone capable of covering his back politically. James, regardless of the success in catching the Southside Slasher, was on his way out.

Unless, they could derail that train.

"Degget is at a table in the back. Just get this done and get the hell out of here before someone recognizes you."

Dickerson looked like he was about to snap a salute and then just turned and walked away. As he went across the room, he slapped a few shoulders and even shook some hands. Mann remembered to breathe when Dickerson finally made it to Flem. Dickerson had a short conversation with the Inspector, shook his hand and also shook the Mayor's hand. Throughout it all, Mann watched carefully. He wasn't sure whether to be disappointed or relieved when he realized that Dickerson didn't get it.

Dickerson again made his way across the room and leaned down to talk to Degget. He straightened and shrugged. Without another word, he walked to the back of the warehouse and left.

Before he could go over to Degget, Mann jumped when he felt a hand on his shoulder. "Sorry Lieutenant, I just wanted to thank you again for what you did with this investigation, Lieutenant."

Mann turned to Commissioner James. "Thank you, sir, but as I already told you, it was good police work on the part of my detectives that solved this case."

"True but I know a good leader when I see one. I don't need to tell you that my decision to put you on this case was questioned, repeatedly," James said. Both of them couldn't help but look at the Mayor. "You proved me right and have given me some juice. Don't know how much good it will do me but it all helps."

"I, uh..."

"Don't worry, Lieutenant, you don't have to respond to that. I just want you to know that I am grateful. If there's anything I can do for you, don't hesitate to contact me."

Just then, the Mayor moved up to the microphone and asked for everyone's attention. He began to thank everyone connected with the investigation. Regardless of his total lack of any contribution, Flem was the first one to be thanked – which wasn't lost on the Commissioner. "Anything I can do for you," James repeated, shaking Mann's hand. "Just don't wait too long."

The Commissioner moved off to the front of the room. Mann caught a glimpse of someone brushing lint off Flem's immaculate uniform. As the toady officer stepped away from the Inspector, he looked directly at Mann. He smirked and brushed his finger across his nose. Mann recognized the second brother. Damn, those boys were good.

Mann listened to the Mayor and then Flem drone on, both working from small cards they held in their hands. The Commissioner stepped up and was the first to actually name key detectives, including Degget, without the benefit of notes.

As though on cue, Degget grabbed Mann's elbow and guided him toward the back door. "OK, I've had my fifteen minutes of fame. Unless you want to listen to more of the speeches, we have work to do."

* * * * *

"There's only one number that he calls?" Mann asked

"That's it," Dani said. "From what we can tell, he never calls anything but a little grocer on 59th."

"Which I know for a fact is owned by Angelino," Degget said. "It's an information drop. He calls the number and they pass on the information."

"It is pretty thin," Mann said.

"So was the flute. But put the shit all together and it is pretty damning," Degget said. "Early in his career, he makes his mark by busting syndicate guys. Lots of good busts but if you really track them, and I have, most are all beneficial to Angelino in one way or another. And if they didn't help build Angelino's network, they are throw away thugs that don't hurt Angelino's operation. They take the fall, they do the time and come out richer than when they went in. Flem comes on the scene during my investigation and I am burned a couple days later. Finally, he comes into the Slasher thing and all of a sudden we got suspects dropping almost as fast as the victims."

"Look at Flem's first big bust, his career starter – a mid-level wiseguy that rolled over on his bosses. Those bosses were Angelino's main competition at the time. They went away. Saved Angelino some bullets and propelled Flem on his way toward Inspector. Angelino was with him the whole way. And this time next year, he'll be Commissioner."

"OK, OK, I said it was pretty thin but I'm still thinking about skating on it," Mann said. He looked over at Davis who nodded.

"Really?" Dani asked. "This is putting your ass out there."

Mann looked at Dani for a few seconds. She was right. A misstep with this and Mann would fall so far, he would never get back. Even if he didn't end up in jail, he would never work for the Kesle PD again. He'd be lucky to trade his badge for a cheap uniform and a cloth patch that said Gregg – Mall Security.

Mann turned from Dani's concerned look to Degget's determined face. He knew that look from his own face. He still saw it most days in the mirror and now wasn't the time to retire it – especially when he was this close to a shot at Angelino.

"Screw it…William Harrison Flem is going down."

"William Harrison Flem?" Dani asked. "Of course! WH stands for William *Harrison!*"

"Sure, William Harrison Flem. Why?"

"Remember what Angelino calls his snitch?" Dani asked.

"My Tom Dick," Mann said slowly. He started to smile, which looked more like a grimace. "Tom, Dick, and Harry."

"Tell me this isn't our man," Degget said.

Mann waved it off. "Now we are in a bad spot. Flem is truly connected. Forget Angelino, Flem has some major political weight behind him."

"Untouchable," Davis added. "And an illegally obtained phone and a nickname aren't going to convict him."

"We can't just let him walk away," Degget said. "We know the guy is dirty. All we have to do is prove it."

"What if you didn't have to prove it?" Dani asked.

"Meaning?" Mann asked.

Dani looked at Mann. "How far can we go with this?"

"What do you mean?" Mann asked.

"You know what I mean" Dani answered. "I'm talking about the boys."

"This blows up, it's going to be one more nail in the door between you and the boys," Davis agreed. "She'll have even more ammunition against you. They will hate you forever."

"You got a way to get him, let's hear it," Mann said to Dani.

Dani shrugged and turned her iPad so they could all see the screen. "OK, see that list of files. Those are the dates of Flem's appearances on the nightly news. I can access any of those dates for a brief summary of the interview. The main interviews are all digitized on our network at the station."

"So, you have every one of his appearances?" Mann asked.

"That's right. Every piece of tape that egomaniac has made."

"So?" Degget asked. "That helps us how?"

"Gregg, remember when you said that if the news ever got out about the leak, the guy would be as good as dead?"

"There wouldn't be a hole deep enough to hide in."

"Ever see the *Running Man?*" Dani asked.

"Ya, that Schwarzenegger movie about the game show," Degget said.

"Remember the bit when they showed Schwarzenegger getting killed only they mapped his face onto another guy?"

"No way!" Degget said.

"Way," Dani said. "We've got hours of audio that I can work with."

"Can you do the video?" Mann asked.

"I could use a friend."

"Can you trust him? Would he do it?"

"He's underground. He's a throwback to the sixties with a techno fetish. If it screws up a cop, he'd do it for free."

Mann looked at Dani, Degget and Davis. But he was thinking about his sons. Once again, he was doing exactly what his wife always accused him of – cutting corners on the system he supposedly stood for. But he was getting the job done and the ends *did* justify the means. Besides, the boys had to love him as he was – not some ideal political bureaucrat that their mother wanted him to be. And then there would be the satisfaction of knowing he had seriously screwed the Hinge.

Now he just had to get Flem alone and controlled. He knew exactly how to do it.

* * * * *

Mann stood in the pool of light in front of the large double doors. He couldn't help but look over his shoulder but he needn't have worried. He couldn't even see the street from where he stood. The door finally opened and Commissioner James looked surprised to see Mann.

"Lieutenant? Is this something that can wait until my office tomorrow?"

"Frankly, sir, you don't want me in the office with this," Mann said.

The Commissioner smiled. "I think I should tell you to just get back in your car. It hasn't even been twelve hours and you are already cashing in your chip from this afternoon? When I said don't wait too long, I thought you would have more faith than six hours."

Mann just shrugged and James stepped back to let him in the door.

"Follow me. My office is just up here on the left. My wife wants me to call it the study but I can't do it. I married into money pretty late in life. The only time I was in anything called a study, it was detention in study hall with Sister Theresa Marie. Not a memory I want to relive every time I work at home."

On the way behind his desk, James motioned to the sideboard. "I'd offer you a drink but I'm a Coke man, myself."

The Commissioner laughed at Mann's expression. "Don't look so surprised. I was in the task force fridge and saw all those red, white and blue cans. Patriotic as I am, I was appalled at the sight. Blaak ratted you out. OK, so since you arrived, I have done all the talking. I think it is time you started doing some."

Mann nodded. "Then I won't waste anymore of your time and get right to it."

An hour later, Mann left the Commissioner's house with a promise to have Flem at the warehouse by three in the afternoon on the day after tomorrow. And he would be alone.

Chapter 84

"Inspector."

Inspector WH Flem walked into the cavernous room. Without the desks and chairs, the warehouse seemed enormous. Flem walked slowly across the cement floor toward Mann standing in the half shadow. His hard shoes clicked harshly, sending echoes bouncing off the walls.

"What is this all about, Lieutenant? Who is that behind you?"

Mann turned around and Dani moved out from behind the television monitor. Flem stopped until he could see her fully. Her red hair flashed as she stepped into the full light. "Danett Wood, Inspector."

"Ah, the famous Flashcam and bedmate."

Mann did not respond and Flem continued forward. "You only answered one of my questions. Why am I here? The message from the Commissioner seemed urgent."

"Simply put, Inspector, we want you to testify against your employer, Giovanni Angelino."

Flem did not flinch or so much as pause. "And what would I be testifying about?"

"The years that you have been working for Angelino, misdirecting investigations, informing of pending searches and arrests, helping hit men get rid of witnesses. That sort of stuff."

Flem walked toward Mann, his eyes still flat, almost bored.

"You don't deny my accusation."

"Why bother? It is ludicrous. I am only staying because I want to see you hang yourself. You seem determined to end whatever bit of career you have left."

"It isn't my career that is over."

Flem's eyebrows went up, wrinkling his forehead high into what was once his hairline. He had arrived beside Mann. Dani had moved off to the side.

Mann bent down and pressed the button on the DVD player. The television whined for a minute and then the picture solidified into a full face shot of Flem in his uniform. Dani's voice could be heard off camera.

"Tonight, we bring you an exclusive interview with Inspector William Harrison Flem who has a shocking announcement. The Inspector is a veteran of the Kesle police force, winner of the medal for conspicuous bravery, appointed head of the Mayor's Special Organized Crime Unit, well respected both within the force and in the civilian population. How could this officer become linked with the Mafia? How could this decorated veteran become an informant on his own brother officers? Inspector, how did it all begin?"

"At first, it was innocent," Flem answered. "It was something that everyone did more or less. Turn a blind eye to this crime or that, just to help out a friend. Take a free cup of coffee, a bottle of Scotch."

"But, you did more, did you not, Inspector?" asked Dani, as the camera shot flashed to her. "Did you not interfere with other officers and ongoing investigations?"

"Yes. Over the course of several years, several undercover investigations were jeopardized. However, no officers lost their lives as a result."

The camera continued to go back and forth from Dani to Flem. Even Mann, knowing what to look for, barely saw the subtle changes from one shot of Flem to another. Dani's video tech was a genius especially considering how quickly he put it together.

"But," Dani said severely, "several almost died. In fact, only recently, a contract was taken out on an undercover detective you fingered. He was injured and there have been six deaths as a result of the contract on his life."

"That was regretful. However, the deaths were men who were anything but innocent. Nobody likes to see anyone get hurt. However, that is the nature of the job."

"But, betrayal by your own commanding officer is not part of the job. Why have you decided to come forward?"

"The opportunity to turn State's evidence has been offered."

"So, you were the object of an investigation? In fact, you were caught."

Flem did not respond and the picture returned to Dani. "And after this taping, you will be going into hiding?"

"Arrangements are being made."

"And can we assume that the indictments brought down by your information will involve high ranking members of organized crime?"

"I can tell you this. Before I'm finished, I will have put Giovanni Angelino behind bars."

"Thank you, Inspector. Or should I say ex Inspector Flem? We will have further updates as more information becomes available. And now, back to you Mark."

Flem lightly applauded, his hands coming together in slow, measured applause. "Excellent work."

"It airs at six."

"The video is good but anyone can tell it was doctored. And the audio? Christ, I could identify each one of my appearances. Nobody will believe it. You show that tape and I'll sue you and your station so dry, you'll be farting dust."

"Very picturesque," Dani replied. "The tape still airs."

"Nobody will believe it. It won't stand up under analysis."

"It won't have to," Mann said. 'You won't live to see a courtroom."

Flem stared at Mann, a puzzled look crossing his face.

Degget stepped out from the shadows and laughed.

"You don't get it, do you, you sorry sack of shit." Degget said. "We don't have to convince a court. We only have to convince Angelino of the possibility. Do you think he will take time to analyze the tape before he wastes your fat ass?"

Flem swallowed hard, realization sinking in. Then, his confidence returned. He squared his shoulders. "I can end this with a single phone call."

"If you could make the phone call," Degget said.

Flem turned and stared at the gun in Degget's hand. Seeing the hatred in Degget's eyes, even Mann took an involuntary step forward. Degget's hand was rock steady as he pointed the automatic at the shorter man's head. Flem made a gurgling sound that Mann thought was some sort of a plea.

"Angelino will be especially anxious to talk to you when he discovers you have disappeared for several days. When his snitches do find you, and they will find you, do you think he'll ask you if it's true? Then again, you could just disappear permanently and we won't have to worry about any of this. Really depends on how cooperative you are."

For a moment longer, the tension hung in the air and then Degget raised the barrel of the gun until it was pointing at the ceiling. He carefully released the hammer and put the gun in his shoulder holster.

"Nah. It's going to be more fun watching you try to dodge Angelino. How long do you think you'll last?"

Flem's knees buckled and he sank to the ground. None of the three bothered to try and catch him.

* * * * *

Dani was setting up her camera on the tripod while Flem sat in a chair – a blank look on his face. Behind him, Mann, Degget, Davis and Commissioner James were talking quietly.

"I wasn't sure if you were going to pull the trigger," James said.

"You know," Degget said, with a smile, "neither was I."

James laughed. "The Mayor is going to stroke out when he sees this."

"What's he going to do to you?"

"What can he do? He'll be so busy trying to distance himself from Flem, he won't have time for me."

"I think I should have a lawyer."

The three looked at Flem in his chair. They looked back at each other and laughed. James walked up behind Flem and leaned down close to his ear. His voice dripped with the disdain he felt for Flem.

"You are not getting a lawyer. You are going to sit and answer the nice lady's questions so we have a proper tape to air tonight. You will turn over on Angelino and give us everything you've got. You understand?"

"I'll get you for this," Flem said.

"Do you really think we are the ones you should be threatening?" James asked, slapping Flem lightly on his cheek. "We are your new best friends. None of your old buddies will come within a mile of you once we're done. We are your only protection. You understand that, right? Your life is in our hands."

James stepped back and straightened.

"In fact, as Commissioner of the Kesle Police Department," James said, stressing his position, "I am officially assigning Sergeant Davis and Detective Degget to your protection detail. His life is in your hands, Detective."

Flem whirled in the chair and jumped to his feet. Hatred burned in his eyes. James looked down at the overweight, balding man. Scorn met hatred until Flem finally backed down, beaten.

"Right then, gentlemen," Dani said. "Let's get this thing done."

Mann stepped back and watched Dani fine focus the camera but what he saw in his mind was Angelino finally heading behind bars. Dani stepped forward with the mike and had Degget move the chair out of the way. Smiling with satisfaction, Mann leaned against the wall and listened to Dani start her interview.

Coming in 2012

Too Many Graves

A Kesle City Homicide Novel

D. A. Graystone

There's a new killer in Kesle and he knows where all the bodies are buried because he put them there.

Coming in 2012

Kesle has another killer and he knows where all the bodies are buried!

Too Many Graves

A Kesle City Homicide Novel

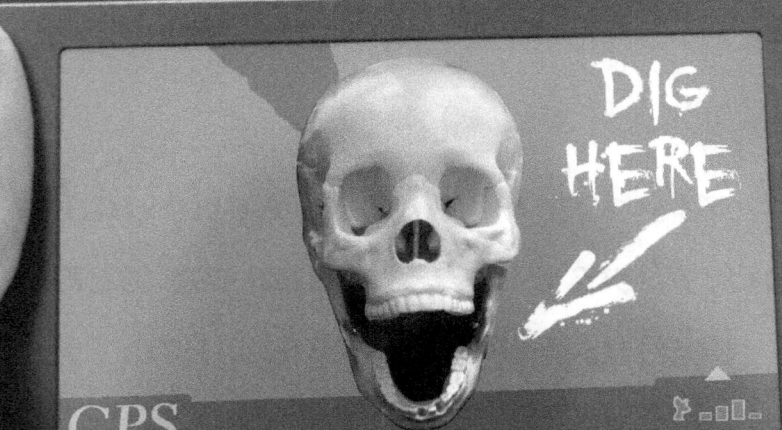

GPS

DIG HERE

D.A. Graystone

www.ingramcontent.com/pod-product-compliance
Lightning Source LLC
Chambersburg PA
CBHW071248170626
46809CB00001B/122